SAWBONES

A PATRICK FLINT NOVEL

PAMELA FAGAN HUTCHINS

SKIPJACK PUBLISHING

FREE PFH EBOOKS

CHAPTER ONE: WRECK

Patrick

"**M**ake a wedge with your skis, Susanne. Like a piece of pie." *With whipped cream on top,* Patrick Flint thought, looking down at the fluffy spring snow. He lost sight of his wife for a moment as he fought to control the demon sticks at the end of his own legs. He'd just recovered from a faceplant after an early and imprudent exit from the Poma lift.

The Poma lift. It was 1977, for goodness sakes, and ski resorts worldwide were moving toward chair lifts, even enclosed gondola lifts, or so he'd read. The Poma lift was a throwback, like Wyoming itself. Everything about the damn contraption was unnatural to Patrick. The smell of diesel in his dry nostrils, in the middle of otherwise pristine winter wilderness. Scrambling into position as if he were a fawn on roller skates. Grabbing the pole, similar to the ones strippers used in movies, only this version swung freely from an overhead conveyor cable and ended in a hard rubber disc at knee-height. Jamming the disc between his legs. Learning not to lean back into it or, God forbid, sit on it and end up butt first in the snow. Trusting it to drag him by the rump slowly up hill. Fighting the opposing force of gravity when the lift strained against the steepest stretches, as if it were being powered by a team of elderly and infirm mice.

On his first lift ride, the engine had shut down with a shuddering moan while he was still mid-slope. *Some poor schmuck probably bit the dust loading or unloading.* He thanked the good Lord it wasn't him and marveled at the view. The snow-topped Bighorn Mountains around him. Frozen Meadowlark Lake below him at eighty-five hundred feet. The elevation this far north was analogous, weather-wise, to something one thousand feet higher in Colorado, and two thousand feet higher in New Mexico. The rivers flowed north. The Rocky Mountains themselves—of which the Bighorns were a part—extended three thousand miles from northern Alberta down into New Mexico. The size and scope took his breath away. But there was majesty even in the small details. A magpie chattering in the distance. Snow falling from tree limbs. A snowshoe hare juking and jiving. It energized him. Made him feel completely alive and in touch with his senses in a way he didn't feel back in town.

After ten minutes waiting, though, he grew impatient. He decided the lift must be broken. He surveyed his surroundings. The snow to his left looked perfectly skiable. There was no reason to stick around unless he just wanted to freeze his tush off. He let go of the bar and skied over what appeared to be a gentle hump.

It wasn't.

Five sweaty minutes later, he'd finally extricated himself from a deep drift of heavy snow. A very humiliating five minutes during which the re-started lift dragged a captive audience uphill past him, including his amused wife, who had been vocal in questioning his decision from her perch safe on her own disk.

So, standing here beside his wife now and struggling to stay upright, he was determined. He *wasn't* going to fall again so soon.

"We should have taken lessons." She sounded testy, and when she looked up at him, her doe-like eyes flashed with heat. But even in irritation she was so adorable that he would have given in to the urge to hurry over, bend down, and kiss her, if only he were certain he could have gotten back up afterward. He loved this feisty Southern beauty, with her slap-red checks and strands of long brown hair blown into her mouth. She pushed at the hair with her bulky mittens, not that it did any good. "The stupid skis won't do what they're supposed to."

Teaching himself and his wife to ski wasn't going as easily as Patrick had planned. He'd been offered a chance for them to ski free of charge today thanks to Meadowlark Ski Lodge's "Doctor of the Day" program, and he'd jumped at it. The ski resort was forty-five miles on wintery mountain roads from the nearest hospital in Buffalo, so they offered family lift tickets to doctors who would spend the day onsite and on call. Patrick had been careful not to mention they were beginners when he'd picked up their lift passes and equipment, without outright lying about their levels, even though this was the first time skiing for all the Flints—Patrick, Susanne, their sixteen-year old daughter Trish, and their newly-thirteen son Perry. Patrick had read a book on alpine skiing the week before and passed the information along to his family, under the theory that they could learn to ski at a fraction of the price that expensive lessons would cost at the slope. His mind returned to his less than masterful debarkation from the lift. As a doctor, he'd grown accustomed to being skilled at his profession. To knowing more about his field than anyone else in the room. This experience—being a rank amateur—was the pits, but it was a temporary condition. Hadn't most of his time in Wyoming been a study in this exact same phenomenon? All he needed was practice and willpower.

He was about to say *mind over matter* to Susanne in an encouraging voice, when the tips of Susanne's skis crossed. Down she went, her wail cut off by an *oomph*. She landed awkwardly, like a pretzel in her brown and yellow jacket and matching snow pants. He almost laughed, but it died on his lips when she didn't move or make a sound.

"Are you okay?" he shouted.

She didn't answer.

He went through a mental checklist of possible injuries. The head—a concussion or an intracranial hemorrhage. A broken bone. A sprain. Even a puncture or other damage to the spleen.

"Susanne, if you can answer me, are you all right?" He moved as quickly as he could toward her, heart rate accelerating.

Then Susanne lifted one of her ski poles and shook it, like a fist. Or a middle finger.

She was conscious, anyway. That was good. So far, assuming Susanne was okay, Patrick hadn't had any patients. He hoped he didn't get any. Not just because of well wishes for his fellow skiers, but because his own family needed to spend some peaceful time together having fun. Trish and Susanne were the star witnesses in a death penalty trial that was starting soon, where he and Perry would play supporting roles with their own testimony. It would be one long, hard flashback for all to them to their ordeal with Billy Kemecke, a convicted murderer who'd busted free during transport to the state penitentiary. After his escape, he'd held Susanne hostage while he ransacked their family home and pried information from her about Patrick's whereabouts. He'd kidnapped Trish from a campsite in the mountains and dragged her up into rugged and remote Cloud Peak Wilderness. He'd even slit the throat of his own cousin right in front of Trish, and he'd attacked their friend Deputy Ronnie Harcourt. He'd only stopped his reign of terror when Susanne put him down with a bullet through his shoulder. And all of this was because Kemecke wanted to punish Patrick. He believed Patrick had caused the death of his mother, although she'd been too far gone with sepsis for Patrick to save her when she'd arrived at the emergency room in Buffalo a few weeks before. Kemecke hadn't acted alone on his rampage, and Patrick had been forced to kill Chester, Kemecke's brother and accomplice, during the showdown. Kemecke's teenage nephew Ben was currently residing in juvenile detention for his role—albeit coerced —in Trish's kidnapping. Since then, Kemecke's family, especially his sister Donna Lewis, had made things uncomfortable for the Flints in Buffalo. Donna didn't just hold Patrick responsible for the death of her mother, like Kemecke did. She also blamed the entire Flint family for the fate of her brothers and nephew.

Patrick expected the proceedings to put them all under a lot of stress and pressure.

"What hurts?" He stopped to retrieve Susanne's other ski pole a few yards up the hill from her.

Something whizzed past him so close that he gasped and nearly lost his balance. It was low to the ground—short and pudgy—and hatless, with blond hair sticking up and out from under a goggles strap.

It shouted, "Hey, Dad."

His son, Perry, skiing like he'd been doing it all his life.

"Where's your sister?" Patrick shouted after him.

His son vanished behind a rooster tail of snow. It was hard to hear him, but Patrick thought he heard him say, "I dunno," before the tail disappeared around a bend in the trail.

They hadn't seen Trish since five minutes after they got to the slopes. Patrick tried to block thoughts of the current Trish out of his mind in favor of the sweet little girl she used to be. The one who'd curled up in his lap and listened to him read his medical school texts aloud—his personal blend of parenting and studying. She was erratic now. Hormones, mostly, but also a result of what she'd been through, and was still going through, thanks to Kemecke. Of course, she didn't make things any easier on herself or the rest of the Flint household by dating Donna Lewis's son Brandon. Donna had forbidden Brandon from seeing Trish, and Patrick and Susanne did their best to keep the lovebirds apart, but the two were doing their Romeo and Juliet best to stay together.

Which meant that since Trish wasn't with her parents or Perry, there was a better than even chance she was with Brandon. Well, Patrick couldn't do anything about it up here on the mountain. He and Susanne could deal with Trish at lunch.

Patrick crept closer to his wife. His downhill ski lost traction and sent him into a standing split, but he clenched his gluteus maxiumus and stayed upright. It wasn't okay to grab the parts that hurt, so he kept a stiff upper lip. When he reached Susanne, he planted his pole tips deep in the powder, into the packed accumulation below it, and leaned on them. He pulled off his gloves and stuffed them in his pockets. His wedding ring glinted bright gold against the stark white of the snow. He'd only started wearing it a few months before—after nearly seventeen years of marriage without one—and he still hadn't gotten used to it. He kept expecting to catch it on something and rip his finger off at any minute.

Wind whipped snow off the ground and around them as Susanne tilted up her tear-streaked face.

The sight of it almost did him in. "What hurts?" He laid the back of his fingers against her cheek.

"Skiing gives me a headache." Her teeth chattered. "These clothes aren't waterproof. I'm freezing, and I can't get up."

He made a show of checking her face and ears. "I don't see any signs of frostbite." They both knew she hadn't been out long enough, and that it was actually too warm for it. But given that he hadn't sprung for ski wear for any of them, he didn't mention it. His own Scotch-guarded blue jeans felt a little damp. "Are you injured?"

"I don't know. I don't think so. Just uncomfortable. And frustrated."

"Okay." He made a grab for one of her skis, ready to turn it, but he lost traction and went into a split with the other leg. He didn't handle this split as well as he had the one on his other side, and he fell like a rifle-shot bear. He rolled to his back. He definitely needed a lot more practice. Maybe being twenty years younger would help, too.

Blowing snow dusted his face. He stared at the blue sky, startling in its intensity, thanks to winter's lower temperatures and humidity decreasing the water vapor in the air. He rested, thinking and blowing warm breath on his icy cold fingers. Helping Susanne would go faster and more safely without his skis on. He sat up, released his boot bindings, and unfastened the straps from around his ankles that kept his skis from running away. When he was done, he stuck the butt of the skis in the snow so they wouldn't glide off. Kneeling beside Susanne, he lifted one of her skis with her foot still attached and turned it around one hundred and eighty degrees, in line with the other.

"Is that better?"

She sighed. "Much."

"Why don't you sit up and swing your legs around so they're perpendicular to the incline. If they're pointed downhill, they'll spurt out from under you when you try to stand up."

Susanne tried, but it wasn't pretty.

Maybe he should have coughed up the money for ski lessons. He could sign them up when they got down the mountain. He looked around, hoping they were close. The lodge was nowhere in sight.

Make that *if* they ever got down the mountain.

Susanne cocked her head. "What are you mumbling about?"

Patrick clamped his lips together. He had an incurable habit of talking silently to himself. A man's voice from above them saved him from admitting he was about to cave in for lessons.

"Need any help?"

Patrick recognized the voice and turned toward his friend Henry Sibley. "Hey, Sibley. Haven't seen you in a while." Henry was skiing in Levi's, a felt cowboy hat, sunglasses, and an oil cloth jacket. Even on skis, he looked like a rancher.

Henry did a double take. "Patrick? I hardly recognized you with that molting marmot attached to your face."

Patrick rubbed his sparse whiskers, dislodging chunks of ice. His beard was kind of marmot-orange. In contrast, Henry had a thick black beard, neatly trimmed. Patrick's hadn't gotten long enough for scissors yet, even though he'd been babying it along since New Year's Day. *It's just in its training phase.* He winked. "Winter's long. Gotta do something to stay warm."

Susanne piped in. "He'd grow it on his back if he could."

"Hey, it works for bears."

"They hibernate in caves in the mountains, which may be where you end up if you don't let me shave it off soon."

Patrick grinned. So far, she hadn't attacked his beard with a razor in the middle of the night, but he knew the day was coming. "Hey, where's Vangie?" Vangie was Henry's very pregnant wife, and Susanne's good friend.

"She's down at the lodge having hot chocolate and told me to go on without her. We're shorthanded at the ranch, so I haven't gotten out on the slopes much lately." Henry expertly positioned himself downhill of Susanne and grabbed her hand. "Here you go." He pulled her to her feet.

She leaned against him while she steadied herself. "Thanks, Henry. You don't happen to teach skiing, do you?"

Loudspeakers crackled from one of the poles supporting the cables of the Poma lift. After a piercing squelch, a woman's voice boomed, "Doctor of the Day, you're needed at the base of the main run. Doctor of the Day, report to the base of the main run."

Patrick raised his hand. "Duty calls." He glanced down the hill. The slope was daunting. He hoped whoever was hurt wasn't in need of immediate assistance. It would take a while to get Susanne there.

Henry nodded. "Me, too. I'm giving Susanne a lesson. We'll all see you at the bottom."

Susanne and Patrick said, "Thank God," at the same time.

"You're a good man, Sibley." Patrick saluted with two fingers to his forehead. Then he put his skis back on and pointed them across the mountain.

Take it slow, he coached himself. *Traverse the mountain. Don't fall— it's easier to stay up than get up.* Luckily, there wasn't much traffic on the run, so he was able to control his speed by making the wide turns his book had recommended for beginners. *I'm getting the hang of this.* Maybe the expensive lessons wouldn't be necessary after all.

He glided shakily into a curve. Movement in the trees to his right drew his eyes. He saw something tawny and low slung with a twitching black-tipped tail. Mountain lion—here and in broad daylight? He knew they lived up in these mountains, had his own up-close-and-personal experience with one. As quickly as it appeared, though, the animal was gone, and he couldn't be sure he'd seen it at all.

He returned his concentration to finishing his turn. The imposing lodge and its wide wooden deck came into view. Relief flooded through him. He could hear the din of happy voices as clearly as if he was standing in the middle of the crowd. *Lunchtime?* He was feeling more confident, and he hated looking like a loser, so he tightened his turns and fought his skis out of the snowplow position and into something more respectable. His speed picked up. Despite his sunglasses, the wind teased tears from his eyes and burned his cheeks. His confidence grew. He was skiing. He was *really* skiing. As he neared the bottom of the run, he saw a group of about ten people clustered, their backs to him and eyes on a person reclined in the snow. That had to be his patient.

He planned his approach, and, more importantly, his stop. His ski instruction book recommended a deep snowplow for beginners, but he was no longer skiing like a beginner. His turns had gotten pretty good, if he did say so himself. Intermediate skiers stopped by turning against the hill and digging in their edges. That is what he would do.

He started looking for a place to initiate his turn, one that would leave him well short of the group. The slope had been swept bare of powder by the wind and a multitude of skis, and he couldn't find a spot to his liking. The run was wider down here, and the longer he traversed it without a turn or a wedge, the more speed he built up. He saw that he was drawing too close to the lift. He had to turn immediately, or he'd career across the tow line. His stomach fluttered, but he ignored his nerves and threw himself into his turn. His skis slid sideways out from under him. He heard the sickening sound of their metal edges scraping against ice, felt the sensation up through his legs. He didn't fall, though, and he only flailed his arms a little.

But now he had a long stretch of real estate in front of him before he reached his patient, and no more room on his downhill side for another turn. To his dismay, he was picking up speed much more quickly on the packed snow. As he barreled toward the group, he shifted his weight uphill to dig in his edges, but that only seemed to make him go faster.

He was out of control, with only fifty feet to go.

In sheer desperation, he shifted deep into the snowplow position, with his legs bent and his front tips together and back tips wide apart. His skis knocked against each other, and within seconds, his thighs were burning. He sunk deeper, praying. *Dear God, please help me not make a buffoon of myself in front of all these people.*

His prayer went unanswered. He rode over the backs of the first person's set of skis, which brought him to a grinding halt, and he straddled the legs of the next skier. One by one, people tumbled like dominos until he'd taken out everyone in the group beside his patient, except for one woman. For a moment, there was complete stillness and silence. His brain went silly on him, and he thought, *Maybe the game is bowling instead of dominoes. I'm only one pin short of a strike.*

He cleared his throat. "Sorry. Is everyone okay?"

A man under him shouted, "What the hell? You skied over my wrist. Could have chopped it off. Those things don't grow back, you know?"

"Belongs in ski school," another muttered. "A danger to himself and others."

"My son is hurt, and you almost skied right over him," a woman said from the ground beside him. She lifted her face. Her eyebrows were frosted in snow crystals. "You shouldn't be out here if you can't control yourself."

Patrick closed his eyes. If he was hurting anywhere, the sting of mortification distracted him from it. This wasn't good. Not good at all. But he had to tell them who he was, so he could help his patient.

He opened his eyes, smiled grimly, and said, "Did someone call for the Doctor of the Day?"

CHAPTER TWO: DIVERT

Bighorn Mountains, Buffalo, Wyoming
Saturday, March 5, 1977, 11:15 a.m.

Perry

Perry pointed his wedge downhill and let the wind buffet inside his jacket and tickle his nose. The trees were a blur on either side of him. He'd never gone this fast before, except in a car, and it was amazing. He liked this skiing thing. He was just glad his dad hadn't made them sign up for ski school where he would have had to hang out with a big group of babies all day. Skiing was easy. Why hadn't they come before? They'd lived in Wyoming for two years, and he could have been skiing all winter that whole time. He could have even had his January birthday party up here. Next year, he would for sure.

He thought about his athletics schedule for a second. Football season would be over by the time ski season started, so the coach couldn't tell him not to ski. Did Buffalo High have a ski team? He hoped he wasn't getting too late of a start at it, but he could learn fast, like he'd done with football. A little thrill ran through him. He could be a racer. A downhiller like Andy Mill. He'd cheered hard for him during the Olympics. Even though Andy had been hurt, he'd wanted to race so badly that he'd stuck his leg in the snow until it was numb before his event, and still finished in sixth place. He was tough, like Perry's dad. Like Perry wanted to be.

When you aren't tall, you have to be tough, and Perry was definitely short. His sister never got tired of reminding him what a shrimp he was. "It's not the size of the dog in the fight, it's the size of the fight in the dog," his dad always told him. His dad was sort of right, but a big dog with big fight in him was still best, to Perry's way of thinking. That's why he had asked for barbells and ankle weights for his birthday. He'd been using them, too. It wasn't fair. All his friends were shooting up like weeds. Perry measured his height against a goal mark he'd made inside in the door jamb of his closet every day—the height of his best friend John, at the end of football season—and, to his great disappointment, he didn't seem to be gaining on it. Or growing any whiskers or chest hair, either. He'd know if he had, because he used a magnifying glass to look every night.

He snowplowed to a stop. His ankle was shaking and it ached. He'd broken it in football last fall, then hurt it again in December, and he'd only gotten the cast off two weeks before. Skiing with a barely-healed broken ankle? Good thing he'd been using his ankle weights. He grinned. So maybe he was a little tough.

He looked around him. He could see the big, blocky lodge at the foot of the mountain. He was on the last pitch before the wide-open slope down to its wooden deck. Did he have time to ride the lift up for one more run before lunch? His stomach growled. *Nope.* He was definitely eating the sandwich in his pocket when he got to the bottom. But he didn't have to be in a hurry to get there.

His lips stung and he ran his tongue over them. Cracked, dry, and bloody. Setting his gloves in the snow at his feet, he pulled his Chapstick out and rubbed it on. It was too cold to spread well, and it tasted waxy. He kept rubbing until he got a little bit on. As he reached to drop it in his pocket, the stick slipped out of his fingers. It disappeared into the powder by his gloves. That was okay. It hadn't been doing much good anyway. He slipped a hand back into one of his gloves, wiggling his fingers and pulling it on, then repeating the process on the other side.

A set of ski tracks headed off the run and into the forest, wide apart, like someone was skiing with their legs in a big V. The trail looked pretty flat and really fun. He could do it. His only worry was if he got stuck. His parents hadn't let him rent poles, at the recommendation of the old man doling out the equipment. If there were any flat stretches, Perry would have to take off his skis and walk. No problem, he decided. He was going for it.

First, since his dad was always lecturing him on wilderness survival, he thought through his supplies: one sandwich and his pocketknife. That was it. Not even a Chaptstick anymore. Probably not everything he would need if he was caught in an avalanche, attacked by a moose, or fell and broke his leg. But none of those things were going to happen.

His dad had a tendency to overreact to little things. How much school supplies cost, taking out the trash a day late, or losing stuff. So, sometimes his mom, Trish, and Perry kept secrets from his dad because, as his mom always said, "What your dad doesn't know won't hurt anyone."

Like now, when Perry knew he would be fine.

Staying in his wedge, Perry turned by taking little steps until he was pointed in the right direction. Then he bent his knees and leaned forward. He gathered speed quickly until he hit the powder. Once, he'd mashed the brakes too hard on his bicycle and gone right over the handlebars. This was almost that bad. He jerked backwards with his arms out to keep from falling on his face. His position made him think of the ski jumpers he'd watched in the Olympics. Those huge jumps were definitely not something he wanted to try, but a small one would be okay.

Trees flashed by him on either side. Tall ones with thick piney branches and baby ones with just their tops sticking out of the snow. He ran over one of the baby ones. A pinecone fell silently to the snow beside him. It was so quiet that the silence seemed loud. All he could hear was the wind in his ears and the chittering of an angry squirrel.

Every now and then his tips would go under deep powder, and he'd have to fight to stay upright. A few times he almost hit a tree, which was a little bit scary. But mostly he just felt strong and free. His dad had never skied through a forest before, or at all. Perry was the first one in his family to do something this cool.

A reverberating crack ripped through the silence. It felt like something had punched his eardrums. His heart started beating like a bass drumroll. He snowplowed so hard that his butt nearly hit the ground, but he couldn't stop, not until his skis wedged against trees on either side of the trail.

The silence was even louder now, except for his heavy breathing. He tried to slow it down, but it didn't do much good. He still sounded like his dog Ferdinand after he'd been chasing a jackrabbit.

What had made that noise? Had a tree split from the cold? He'd learned in school that they could do that. If that was what it was, it could have fallen on him. He scanned the forest, looking for a fallen tree or anything out of the ordinary. About one hundred feet away through the trees, he saw something move. It was a person in a white camo snow suit, wearing one of those caps with an attached face mask that covered up the neck. The person slung a long narrow bag of gear onto the back of a yellow snowmobile and mounted up. *What's in the big bag?* This wasn't a great place for a picnic lunch. Or for trapping, and the only thing still in season for that was weasel—which Perry only knew because John's dad was into trapping and talked about it all the time when Perry spent the night at their house.

The person turned and saw him. Perry waved, but the person didn't wave back. Perry almost shouted a greeting, thinking maybe the person couldn't see Perry because he was blending into the forest, but then he realized that didn't make sense. His coat was red and yellow. He would stand out against all the snow, not blend in. Then he considered warning the person about the crack he'd just heard, but, before he could, the person looked away.

His stomach did a funny flip and started hurting, something it was doing lately whenever he got nervous. He jerked his hand out of the air and turned as fast as he could, ready to ski like mad out of there. But the path back to the ski run was more uphill than he'd thought when he was skiing out. He groaned. It wasn't steep, but it definitely wasn't flat. He'd have to walk up it. He slid one ski forward, which sent him backwards instead of forwards. He tried it again with the same result. It felt like there were eyes drilling into his back, and, for all he knew, the person was getting closer to him. He needed to get back to the trail, ASAP. Suddenly, he knew what he had to do. To keep himself from going any further downhill, he put his skis in a reverse wedge, with the front tips out and the back tips together. It worked. His backward momentum stopped, and he was able to take a few tiny steps up the slope.

Then he heard the snowmobile fire up. He was close enough to smell exhaust blowing toward him on the wind. It revved a few times, and, after a couple of seconds, the engine noise caught and held. The snowmobile was moving, hopefully going in the opposite direction from Perry. Perry kept creeping slowly up the hill. The engine sound grew fainter. He leaned against a tree to rest, sweat dripping down his back. He felt strangely lighter. Relieved.

The person hadn't been friendly, but there had been nothing to be scared about. He was just being a big fraidy cat.

Still, he was all alone out here, and no one knew where he'd gone.

Perry started inching up the path again, a little faster this time.

CHAPTER THREE: SKIP

Trish

"**A**re you, like, even going to try skiing?" Brandon Lewis tugged one of Trish's long, blonde braids.

Trish tilted her head and looked at him from under her eyelashes. She was sitting on the bench of a picnic table out on the deck, facing him. The ski chalet blocked the wind. People were milling around without their jackets in the bright sun. She could almost imagine she and Brandon were on their honeymoon at a fancy European ski resort, as long as she didn't look too closely at the attire of the people around her, which was mostly blue jeans and Carhartt.

"Not without you," she said.

"I can't ski. The finals are really important to me, you know?"

"It's okay. I'm having fun." She raised her cup of hot chocolate to her mouth.

The state finals basketball tournament was the next weekend in Laramie, and Brandon was a starting forward on Buffalo's boys' team. He wanted to go to the University of Wyoming, but he really needed scholarship money. It was important that he play well in Laramie in front of the Cowboys coaching staff. The boys' team had won state two times in a row only a few years back, too, so they were determined to take back their title, even if it meant sacrificing winter sports. He couldn't risk an injury on the ski slopes.

The girls were defending their own state title, too. Trish would have loved to be playing, but she was languishing on second team junior varsity. Coach Lamkin didn't even seem to know she was alive most of the time. The bajillion games of horse Trish had played with her dad didn't seem to be paying off, although jogging with him had—she always lasted longest in conditioning drills. And conditioning was important now that all the girls' games were full-court like the boys.

Trish gave her boyfriend the once over. She loved watching him play basketball. She loved watching him do anything, really. He had curly blond hair that almost touched his shoulders in the back. He was tall, and, while there wasn't an ounce of fat on his body, he had nice muscles in his arms and shoulders. When she had seen him in swimming trunks at the town pool last summer before they were dating, she'd been mesmerized by his six-pack abs. She couldn't believe how lucky she was to be dating such a fox.

They'd broken up for a while before Christmas. And he'd even gone out with her archrival Charla Newby. But only once. Trish had called him and told him she missed him, and they'd gotten back together. Things weren't exactly the same as before, though. He made her promise she wouldn't boss him around and embarrass him in front of his friends, for starters. That was no problem. She could admit that she hadn't been the easiest girlfriend before, and she would have walked across glass to get him back. Also, he was a little more stressed out, working hard like he was toward a scholarship, and occasionally that made him less patient with her. But he was her soulmate, the boy she was going to marry, and she was willing to work for their relationship. He'd given her his letter jacket and class ring. That meant something, right? She kept them in her locker at school, though—a secret from all of their over-protective parents.

And the parents were their major problem, especially Brandon's mom. Mrs. Lewis blamed Trish's family for her brother being on trial for murder, and she'd blame them even more if he was convicted, because Trish and her mom were the star witnesses against him at his trial. Brandon wasn't allowed to see her outside of school, although that didn't stop them. They found ways to be together. Like they'd done today.

Trish and Brandon avoided talking about his relatives or the trial. It was better that way.

A short, slim man in a shiny gray business suit passed by their table. He slipped and caught himself on Brandon's shoulder. "Sorry," he said.

Brandon nodded. "It's cool, man."

Trish looked down at the man's feet. He was wearing narrow, lace-up loafers with smooth soles. Not the right footwear for icy decks at ski lodges.

Another voice turned her attention away from him. "Trish Flint, is that you?"

Vangie Sibley had a strong Tennessee accent, so her voice was pretty easy to recognize. Trish turned toward her. Vangie and her mom were basically best friends. Trish hadn't seen Vangie in a while and couldn't believe how much her belly had grown. She was so pregnant that it looked like her stomach was about to explode. "Oh, wow, Mrs. Sibley, you look . . ."

"Like I'm hiding a watermelon under my shirt?"

Trish's cheeks grew hot. "I'm sorry. I didn't, I guess, um, I mean you look great." And she did. Her dark eyes sparkled, and her black hair looked super cute in its pixie cut. She looked almost young enough to be a student at Buffalo High, but she was old. Nearly thirty probably. "When is your baby due?"

"Hank will be joining us in a few weeks. Or any time he feels like it now, I guess."

"How do you know it's a boy?"

She smiled. "I just have a feeling." She winked, then turned to Brandon. As a Buffalo Elementary school teacher, she'd taught all the kids in town. "Hello, Brandon. Good luck in the state tournament next week."

He shrugged. "Thanks, Mrs. Sibley."

Trish glanced at the ski slope just in time to see a man wipe out and knock down a whole row of people.

Brandon whistled. "Whoa. That was far out."

Trish peered more closely, frowning, and recognized a flannel jacket and thinning brown hair. "Oh my gosh. That was my dad." Then she laughed. "Man, I'll bet he's embarrassed. I hope he didn't hurt anyone."

Mrs. Sibley tented her eyes and stood on her tiptoes. "One of the people he knocked over may be Judge Renkin. That's his wife standing to the side wiping something off her jacket."

"Coffee," Brandon said. "She's still holding the cup."

A loud crack sounded, then echoed across the lake. Brandon and Trish raised eyebrows at each other.

"A rifle," he said. "A big one."

"It's not hunting season," Mrs. Sibley mused.

Trish looked around. Where could the shot have come from?

Then one person screamed, followed shortly by another, and another.

"Oh, my God." Mrs. Sibley's hand flew to cover her mouth.

"What is it?" Trish asked.

"Someone at the base of the slope has been shot."

Trish craned her neck toward the base of the ski slope. People were standing and pointing, blocking her line of sight. She jumped to her feet. Her dad. Her dad was down there.

"Daddy," she shouted. "Daddy."

And then she was running and stumbling awkwardly in her ski boots, toward the spot she'd last seen him.

CHAPTER FOUR: AID

Susanne

Susanne kept her eyes on Henry Sibley's back as she followed him slowly down the mountain. He made it look so effortless.

He pirouetted around and skied backwards. "Am I still going the right speed? I don't want to lose you." Without taking his eyes off her, he executed a wide turn, still gliding the wrong way.

"I'm good," she said, then wobbled.

"Put your arms out. Like you're walking on a log across a creek." He pronounced creek as "crick" like everyone else did in Wyoming. She still thought it sounded strange even after a couple of years in the state. It made her feel like exaggerating her Texas accent, too. She didn't want to lose her roots, even if she and Patrick had recently moved into the home of her dreams on a bluff above Clear Creek, just west of Buffalo.

She lifted her arms like she used to do on the balance beam in gymnastics as a girl. It worked, and she stayed on her feet.

"See? Doesn't that help?"

"It does. Thanks."

"That's for balance. Now, if you want to make the turns easier, move those arms in front of you and kind of point them in the direction you're wanting to go. Like you're steering a bicycle. I'll show you."

Henry swiveled around to face the correct direction again, with his hands in front of him. He turned again, following his arms like he was steering a bicycle. Or a boat.

Susanne tried it. Her body followed her hands, a little. "Wow, I think that helped, too."

Over his shoulder, he grinned. "You're a natural."

She knew that wasn't true, but it was nice of him to say.

Below them, the trail widened out and ended at the base of the resort. She could see the dreaded Poma lift, the lodge and its broad deck, and the parking lot beyond. It seemed a long way down, still, and she ached with the desire to be there already. She could put her feet up and drink hot cocoa with Vangie. Or a hot toddie. She deserved one after this. But how was she going to convince Patrick that she'd had enough of skiing for one day? She could hear him already. He'd tell her how the cost per hour of her lift ticket and skis went up if she only skied half the day. But they hadn't paid for them, so she didn't care. The thought of going up that lift again gave her the shivers, much less skiing down the mountain.

A loud crack startled her. She looked toward the sound, away from her path, and the tips of her skis crossed. She went down in a graceless heap. Like a hippopotamus on roller skates, she imagined.

Henry turned around and skied uphill to help her. Her skis hadn't popped off, so he hauled her up by one hand, holding on until she was steady.

"What was that sound?" she asked.

"Rifle, sounded like. Although it's out of season. Maybe someone was scaring off a cranky bear that should have been sleeping." He gave her a thumbs up. "Last stretch. Are you ready?"

She couldn't really lift her thumb in her mittens, but she gave him something close to it. "Ready."

They skied quietly for several minutes. Susanne focused all of her energy on no more falls, even though her thighs were quivering, and it seemed like everything she was wearing was wet from sweat and melted snow.

"Something's going on." Henry stopped and pointed at the crowd at the bottom of the hill.

Susanne managed to pull up beside him. Voices buzzed around the lodge as if it were a hive of bees. People were running around, agitated. No one was on the lift. And the crowd in front of the deck had swelled. Something was going on. "Maybe this has to do with the Doctor of the Day call."

"That call was closing in on half an hour ago." Henry frowned. "Come on. I don't feel good leaving Vangie alone down there."

His unease was contagious. Patrick was down there, too. And maybe Trish and Perry. She followed him, skiing faster than she'd thought she could, and snowplowed to a stop about twenty-five feet from the ever-expanding crowd on the snow.

"What's happening?" Henry said to a man who was walking back toward the parking lot.

The man's eyes were wide. "Somebody got shot. I'm out of here."

Panic mushroomed in Susanne's chest and rocketed, tingling, through her body. She wrestled out of her ski bindings, leaving the skis and poles on the ground. She rushed toward the deck, clumsy in the stiff, heavy ski boots. She needed to find her family.

"Mom!" someone screamed. One of *her* someones.

She looked up to see Trish hurrying down the steps from the deck.

"Dad was there." Trish reached her and pointed.

Susanne's hand flew to her throat. Patrick. Trish grabbed her arm and dragged her back toward the cluster of people on the snow.

Henry appeared on her other side. "Come on." He shouldered into the crowd, and they followed.

Susanne's heartbeat was deafening, and her vision had narrowed. "Patrick! Patrick, where are you?" Her husband. The love of her life. The man she'd die for. He couldn't be hurt. Shot. Dead. He just couldn't. They'd been together since their early teens, married before they turned twenty, and had kids before he'd graduated from medical school. He was cheap, he was exacting, but he was loving, loyal, and he was the only one for her. She couldn't lose him.

She was trapped in a maze of people now. She shouted louder. Why wouldn't he answer her? And why wouldn't people let her through?

But Henry was a head taller than her. He stopped suddenly. "I see him."

She clutched his wrist. "Is he all right?"

"Where is he?" Trish wailed.

Henry pointed. "He looks all right. He's down on the ground

tending to someone. There's a lot of blood, so I'm guessing it's the person who was shot."

Susanne still couldn't see her husband, but she gathered Trish in her arms. "Thank God, thank God," she whispered into her daughter's hair.

"He's okay?" Trish repeated.

Henry nodded. "Yes. Let me see if I can get us closer. Then I've got to go check on Vangie."

"I was with her when this happened. She's up on the deck," Trish said.

Henry heaved a sigh. "Good." Then he raised his voice. "Coming through, people. We're with the doctor. Let us through."

The seas parted, a little. Enough to pass. And at the end of the human tunnel and slightly downhill from her, Susanne saw him. Her husband. Her handsome, compassionate, gifted husband. He was kneeling beside a woman in black whose long gray hair was fanned around her head and shoulders. Her neck and chest were covered in blood. As Susanne walked toward them, Patrick yanked off his plaid flannel coat, then pulled his pocketknife out of his jeans.

She fell on her knees beside him. From a quick glance, she could tell the woman was in very serious condition. Thank goodness Patrick had been here. But where were the woman's loved ones? There was no one hovering or keening over her. Had she been alone?

Keeping her voice low and trying to control the emotion that was threatening to spill out in public, Susanne said, "I'm so relieved you're okay. I thought you'd been shot. How can I help?"

Patrick's face was tight, his light blue eyes focused on his patient. "Can you cut my coat into strips for me? I need to try to stop her bleeding."

"Yes. Of course."

He handed her the knife and coat. Wasting no time, she sliced and tore his favorite garment into long sections. When she was done, she looked more closely at the woman. Her hands were bare of gloves. An ostentatious ring on her wedding finger was drenched in blood. It was a big diamond with lots of smaller diamonds around it set in a thick gold band. Susanne's eyes traveled up the woman's body. Patrick was pressing into her neck, where she was bleeding profusely. Then she saw the woman's face.

A little yelp escaped Susanne before she put a fist to her mouth. "It's Jeannie Renkin."

"Yes," Patrick said.

Harold and Jeannie Renkin were their closest neighbors on Clear Creek. Or, at least, they were the people who lived closest to them. There was nothing neighborly about the Renkins, in a state known for its over-the-top neighborliness. Life and conditions here could be harsh. People stuck together and helped each other out, even if that meant sometimes they got a little too far into each other's business.

But not the Renkins. Jeannie had been cool bordering on unpleasant when Susanne had stopped by to introduce herself shortly after the Flints had moved into their home. Then, later, Harold had mailed them a letter complaining about how fast Patrick drove, never mind that it was in response to emergency call outs. The irony of Patrick caring for Harold's wife now that they were facing their own emergency wasn't lost on Susanne. She stared at Jeannie's ashen face. Her normally bright red lips were a pale pink. Her eyes were closed and fake lashes fanned the crepey, lined skin around them.

"Who was the Doctor of the Day call for?"

"A kid. Not a life-threatening injury, so Jeannie has to come first."

"Can I help?" Trish asked. Susanne had forgotten she was there.

Patrick grunted with effort, then answered his daughter. "I need a stretcher. Someone is supposed to be bringing one. We have to get her out of here. See if you can hurry that along."

"Yes, sir." Trish disappeared.

A shadow fell across the snow. Susanne looked up to see Judge Renkin. He was an imposing man, tall and broad shouldered with the beginnings of a belly. He was dressed in unscuffed cowboy boots, a clean hat, a long, new oilskin duster, and jeans with an ironed crease. He was whispering urgently with a man dressed completely inappropriately for the weather. A thin business suit and shirt with no winter jacket. Wingtips on his feet. No gloves on his hands or warm cap on his wiry black hair. The fabric of his suit was shiny. *Smarmy*.

Patrick grunted. "Judge Renkin, could you crouch down here with me for a second?"

The judge and the man in the suit exchanged an unfriendly glance.

"This isn't the end of it," Suit Man said. "Or do you want me to have a little chat with Rawlins or Ochoa?"

"It's over when I say it's over, Peters. And it's over." The judge took two steps, closing the gap between him and Patrick. His body blocked Susanne's view of Suit Man.

"My knees," the judge said. The expression on his face suggested people usually did what he asked and not the other way around.

"I understand, sir, but I'm afraid if I take the pressure off your wife's wound, she'll bleed out, and I really need a word with you."

Renkin squatted on the opposite side of Patrick from Susanne. He didn't touch his wife or even look at her. "Yes?"

Susanne peered around, searching for the man in the suit. She wondered if he was family, but he'd disappeared.

Patrick kept his voice low. "If we wait on the ambulance, your wife is going to die. I'd like to take her down the mountain myself."

"Will she live if you do?"

Patrick closed his eyes. "Maybe. Or maybe not. She's lost a lot of blood, and she's going into shock. But she has a chance if we hurry, and I'd like to try."

The judge nodded, his eyes hooded. "Go, then."

"Would you like to ride with us?"

Renkin glanced at his wife's face. If he was feeling any emotion, he was really good at hiding it. "No. I'll meet you at the hospital." He stood.

Susanne recoiled from him. His wife was *dying,* and he didn't want to be with her, to hold her hand?

Patrick was brusque. "All right, then."

A high-pitched male voice shouted, "Coming through with a stretcher. Pardon me. Pardon the stretcher, please." A young man—early twenties, maybe?— in ski pants and a burnt orange turtleneck sweater was carrying a stretcher over his head, with Trish running to keep up with him. The bystanders surged back as he lowered it to the ground. For the first time Susanne realized how close to them everyone was standing. It was claustrophobic. Voyeuristic.

"I'm back, Daddy," Trish said.

"Good. I need both of you to apply pressure to Mrs. Renkin's wound with these folded strips of cloth," Patrick said to Trish and Susanne. "I've got to get her on the stretcher. You're going to have to press pretty hard."

"Okay." Trish's voice squeaked.

"I've got the first aid kit, too," the young man said.

Patrick nodded. "We need to apply a pressure dressing. Quickly."

The young man threw open the kit and tore into a package of bandages. "These?"

"Yes. I'll need several of the gauze sponges and one of the nonadherent." Patrick took the bandages he held out. "Be ready with the tape."

"Got it." The young man started working the end of the tape away from a roll.

Patrick pulled the bloody tatters of his coat away from Jeannie's neck. Blood gushed from the wound. He pressed the bandage over it. "Apply the tape, please."

The young man licked his lips. He tore a long piece with his teeth and applied it over the bandages, firmly, repeating the process several times.

"Pressure here, Susanne, Trish."

Susanne nodded and pressed her hand down on the bandage and Jeannie's neck underneath it. Trish reached out, hesitated, then gulped and added her hand to the pile on top of Susanne's.

"Good." Patrick huddled with Henry and the young man who brought the stretcher. Then he was on the ground again, this time on the opposite side of Jeannie, tilting her body while Henry and the young man slid the stretcher under her. Blood seeped through the bandage and trickled down Jeannie's neck.

Patrick saw it at the same time Susanne did. "More pressure."

Susanne pressed harder.

Trish paled. "I feel woozy."

Patrick seemed aware of everything and everyone at once. "Have you got it, Susanne?"

Susanne nodded. "I do."

"Put your head between your legs, Trish."

Trish didn't need an engraved invitation. She scooted back on her rear, then bent her legs and put her head between her knees. Patrick hustled around beside Susanne again and slid Jeannie the rest of the way onto the stretcher.

He checked the wound. "Just like that, honey. Stick with it. I'm running to move the car as close as I can. Guys, meet me at the edge of the parking lot?"

Trish got to her feet.

"See you in a minute," Henry responded, and he and his partner lifted the stretcher and began walking it carefully across the snow.

Susanne rose with the stretcher and paced it, bending over Jeannie and pushing as hard as she dared. "Sorry," she said to the men.

"You're fine," Henry said. "Do what you've got to do."

Trish followed. A woman with a large wad of chewing tobacco was suddenly in their path. She was wearing a blue chambray shirt with Meadowlark Ski Lodge embroidered in gold and green on the front pocket, and she was coatless. She spat.

"Excuse us, ma'am," the young man said.

"Is she going to make it?" the woman asked.

"Dr. Flint isn't sure," Susanne said. "We're taking her to Buffalo."

The woman nodded. "Thank you. Damnedest thing." Tears welled in her eyes. She wiped them away with the back of a wind-chapped bare hand. "Sheriff's crew is on the way. Now I've just got to figure out how to get everyone to stay off my mountain yet still stick around the lodge to talk to them."

"Free drinks." Henry suggested. He stepped around her as Patrick pulled their recently-repaired Suburban to the edge of the parking lot. Trish had smashed it into a barn over Christmas—on purpose, to catch a killer. Add that to their totaled station wagon and Patrick's crushed Porsche, and it had been a rough year on vehicles at the Flint house.

Patrick jumped out and made fast work of putting seats down and stuffing odds and ends into the floorboards. He threw open the rear doors and jerked out his container of disaster-preparedness gear and tools. He slipped, and the box fell to the ground. He caught himself on the door before he fell on top of the box. The lid came off, and out tumbled canteens, matches, an ax, jumper cables, tow rope, and various other paraphernalia largely inspired by his adventures with his friend and co-worker Wes Braten.

"I've got it." Trish was already on her knees stuffing items back in the box.

Henry and his partner nestled the stretcher into the back end of the vehicle under Patrick's direction, while Susanne crawled in beside it without ever letting up on Jeannie's neck.

"Where should I put the box?" Trish asked.

"Front seat," Patrick replied.

Trish did as she was told. It wasn't often at her age that Trish was helpful and cooperative. Other adults bragged on Trish to Susanne, but there was a big difference, in Susanne's experience, between how her children acted for her and for other people. Susanne could cajole and threaten Trish to do the dishes to no avail, but when she babysat for other families from their church, they reported that she did the dishes and the laundry and left the house spic and span. Susanne's heart warmed to see that in a crisis, Trish came through, even with her parents there to witness it.

Vangie walked up, and Henry encircled her with his arms.

Trish leaned her head in the back of the Suburban. "Hey, Mom. I should probably get a ride home."

"What about Perry? Has anyone seen him?" Susanne felt like a bad mother. She'd only now thought of her son.

Trish crossed her arms. "Not me."

Vangie raised a hand to get their attention. "We can give Trish and Perry a ride home."

"Uh . . ." Trish seemed flustered, but Susanne didn't have time for it.

"Thank you, Vangie. If you can find Perry, that is."

Vangie gave a half smile. "Neither deer, nor elk, nor coyote, nor any one of God's creatures can remain hidden when my husband is on the trail. Even a teenage boy. We'll get him."

Doors slammed and Patrick climbed into the driver's seat. "Susanne, you okay back there?"

"I am."

"If your arms get too tired, we can trade off."

"Okay." Susanne sucked in a deep breath. *Dear God, give me the strength and courage to do what needs doing for Jeannie.* She readjusted her hands and applied more pressure to Jeannie's neck as Patrick accelerated. The tires spun without catching for a few sickening rotations, then found traction. They shot out of the parking lot and onto the road down the mountain.

CHAPTER FIVE: RETURN

Perry

A s soon as he cleared the drifts between the edge of the forest and the ski run, Perry flopped to his back in the snow. It had taken a lot longer to climb back up the trail than he'd imagined it would. He was so hot that he'd tied the sleeves of his coat around his waist. His sweater and wool cap were soaked from sweat. A stomach rumble reminded him that he hadn't eaten lunch. He pulled his glove off with his teeth and rummaged in his pocket for his PB&J, but came up empty. No PB&J or pocketknife. His dad was going to be mad. Patrick Flint didn't believe in wasting food or money. But even his dad wasn't hard core enough to make him go without lunch. Or at least Perry hoped he wasn't.

He climbed to his feet and squinted at the lodge. A stream of people was walking away from it to the parking lot. Eyeballing the route, he noticed something funny. No one was on the lift. Maybe people were just eating, though. He looked around him on the ski run. There were no other skiers on the slope. That was even weirder.

He was all alone.

His stomach started feeling weird and jumpy. Something was wrong, and he needed to go find out what it was. He was half anxious to find out, half dreading it. He took a few steps to get his speed up. He didn't even think about his turns, just pointed his skis toward the bottom. It took less than a minute for him to get down, where he crash landed face first twenty feet from the lodge deck. His goggles got knocked off his face. When he pushed up on his hands, his right one was freezing cold. His glove. He'd forgotten to put it back on. After he wiped the snow out of his eyes, off of his face, and out of his goggles, he checked his pocket for his glove. It was definitely missing. It was somewhere way uphill from him, and there was no way he was walking back up there to get it.

If his dad wasn't mad about the sandwich and the pocketknife, he would for sure be pissed about the glove.

"Perry?"

His mom's friend, Mrs. Sibley, was standing beside him, holding up one of his skis. She was a teacher in town, but for the little kids. He'd never been in her class. Then he noticed her stomach. It was enormous. He tried not to look at it, but he couldn't keep his eyes away. Away and back. Away and back. Away and back, where they stayed.

"Hey, Mrs. Sibley. Where is everybody going?"

A funny look crossed her face, like she was sad about something. "There was, um, a bad accident. Your parents had to take someone to the hospital, and the ski resort owners decided it was best to just shut down for the rest of the day."

He stood up, scrunching his forehead. *My parents just left me?* "What about Trish?"

Mrs. Sibley tousled his hair. He forced himself not to duck away, even though he hated it when people rubbed his head like he was a baby. He was thirteen. Almost a man, if his growth spurt would just start. And his voice would get deeper. And his whiskers and chest hair would come in.

"She's with Henry. We're giving you guys a ride home."

"Okay." He took off his other ski, retrieved the one Mrs. Sibley was holding for him, and tucked both of them under an arm. "Who got hurt?"

The two of them started walking past the lodge together. Perry's feet clomped in the ski boots. Snow started building up on the bottom of them, and it was hard for him to keep his balance.

"Jeannie Renkin. Do you know her?"

"Does she go to my school?"

"No, she's older. Older than your parents."

He shook his head. He was glad it wasn't someone he knew.

Mrs. Sibley guided him toward the ski rental shop. "This way. We have to return your equipment."

"Okay." He reached a wooden walkway and stomped his feet to get the slick snow pack off his boots.

After they turned in his stuff, they headed for the parking lot. Perry saw Mr. Sibley standing by a truck talking to two men in deputy's uniforms. The men shook hands with Mr. Sibley, then they walked off.

"She found you, Perry. You all set?" Mr. Sibley clapped Perry on the shoulder.

That was more like it. A masculine gesture, from one man to another. He nodded at Mr. Sibley. "Yes, sir."

Mrs. Sibley rotated in a circle. She wobbled, a little like a Weeble. "Is Trish in the bathroom or something?"

Mr. Sibley opened the passenger side door and took her elbow. "I let her ride home with her boyfriend."

Mrs. Sibley froze. "We don't have permission to let her do that."

"She said it was okay with her parents. I thought that meant it would be fine."

Mrs. Sibley raised her eyebrows at Mr. Sibley. The look she gave him reminded Perry of how his mom looked at his dad sometimes. It meant, "That's what you get for thinking." Or so his mom had told him.

Perry opened the back door. As he climbed in, he realized Trish was going to get in trouble with their parents. She was mean to him most of the time, so he grinned. "Trish always *says* that."

"So, she's not allowed?" Mr. Sibley paused with his hand on the door frame.

"Most definitely not." Mrs. Sibley harrumphed. "I keep telling you, this parenting thing is harder than it looks."

Mr. Sibley shut the door. Through the window, Perry thought he looked like he was going to throw up.

CHAPTER SIX: STRIVE

BUFFALO, WYOMING
SATURDAY, MARCH 5, 1977, 12:10 P.M.

Patrick

P atrick jumped from the Suburban and ran beside Jeannie
Renkin's stretcher through the hospital parking lot. Two emergency medical techs were pushing the stretcher, one a woman who walked stiffly on the back of her feet, the other a man with a gray beard and tattoos showing above the top button of his shirt. Wes Braten, Patrick's tall, lean buddy and an x-ray tech for the hospital, appeared beside them.

"Where to, Doc?" the male EMT asked.

"Best to take her to the OR where I can evaluate the wound and see if we can stop the hemorrhaging. She's lost a lot of blood." To Wes, he said, "We started fluid resuscitation in the ambulance, but her blood pressure keeps dropping. Do we have any O negative packed red blood cells here?"

Wes fell in to help with the stretcher. "No, Doc, we don't. We used our last unit yesterday on an OB patient from Gillette."

That was very bad news. Emergency surgery, and fast, was Jeannie's only hope. If there was any hope at all, he had to find a way to stop the hemorrhaging before she bled to death. He prayed it was an external vein injury and not an injury to the internal jugular vein or carotid artery. He would be taking a huge risk clipping or tying off either of those vessels. But his intuition told him it was an arterial bleed.

He hoped operating on her wouldn't do more harm than good. Because that was his goal today and every day. First, do no harm—the common shorthand of the Hippocratic oath for physicians. Some days it was more challenging than others. He'd received the best in medical training in school at the University of Texas Southwestern and in his residency at Minneapolis General. He'd added the experience of close to a decade of emergency room and family practice. Yet each day made him more aware of what he and the rest of the medical community didn't know. They were barely past bleeding with leeches and administering strychnine as a remedy for heart and respiratory complaints in some ways. He shuddered. And to think he'd been poisoned with strychnine only a few months earlier. It had nearly killed him. So, every day he reminded himself to do no harm. And every day since he'd been forced to take a life, however unintentionally, to save his daughter, he reminded himself he was in the business of saving lives, not taking them.

In other words, do no harm. Full circle. *Jeannie will die without the surgery*, he reminded himself. Any harm from the surgery wouldn't be caused by him. It would be because she was marked for death by the killer's bullet.

The four of them hustled their patient through the door and the waiting room of the ER, quiet except for the squeak of a door in need of a good greasing and the buzz of fluorescent lights. They passed the receptionist—a new employee, fresh out of school and eager to do a good job.

"Has Judge Renkin arrived yet?" he asked her.

She stood as if coming to attention, but she didn't salute. "No, sir."

"Let me know when he arrives." He needed to talk to him about Jeannie's prognosis. It wouldn't be an easy conversation.

"Yes, sir."

"Thank you."

As they wheeled onward to the OR, Patrick's brain processed the information about Jeannie's condition like a mainframe computer. Unfortunately, besides the surgery, there was probably nothing more they could do to save her. She'd been bleeding so profusely from the get-go that he'd known her carotid or jugular had at least been nicked.

Another of his fears had been injury to her cervical spinal cord or lower brain stem, but, if the latter had taken the hit, she would have died before they'd ever left the ski resort. Honestly, he wasn't even sure how she'd lived as long as she had. Or how he'd kept the Suburban on the road on the way down the mountain. Certainly, he couldn't have covered the distance any faster. By the time they'd come upon and flagged down the ambulance from Buffalo, he'd made it fifteen miles from the ski resort, all the way to the turn-off to Hunter Corrals. Jeannie was already in shock by then. Susanne had taken the wheel of the Suburban, and they'd loaded Jeannie. He'd waved goodbye to his wife as the doors to the ambulance had shut behind him.

Patrick, Wes, and the EMTs arrived at the OR, where they were met by Kim, an efficient duty nurse who wore her gray hair in a low bun and looked like she could play fullback for the Wyoming Cowboys.

The female EMT started rattling off an update on Jeannie's condition. She was out of breath and talking fast. "Patient has endured a massive hemorrhage. Blood pressure is 70 over 30, pulse rate is 130. She's in shock, with diminished capillary refill, and has never regained consciousness."

Patrick already knew all of this, but he appreciated her following procedure, and it saved him from repeating the information himself. "Thank you."

"Of course."

They transferred Jeannie onto the OR table. The EMTs bade them farewell and headed back toward the exit with their stretcher.

Patrick issued orders to the OR staff. "Please get me the vascular tray. Hang another liter of Ringer's and run it wide open for now. She's in serious hypovolemic shock, and we have to try to support her blood pressure until I can stop the bleeding. We're going to try to repair or tie off the bleeding vessel."

Kim started hooking Jeannie up to the monitors and preparing her for surgery.

Patrick leaned over Jeannie, prying open one eyelid and shining a penlight into it. He lowered the light to his side. Suddenly, Jeannie's eyes opened, and her fingers clamped onto Patrick's wrist with an icy grip. Her lips opened and closed. She was trying to talk. He needed to go scrub in and take a few deep breaths. But he couldn't run out on her when she wanted to say something. She deserved a few moments of comfort. He leaned close to her, listening.

Her words sounded like she was gargling, but he understood enough combined with reading her lips to guess what she was saying. "My . . . husband."

He squeezed her hand. "He's on his way. You've been shot, Mrs. Renkin. We're taking you into surgery now to fix you up. Do you want me to bring him to see you?"

She closed her eyes. "No. His fault. His." Then her hand went limp, and her eyes rolled back in her head.

Kim broke in. "She's coding, Dr. Flint."

"Dammit." He placed his hands on her chest and started compressions. The surgery was a long shot as it was, but it was a no-go if she didn't have a heartbeat before they went to work on her.

Kim placed a bag-valve mask over Jeannie's nose and mouth, tilted her neck to open her airway, and begin ventilating her. Then, with her other hand, she pressed into the side of the neck opposite the wound, checking for a pulse.

Patrick stopped the chest compressions. "Anything?"

She shook her head.

Patrick restarted. So did Kim.

After another two minutes, they repeated the process. Compressions stopped, Kim palpated for a pulse.

Kim said, "Still nothing, Dr. Flint."

He nodded. They both kept going anyway. Sweat dripped down Patrick's forehead.

Wes said, "Let me take a turn, Doc."

Patrick made room for Wes. "How long?" he said to Kim.

"It's been nearly five minutes."

The two men continued trading off on compressions until Kim told them fifteen minutes had passed. By then, Jeannie's pupils were fixed and dilated and didn't respond to Kim's penlight.

Patrick lifted his hands from Jeannie's chest. "Time of death 12:30 p.m."

CHAPTER SEVEN: SNEAK

BUFFALO, WYOMING
SATURDAY, MARCH 5, 1977, 7:30 P.M.

Trish

Trish wrapped her arms around herself. It was cold outside the theater where she was playing hooky from *Rocky*, the movie she'd told her parents she was going to see with her best friend Marcy, when what she was really planning to do was hang out with Brandon. They did this every Saturday night. They would park one street over, sing along to the songs on the radio in his truck, and steal kisses. He would try for more, she would fend him off. She couldn't believe her parents hadn't figured it out yet. Or that they'd let her go out at all after her mom had blown a gasket over Trish riding home from Meadowlark with Brandon.

She blew on her hands and stomped her feet. What had happened to the stupid groundhog seeing his shadow and the short winter it was supposed to mean? It had been nothing but cold here in Buffalo since *forever*. October or November at least. If Brandon didn't show up soon, she was going to turn into a human popsicle.

She was starting to get concerned about him. He was never late. They always timed their meet-up so people weren't coming in or out of the theater—after the feature started, plus a few extra minutes to dodge the latecomers. That way no one would tattle to their parents. If she stayed outside much longer, someone arriving early for the next movie was going to see her.

After another five minutes freezing her tush off, she decided to hide out in the theater bathroom and read. Her parents had given her *Roll of Thunder, Hear My Cry* for Christmas, and she was just now getting to it. Between basketball, school, Brandon, friends, and her horse Goldie, she'd been busy. But as she pulled the door to the theater open, she heard the distinctive thumping noise of Brandon's truck. He needed a new muffler, but he didn't have the money. The truck was not only loud, it stunk like gasoline all the time, too. Brandon suspected the carburetor was behind the odor. That cost money to fix, too. He planned to get a job after basketball season ended. Then, after he'd fixed up his truck, he was going to take her out to dinner at a real restaurant in Sheridan, where no one would recognize them.

Releasing the door, she tried to contain her goofy grin. The brown truck bounced over a pothole and into the parking lot. When the street-light backlit the truck cab, she frowned. There were two heads inside it. Who was with Brandon?

Brandon parked and hopped out. He loped over and put his arms around her waist. He swung her in a circle then kissed her right on the lips, in public. "Hey, baby. I have a surprise."

Her smile broke through her best efforts. Brandon was way cooler than anyone else at her school. Big city cool. "A good one or a bad one?"

"Like, good, I think." He released her and turned toward his truck.

A tall boy, thicker than Brandon and with dark, straight hair, walked over from the passenger side. Trish's mouth went dry. It was Brandon's cousin Ben Jones, who she'd thought was still in juvie. She'd just been with Brandon that afternoon, and he hadn't mentioned anything about Ben getting out.

The last time she'd seen Ben was at his sentencing. She'd given a statement on his behalf, explaining that when he'd helped kidnap her and later buried a man on the mountain, it was only because he was forced into it by his lunatic father and Uncle Billy. At the time, she'd thought she was doing the right thing, even though her parents hadn't agreed. Since then, she'd started to see their side of things. Maybe someone who grew up used to kidnapping and murder needed some time locked up where he could learn right from wrong.

Now, seeing him out of custody, she was nervous. Not just because he had helped kidnap her, but because *her* dad had killed *his* dad during her rescue. If she were him, she'd hold a grudge against the Flints.

It took all she had not to turn and run into the theater and call her parents to pick her up.

"Hey, Trish," Ben said. He pushed his hair back, and she saw a scar on his forehead. It was right where her dad had clobbered him with a gun during her rescue.

She didn't know what to say. "Hey." She bit the inside of her lip. "Um, Brandon, can I talk to you for a minute?" She backed toward the theater door.

The two boys exchanged a look, then Brandon followed her.

"Que pasa?" He hunched his shoulders against the cold.

She whispered, "What is he doing here?"

"He got out."

"How? When?"

"He showed up at our place tonight. Isn't that sick? His lawyer got him early release, you know."

"Why isn't he with his mom?"

"She's bad news. That's why he was living with us, like, before. And now he's back. So boss."

Boss wasn't how Trish would describe it. "Did you know about this?"

"Not until this afternoon."

Trish shot a quick glance at Ben. He was tying the laces on his Converse high tops. "He hates me."

"Mellow out. He thinks you're cool."

"Well, he hates my dad then."

Brandon didn't reply.

"Is this your surprise for me?"

"Um, it wasn't really *for* you, but, yeah, like, this is the surprise."

Hot tears welled up in the corners of Trish's eyes. Unexpected, surprising tears that cooled immediately, then rolled down her face in an icy trail. "Well, it's *not* a good one."

He reached for her, trying to pull her into a hug. "Don't be such a spaz."

She made her body stiff and didn't return the hug. "So, right now, our time—it's the three of us?"

He released her and stepped back. "Um, yeah. You got a problem with that?"

"Um, yeah." Trish heard her tone and knew instantly Brandon wasn't going to like it.

His voice turned hard. "I told you when we got back together that things were going to be different, you know. Catch my drift?"

The part of Trish that was angry wrestled with the part of her that was afraid of losing Brandon. She managed to say, "I'm sorry," but her heart wasn't in it.

An old VW van entered the parking lot. Trish stepped into the shadows. They'd been out there too long.

"Whatever. I'm gonna cut out." Brandon stepped away from her.

Trish panicked. The part of her afraid of losing him suddenly won out. Tears sprang into her eyes. "Wait. I'm sorry. I really am."

The van jerked to a stop between Ben and Brandon. A man with stringy hair and a droopy moustache was driving. Trish had never seen him before. But she definitely recognized the passenger. Brandon's mother, Donna Lewis. She rolled down the passenger window and leaned her head out in a cloud of smoke. As mean as the woman was, Trish had to admit she was pretty. She had hair like Dolly Parton, and a body nearly that amazing, too.

"Stay away from that girl, Brandon." Her voice was raspy, like she'd smoked a million cigarettes in her life. Which she probably had.

Brandon held his hands up. "Chill, Mom. We ran into each other."

Trish swiped at her nearly frozen tears. "I was just going."

Mrs. Lewis wagged her finger at Trish. "Tell your parents that your family wasn't able to keep Ben locked up, and they won't be ruining my brother's life either."

From inside the car, Trish heard the man laugh. He sounded like a hyena.

Mrs. Lewis's brothers were bad people, and Billy Kemecke had done horrible things. He deserved to be punished. It wasn't Trish's or her mom's fault that he got caught, and if they didn't testify, then what would happen? Kemecke might not be convicted. Trish felt a responsibility to testify, and, whether she wanted to or not, she had to do it. She *would* do it.

Trish's emotions were amped up. She was worried about Ben's arrival, hurt by how Brandon had treated her, and so tired of Mrs. Lewis's attitude and the things the woman said to her. So tired of it. She blurted out, "You can't keep us from testifying." She wanted to clap a hand over her mouth as soon as she said it, but it was too late to do any good anyway. Her words were already out there.

Mrs. Lewis smirked at her. "We'll just see about that." Then she turned to the driver. "Get me out of here, Stamey."

The van peeled out of the parking lot. Brandon and Ben drove away after it. Trish was left standing alone, with Mrs. Lewis's threat ringing in her head.

CHAPTER EIGHT: GOSSIP

Susanne

Susanne walked arm-in-arm with Vangie from the sanctuary down the hall past the Sunday school classrooms toward the community room in the First United Methodist Church of Buffalo. It was a small church, modest and spartan. Warm and welcoming. The cross in the nave was natural wood, the walls unadorned. The exterior was plain white siding. While it wasn't a replacement for her church back in Texas, she'd learned to love it and the congregation. It was important to her to have a church home. The kids needed it. She needed it.

Henry turned to her and Vangie from the doorway of the adult room. "Have a doughnut for me, ladies."

Henry was teaching a series on handling hardship. Ranchers certainly learned about that honestly, and with Vangie's series of miscarriages, the couple had faced more than their share of heartache. Susanne had tried to talk Patrick into coming to the series, without any success. Patrick wasn't very religious, at least with respect to church attendance. He prayed daily, and he was a better Christian than many of the regular attendees. But with all the time he spent on middle of the night callouts to the hospital, he refused to sacrifice any chance to sleep in or catch up on his endless list of projects around their new house. She had learned to be satisfied that he kept his promise to attend with the family every Christmas and Easter.

Susanne smiled at Henry. "Of course."

He motioned for them to stop, and they stepped through the doorway of his classroom. "Did you hear Judge Ellis in Sheridan died last night? Max just told me." Susanne knew the Max he was referring to was Max Alexandrov, the new attorney for Johnson county.

Vangie said, "He was so young. Only in his forties! And he took care of himself."

Susanne had heard that Ellis was into jogging, like Patrick had been in the last year.

Henry lowered his voice. "He was found in his Bronco, inside his garage, with the engine running."

"Suicide?" Susanne was aghast.

Vangie's face looked stricken. She touched her belly. "But he loved his wife and kids. He was successful. He always seemed confident. What could have possibly been wrong?"

Susanne pursed her lips, disturbed by a thought. "He had the Kemecke trial in his court, didn't he?" Where she and Trish were set to testify.

Henry tapped a finger on his lips. "Had to. He's the county district court judge for Sheridan."

Susanne remembered well the controversy over jurisdiction in the Kemecke case in the first place. With crimes committed in Big Horn, Sheridan, and their own Johnson county, she and Patrick had sweated that one out. They had been immensely relieved when it was first assigned to Big Horn. Then the trial had been moved to Sheridan since the judge in Big Horn county was the father of the deputy Kemecke killed in his escape from custody. That was still better than Johnson county, since the district court for Johnson was in Buffalo—too close to home in many ways. Would Judge Ellis's death mean the trial would move to Buffalo after all? Judge Renkin would need time to grieve Jeannie's death. That could mean a postponement. The uncertainty gnawed at her.

Henry cocked his head. "Are you okay, Susanne?"

She waggled her hand. "Yes. Lost in thought for a moment."

He dipped over from the waist. "Well, ladies, I have to do some last minute preparations for my class. Have fun."

Vangie blew him a kiss from her fingertips. "See you in a few minutes."

As the women reentered the hallway, Susanne changed the subject, eager to think happier thoughts. "Are you having any Braxton Hicks contractions yet?" She'd had the false labor contractions herself for days before she delivered each of her kids. They were nothing to worry about. Just a sign that a woman's body was getting ready for the big event.

Vangie nodded. "Starting to. When I told Henry about them, he said not to worry. He's helped dogs, cats, cows, horses, donkeys, and sheep deliver. That he's short-handed at the ranch, but he can fit me in if he has to."

Susanne's jaw dropped. "He did not."

"He did. But remember, this is the same man that let Trish convince him it was okay for her to leave with Brandon yesterday. He's got a big heart, but he makes some dumb decisions." Vangie grimaced. "I'm so sorry about that."

"Don't worry about it. She's pulled one over on us a few times ,too."

Vangie leaned her head against Susanne's shoulder. "But what if we have a girl? Henry will be the most inept girl-father ever."

"Right in line behind Patrick. Trish has him wrapped around her little finger."

Vangie laughed.

"But even Patrick agrees with me that Trish's relationship with Brandon is a disaster. Especially now, with the trial coming up."

The two friends entered the community room. On one end was an elevated platform used for children's programs. Snacks and coffee were on a credenza at the other end. The center of the room was filled with folding tables and chairs. The coffee smelled burned, but Susanne and Vangie beelined for it anyway, passing by the doughnuts.

"Well, she looks gorgeous as usual." Vangie cut her eyes toward Barb Lamkin, the Buffalo High girls' basketball and volleyball coach. She was nearly six-feet tall, with wavy auburn hair and a posterior Susanne would have died for. All the women in Susanne's family were curvy, especially in the rear. Barb had lean hips and a flat bottom. Susanne knew she couldn't fight genetics. However, Barb also probably exercised a lot more than Susanne. She'd played basketball at the University of Wyoming back in the days of six-on-six. Trish idolized her. Not that it did her any good. Trish warmed the bench for the junior varsity. The poor girl seemed to take after Susanne when it came to athletic ability.

Barb was hugging a shorter woman with light-brown hair pulled back in a clip, large eyeglasses, and a sweater set and skirt that looked prim and old-fashioned. Susanne hadn't seen her before. She must be a visitor. She and Barb separated, and she left.

Susanne studied Barb. Had she put on some weight? If so, it just made her chest look bigger and her angular face softer. Susanne sighed and filled a Styrofoam cup with coffee. "I hate her."

"I know. Me, too. Except that she's so nice. And successful. I mean, her girls did win state last year."

The things to like were exactly why Susanne hated her. She struggled to be more charitable and latched on to a thought. "She *is* unmarried in her thirties. I'm sure that's hard."

Barb walked up behind them. "Hello, Susanne, Vangie."

They shared a wide-eyed look. "Hello," they chorused.

Had she heard them talking about her? Susanne felt a twinge of guilt. She hurried to cover up any awkwardness, just in case. She had been raised Southern, after all, and there was nothing worse than making other people uncomfortable, except for wearing white shoes after Labor Day. "Good luck next weekend at the state tournament. Are the girls excited?"

Barb filled her own cup of coffee. If she'd overheard them, she didn't give any sign of it. "Pretty much. It ranks slightly below being asked to prom and picking out a dress, but higher than fly fishing. If I can just keep their attention for one more week, we have a shot at it. But I'm not as optimistic as I was last year."

"Well, good luck, anyway," Vangie said. "The community is very proud of them and you."

"Are you girls getting a doughnut?" Barb turned back and eyed the table with the food.

A doughnut? Susanne had been planning on having more than one.

Vangie rested her hand on the bulge of her stomach. "I only have a few more weeks to eat for two, so, of course I am."

Susanne followed Vangie to the snack table. Vangie took a chocolate covered glazed. Susanne willed her to take a second one, but she didn't, so Susanne chose only a plain glazed. Barb walked with them to a round table, without a doughnut for herself.

"Aren't you getting one?" Susanne asked.

"I can't eat them. They go straight to my backside. My boyfriend doesn't like it."

Susanne wondered who the boyfriend was—she hadn't heard about Barb dating anyone. She really *did* hate her. But Patrick loved Susanne's figure, *and* she got to enjoy a doughnut, while Barb didn't. She bit into the glazed confection and chewed slowly, making sure to telegraph exactly how much she enjoyed it.

While Susanne and Vangie were chewing, Barb said, "Did you hear Jeannie Renkin was shot yesterday?"

Susanne set her doughnut on a napkin. "We were there. My husband Patrick and I drove her down the mountain."

Barb's green eyes widened. Susanne thought her blue eye shadow was a little much for church. Then she chastised herself. What was it about this woman that was making her act this way, even if only in her head?

Barb said, "Did you see who shot her?"

Susanne pointed at Vangie. "The Sibleys were there, too. And our kids. It was awful. But no one saw the shooter." Then she smiled at her pregnant friend. "I assume Perry didn't see anything. He went straight to his slumber party as soon as you brought him home. We haven't seen him since I dropped him off."

Vangie was chewing. She covered her mouth. "He didn't say anything. But . . ."

"What?"

"We didn't actually tell him what happened. Just said there'd been an accident. I know someone's probably told him by now, but it just felt *wrong* to tell a child something so horrible."

"Don't let him hear you call him a child." Susanne winked. "Ever since his thirteenth birthday, he has insisted I call him a 'young man' or a 'teen.' He says he's sick and tired of being treated like a baby."

"Ah, he's such a sweetie."

"Also a forbidden term."

All three women laughed.

Barb's face grew serious. "I don't mind telling you that as a single woman, this has me pretty rattled. Who would kill Jeannie, and does this mean the rest of us aren't safe either?"

Susanne picked her doughnut up and poised it at her lips. "Maybe it was a poacher. And now he's afraid to come forward because someone died." She took another bite of doughnut and held it in her mouth, letting the sugar dissolve into her tongue. *Delectable.*

Vangie nodded. "Or, who knows? Maybe they weren't aiming at Jeannie. Or even anyone."

Barb looked around, then leaned in and lowered her voice. "Well, that would make more sense. Who would want to hurt a nice lady like Mrs. Renkin? Now, her husband is a different story. I'll bet he's made a lot of enemies as a judge."

As Jeannie's neighbor, Susanne wouldn't have described her as nice, but she took Barb's point.

Vangie licked chocolate from her fingers. "Or even as an attorney. Everyone hates attorneys."

Barb smiled slyly. "I heard he's thinking about running for the U.S. Senate. I wonder if the shooting has something to do with that."

Susanne's eyebrows shot up. Their neighbor was running for Senator? That was big news.

Vangie pushed her chair back. "Well, whoever it is, I'm sure the sheriff will figure it out."

Susanne had a chilling thought. The Kemecke capital murder trial—it was presumably now in Judge Renkin's court. What if the judge in Sheridan had been *murdered* to keep him from presiding over the Kemecke trial? If so, Jeannie's shooting could be related to the trial as well. Kemecke and his family were bad news and certainly no strangers to violence.

Could the man who'd held her hostage and kidnapped her daughter be behind two new murders? And, if so, who else was in his line of fire? She suddenly felt very vulnerable and exposed.

And concerned about her family, especially Trish.

CHAPTER NINE: VIEW

Patrick

When he climbed out of the Suburban, the sun warmed Patrick's face and the glare made him squint. He wished he'd worn sunglasses, but he'd be inside soon enough. He and Susanne were attending the viewing for Jeannie Renkin at Yardley Funeral Home.

He came around the front of the vehicle and took his wife's hand. She flashed him a subdued smile. He understood. It was how he felt, too. He and Susanne had become invested in Jeannie's survival during her final hours. The fact that they weren't friendly with her before didn't matter. There was sorrow for them in her death, in their inability to save her, as there was anytime dying brushed too close to living. He felt it all the time, but more keenly because of sharing the experience with his wife. And, yet, there was also warm sunshine today and her hand in his. Life went on, with reasons for smiling, even in the midst of death.

A few steps later, mud splashed on the hem of his pants. He'd veered off the sidewalk. Melt was the price to pay for spring warmth, as would be ice tomorrow morning. He brushed at the splatter, mostly smearing it, and looked around. Even though the Flints had lived in Buffalo two years now, this was his first visit to the funeral home. It was in a not-too-large old house on a quiet residential street. Wooden siding. White trim. Paint in need of a refresh, but not direly so. A pair of mature red maples that would provide shade and brilliant color once the leaves came back in. The type of place that brought to mind a family crowded around a groaning Thanksgiving table. Or kids playing freeze tag at dusk while their fathers grilled steaks in the backyard and drank the trendy tequila sunrises their wives forced on them when they'd rather be drinking Coors. It wasn't the kind of place that made him think of burial preparations and display. But he guessed that was kind of the point—that funeral homes should be homey. This one succeeded.

He opened the front door and moved aside for Susanne to enter first, his fingers resting in the small of her back. Once they were inside, he took her hand and slipped ahead of her to part the crowd. The parlor was so packed that he couldn't see the walls or furniture. Even the artwork was obscured, except for a painting of a mountain lion fighting off two hunting dogs, hanging above the fireplace mantel. Other than that, the room was just bodies crammed together, giving off humidity and an odor of mingled sweat, molasses, and livestock. They were in ranching country after all.

He stopped and felt Susanne's gaze on his profile.

She said, "You look like you've contracted a bad case of mange."

He rubbed his jaw. The beard was patchy, he'd admit. And itchy, which he wouldn't.

She cocked her head. "How can you have more hair on your neck than your face?"

"Just how I like it."

"As soon as winter is officially over, I am going to take great joy in assisting in your shedding process."

He winked. "Only ninety frost-free days a year here."

"If you're suggesting that you plan to attempt facial hair nine months out of twelve, I'd advise you to consider its impact on your love life."

"Ouch," he said, holding back a chuckle.

She squeezed his hand.

They continued across the room toward a somber throng in the back near Jeannie's open casket. Patrick and Susanne stopped at it, and together they gazed at their former neighbor. The funeral home had done a decent job with her. Her makeup was thick, like it was spackled on. It probably was, to cover the pallor of death. Her gray hair looked stiffly coiffed and darker than it had a few days before. A voluminous pink scarf wound around her high-necked white blouse, covering her neck wounds. The tails of the scarf were artfully arranged against a soft black cardigan. There was no sign of the trauma she'd endured in the last hour of her life.

At the head of the casket, Judge Renkin was holding court with a cluster of men in cowboy boots and western suits. They varied by height, girth, and how much hair they had on their heads, but not much else.

"Do you want to join them for a moment and pay our respects to the judge?" Patrick asked.

"If it's all the same, I'd rather let you do that, and I'll go talk to that group of ladies." Susanne nodded toward three women a few feet away. "I think that's his daughter, talking to Trish's basketball coach."

"Sounds like a good plan." He pecked her on the cheek. "Then we can get out of here. I don't like to think too long about burying wives."

She smiled up at him. "I'm glad to hear that. Ten minutes?"

"If that long."

After Susanne left, Patrick walked with his hand extended to Judge Renkin. "Judge. My condolences."

Renkin clasped Patrick's hand and shook it. The judge's palms were smooth and his nails clipped. He lowered his head. "Thank you for that, and for what you did to try to save my dear, sweet Jeannie. I'm so torn up about her death. Gentlemen, do you all know Dr. Patrick Flint?"

Patrick wondered just how torn up the judge was. He hadn't ridden to the hospital with his wife or made an appearance there in her final minutes. In fact, it was a full hour after she'd died when he'd finally shown up. Patrick had broken the news to him, and the dry-eyed, calm-voiced judge had nodded and said, "I'm sure you did all you could."

But Patrick didn't reveal his thoughts.

The men exchanged rough, scratchy handshakes with him. More than one cheek bulged with chewing tobacco, and hat marks ringed all their hairlines. It was like a who's who convention for the town. The mayor, the county attorney, the county judge, and a few additional elected officials. Patrick had even glimpsed the sheriff across the room a moment before.

Patrick introduced himself to the one man in the group whom he didn't recognize. "Patrick Flint."

"Shep Rawlins." The silver-haired newcomer gave Patrick a onceover that morphed into a toothy grin and longer-than-comfortable contact with ice-blue eyes. His jacket was a better cut, his hair style more expensive, his teeth whiter and straighter, and his face slightly more handsome than those of the other men. His name sounded familiar, but Patrick couldn't place him.

"Where's that lovely wife of yours, Dr. Flint?" the judge asked.

Patrick gestured toward Susanne. "Visiting with some of the ladies." A young woman in boots and a modest yellow dress was hurrying toward the group Susanne had joined. From the woman's attire to her gait to a funny waddle in her behind, she reminded him of a duck. He turned back toward Renkin, stifling amusement.

The judge scowled so quickly Patrick wondered if he'd imagined it. "Oh, yes. There she is. Please give her my best."

"I will."

Renkin angled his body to include the rest of his cronies. "The coroner hasn't issued a report on Judge Ellis's death yet. What are your thoughts, Max?"

Johnson County Attorney Max Alexandrov crossed his arms over his sports jacket. His young wife had recently run back to her family on the east coast, and he still exuded a forlorn air. He pushed back his thinning light hair. When he answered, it was in the slightest of Russian accents, as if he had grown up in a household with Russian speakers. "Too early to say. Right now they're calling it suicide by carbon monoxide poisoning."

Renkin's voice boomed. "What are the odds that the judge set to hear the Kemecke case died by supposed suicide, and, on the same day, the wife of the judge who gets the case when Ellis dies was shot and killed, too? Suicide is bollocks, I say. Someone could have knocked Ellis out. Or drugged him."

"Might be related. Might not. They'll be sending off a blood sample for toxicology. That'll take a week or more, but, if it was murder, they'll figure it out."

"Any leads on who shot my Jeannie?"

"Sheriff Westbury said I'll be the first to know. You'll be the second."

"Either way, the trial is coming to my court."

Buffalo Mayor Martin Ochoa leaned on his crutches, which he was using while his broken leg mended. He was a short, portly man with a curled mustache who had first been elected right after the Flints moved to Buffalo. He'd risen from humble beginnings. His father was a Basque sheepherder without two nickels to rub together. Patrick had voted for him. "I don't like it. Billy Kemecke is poison to this town. Can you refuse the case, Harold? No one would blame you for taking time to grieve Jeannie's death."

Shep Rawlins nodded. "I need you alive, Renkin. You're in year five of six of your term. It's time to be thinking about your transition."

Transition? Patrick had no idea what the new guy was talking about. He tried not to act like an outsider to the conversation, but he wasn't in politics, nor did he enjoy talking about it. Maybe he just needed to collect Susanne and get gone.

The judge pulled a pamphlet from his back pocket, lifting the edge of his suit coat. The pamphlet said YARDLEY FUNERAL HOME on the cover. He tapped it in his left palm, lips pursed. "I appreciate that, Governor Rawlins." *The governor of the state of Wyoming. Of course, that's why his name was familiar.* "I intend to stick around and pursue our plans." He winked. "But a good judge—one the people can count on —doesn't unduly delay justice over personal issues. I like to think I'm that kind of judge." He paused theatrically. "And I know my Jeannie would understand."

Patrick felt a current of electricity course through the men. He'd heard rumors of Renkin running for the U.S. Senate from Susanne. Could those be the plans the judge was referring to?

The governor's face creased with a concern that didn't reach his eyes. "I appreciate your sense of honor and duty. Those are important qualities in a public servant, appointed or elected. And of course, with a case this high profile, the public will definitely take note of your sacrifice. But your safety . . ."

Johnson County Sheriff Cliff Westbury stuck his head into the group. In a surprisingly soft-spoken voice, he said, "Harold, I'm on my way out. My condolences again." The sheriff stood a good three inches taller than Renkin and outweighed him by fifty pounds or more, a lot of it through the midsection.

Renkin took Westbury's hand and held it, while maintaining eye contact with the governor a moment longer. "I'll be extra vigilant, you can be sure of that, Governor." He turned to Westbury. "Sheriff, can you help us keep the court safe until the Kemecke trial is over?"

Westbury clapped the judge on the shoulder. "Already working on it, including 'round the clock protection for you."

The men released each other.

"Thank you, Sheriff."

The sheriff touched two fingers to his forehead and headed for the door.

Rawlins frowned. "At least take the rest of the week off. From everything and, um, everyone. I think the people would expect that. Even demand it."

Renkin made a *hmmm* sound. "I can see how they would." He started nodding. "Yes. I'll do just that."

"The state would be happy to pay for private security as well," the governor said. "Not just because of Ellis and your wife. It's the first death penalty case in Wyoming since the U.S. Supreme Court reversed their ban on them. We could have rested on our laurels with Kemecke—he was never getting out of jail again after he escaped custody—but if ever a man deserved a shot at lethal injection, it's him. And you're well known for your 'hang 'em high' point of view.'" Several of the men chuckled. "You and the trial will attract attention, some of it unwanted. As will those *plans*."

"Thank you, Shep." The judge turned to Patrick. "I'm sure your family will appreciate getting this trial over with. Especially your wife and daughter."

Patrick stroked his whiskers. "They'd be happier if they didn't have to testify at all." It seemed to Patrick like nothing good could come of bringing Kemecke back to Buffalo, for the Flints or the town.

"Unfortunately, Kemecke wouldn't accept a deal for life in prison. This one is going the distance, whatever the cost."

Renkin's words hit Patrick's gut like a sucker punch. He twisted his wedding ring back and forth. Before he could muster a reply, an unfamiliar man joined them. He was outfitted like a city slicker. The judge stiffened and shifted so his back was to him. Patrick was curious about him, but not enough to stay and find out who he was. It was time to go. He offered his farewells to the judge and the other men, then headed for Susanne, mumbling to himself and worrying about the Kemecke trial and the roles his wife and daughter would play.

The last words of the judge still echoed in his mind. "Whatever the cost."

That cost is exactly what I'm afraid of.

CHAPTER TEN: CONFESS

Perry

Perry leaned into the wind as he trailed behind his parents, who were holding hands in front of God and everybody even though they knew it embarrassed him. They were walking in from the parking lot back to the basketball arena. The whole family had taken a break from the state tournament to go to McDonald's for lunch. Since they rarely ate out, Perry had made the most of it. A quarter pounder with cheese, a chocolate milkshake, and a large order of Fat Freds, known as French fries to anyone outside his crazy family.

"Are you sure you want to eat that much, shrimp?" Trish had said. She'd ordered a fish sandwich and water.

Perry straightened his posture. "I've grown an inch and put on ten pounds since the start of the school year."

"All in your butt."

He glared at her. "That's muscle. Dad said so."

Thank goodness, Trish had left lunch early and gotten a ride back to the arena with one of her friends. He couldn't stand listening to her one more second whining about missing all the basketball she'd come to see, when he knew for a fact the only thing she was worried about seeing was *Brandon*.

He didn't know why she had to be such a bad sport and ruin everything. His parents had just been trying to cheer Trish and him up by taking them out to eat. Trish, because the Buffalo teams had lost in the opening round, and because Brandon had sprained his ankle. Their dad was the doctor for the Buffalo teams during the tournament, so he'd wrapped it up. It didn't look like Brandon would be able to play in the consolation round. Perry, because his parents hadn't let him bring a friend with him to the tournament. Not that he whined about it all the time like Trish did, but there was *so* much sitting around and *so* many games. It was no fun when his teams were losing, either.

The truth was he didn't even like basketball very much. He was even worse at it than Trish was, and that was saying something. He'd overheard his dad tell his mom that Trish would be good if only she was quick . . . or coordinated . . . or could jump higher than two inches off the ground. Plus, it was one of the last weekends of the year the ski slopes would be open. As cold as it was in Laramie, he'd bet it was even colder at Meadowlark.

He'd begged to stay and ski, but his parents had turned him down flat.

He shivered and ducked his head, hurrying to catch up with his parents. As they neared the doors to the arena, he saw a flash of white camo in his side vision. It reminded him of the person on the snowmobile at the ski mountain. His stomach lurched, and he turned for a better look. The sidewalk was crowded with people, and all he could see was the pattern of the white camo jacket and, bouncing along above it, a white wool cap.

"That's just like the person I saw back in the forest at the ski resort," he said, mostly to himself but out loud.

His mom heard him, and she stopped. His dad kept walking. "What person?" She gave Perry a weird look, which she did a *lot* lately.

"When I was late coming down the mountain at the ski resort because I went off-trail through the trees and then had to walk a long way uphill back."

"Not when. What *person*? You didn't mention a person when you told me why it took you so long to get down."

"Huh. Well, I saw someone on a snowmobile."

Susanne raised her voice. "Patrick, come here." His dad had made it to the doors, where he was waiting. After he'd walked back over to them, his mom said, "Perry, repeat that for your dad."

"I was late coming down the mountain at the ski resort because I was off-trail in the trees, and I had to walk uphill—"

"The other part."

"I'm getting there, Mom." Perry had always thought Trish was rude when she rolled her eyes at people, but right then he had an urge to roll his at his mom. Then he felt guilty, so, instead, he tried to sound extra cooperative. "I saw someone on a big snowmobile back in the woods."

His parents looked at each other. His mom seemed worried, and his dad made an expression like he'd just taken a big bite of leftover cabbage that had gone bad. Perry had seen him do that once, so he knew exactly what it looked like.

Patrick moved their threesome out of the flow of foot traffic. "Who was it?"

Perry shrugged. "I don't know."

"Man or woman?"

"I couldn't tell."

"Think, Perry. Short, tall? Hair color?"

"Um, medium-height. I couldn't see any hair."

"Did anything else stand out?"

"Why are you asking me all these questions?"

And then it hit him. His parents and the Sibleys had tried to pretend that the ski resort was closed because of an accident, but a shooting and an accident aren't exactly the same thing. The shooting had been all over the news. Everyone at school was talking about it. His friends thought it was cool that he was there. Or almost there, since he'd been stuck up in the woods. And now his parents were asking him questions about it, because *they thought the person he saw might be the one who shot the judge's wife.* That had to be it.

His dad's lips were moving in an angry way, but no sound was coming out. Perry gave him a second for his brain and mouth to sync back up.

His ears felt hot. "Do you think I saw the murderer?"

His mom put an arm around him. "I'm sure you didn't, but maybe that person saw something that would help the authorities catch the killer."

His dad started firing questions at him so fast that it made his ears even hotter.

Perry closed his eyes, trying to remember. He answered his dad the best he could, but he stumbled when he got to the part about losing his pocketknife. "I, um, I'm sorry." He'd lost a glove, too, but he left that part out.

But his dad didn't get mad about the pocketknife. He rubbed at his beard. It was a really wimpy beard. Perry wished he would shave it off. Or just not make Perry be seen in public with him. "We need to take you in to tell someone in the sheriff's office about this when we get back to Buffalo." He looked at his wristwatch. "I'm due inside for the boys' game." He walked off fast, then turned for a second. "We'll talk about that pocketknife later."

Rats. Perry thought he'd gotten off easy about the knife for a minute.

"I need to check on Trish," his mom said. "Before she and Brandon do something dumb and Donna Lewis comes after us again."

Perry widened his eyes at her, trying to look innocent. "Yeah, I think she was going to find him before the game." He actually had no idea if she'd planned that or not. He just liked it better when his parents were grilling Trish instead of him.

Susanne growled, and she hustled Perry inside. His legs felt heavy as he climbed the bleachers, because of the ankle weights he'd strapped on that morning. If he was ever going to be a downhill racer, his legs needed to be stronger. He and his mom sidled down a row and took a seat. It seemed like everyone he knew from Buffalo had come to Laramie, all except for his friends.

His mom stood and scanned the stands for Trish. Perry searched, too, conscious of the squeak of sneakers on the hardwood floor, the smell of buttery popcorn, and a cold breeze coming from somewhere above him. When he turned to look for the source of the air—an open window at the top of the stands—he saw Trish sitting with the girls' varsity basketball team, near the window. They had won their consolation round game that morning, so he knew they had to play again later in the day. He was surprised Trish wasn't with Brandon. Where was he? He glanced down toward the gymnasium floor. Even though he was hurt, Brandon was with his team. He was in a track suit, sitting on the first row of the bleachers, watching them warm up.

Perry was about to tell his mom where Trish was, when he saw something that made his heart pound like a jackhammer. A tall, dark-headed kid was right behind Brandon. Perry had seen him before, two times. The first time was up in the Bighorn Mountains, in Cloud Peak

Wilderness, burying a man in the dark. The second time was in a picture with a newspaper article about his sister's kidnapping ordeal. He even knew his name. Ben Jones.

Wasn't he supposed to be locked up?

Ben wasn't watching the team. He was facing up into the stands, right at Perry. At first, Perry thought Ben was staring at him. Then he realized Ben was staring *past* him. Perry turned in his seat, following Ben's gaze.

Trish was up there. Was Ben staring at Trish? He needed to tell somebody.

He stole a glance at his mom. Someone had taken a seat beside her, and they were yakking. He knew it would be rude to interrupt her, and he couldn't talk to his dad, because he was on the court with the boys' coach. Perry started bouncing his knee.

His mom was talking in a happy camper voice. "Patrick told me that Governor Rawlins and Judge Renkin were talking about their secret plans for Renkin's future the other day. I'll bet it was about that Senate campaign you told me about."

"I'm not surprised," the woman replied. He couldn't see who she was, but she didn't sound like anyone he knew.

Susanne turned to Perry and whispered, "You're bouncing the entire bleachers. Stop it."

He froze, feeling like a baby.

Susanne leaned back toward the other woman. "I've been meaning to ask you, if it's not too personal. At church, you mentioned a boyfriend. Is he someone I know?"

The woman laughed. "We're keeping it under wraps for now. There's quite an age difference between us, and, as a coach, I have to be sensitive to parents' perceptions. But I think you'll recognize his name when we go public."

Boring lady stuff. He couldn't wait any longer. "Um, Mom?" He tapped her shoulder.

She held up a hand. "Just a second."

"It's okay." The woman his mom was talking to leaned around her and smiled at him. "Hi, Perry."

Perry drew in a whistley breath he hoped she couldn't hear. "Hi, Coach Lamkin." All the boys in his class thought Coach Lamkin was super foxy. She was pretty, with her long red hair and green eyes, but also kind of scary. Tall and strong and . . . something he couldn't put his finger on that gave him funny fluttery feelings in his belly. His favorite teacher, Ms. Tavejie, was prettier and a lot nicer. Back when he was little, he'd had a crush on Ms. Tavejie. Now, he realized she'd probably never like him back. Not in *that* way. But he still liked looking at her.

The coach pointed. "What is that you have around your ankles?"

Perry muttered, "Ankle weights." *How embarrassing.*

She nodded approvingly. "Nice. Are you going to play basketball next year?"

"I'm not sure. I'm not very good."

"That's okay. You'll get better if you practice." She kept her gaze locked on his.

It made him nervous, and he blurted out, "I want to ski."

"Oh?"

He couldn't believe he'd said it, but it was true. "I want to be the next Andy Mill."

"You know he grew up here, right?"

"Here, in Wyoming?" Perry's voice squeaked, and he wanted to crawl under the bleachers.

"Here, in Laramie. At least for a few years. I'm from here, and I used to babysit him."

"Really?" Perry no longer cared that he was squeaking.

"Really."

"That must have been so cool."

She laughed. "He wasn't famous then. He was just an energetic boy who didn't want to go to bed."

Perry considered his idol as a boy. If Andy Mill had been ordinary back then, like Perry was now, then maybe Perry could become a great racer, too.

"Where do you ski?" the coach asked.

"Meadowlark."

"Only once," Susanne said. "Last weekend was his first time."

Perry had another urge to roll his eyes. This time he felt less guilty about it.

Coach Lamkin smiled. "You've gotta start somewhere. How did it go?"

Perry shrugged, trying to be as cool a cat as Brandon was when people asked him about basketball. "Oh, pretty good."

Susanne leaned close to the coach. "Other than we think he may have seen the person who murdered Jeannie Renkin."

"What?" The coach put a hand on her chest. "That's terrifying."

Susanne pressed her fingers to her mouth. "I shouldn't have said anything. We haven't taken him in to tell Sheriff Westbury about it yet. Please don't repeat that to anyone."

Perry chewed the inside of his lip. He was pretty sure his mom had just done a bad thing that his dad would be unhappy about. Perry wasn't going to be the one to tell him, though. *What dad doesn't know won't hurt anyone.*

Coach Lamkin made a zipping motion across her lips. "Mum's the word."

Perry decided it was time to point his mom's attention elsewhere. "Hey, Mom, there's Trish." He pointed.

"With Brandon?" Susanne craned her neck to see.

"No. Brandon's with his team. She's with the girls' team. But I think there's something you need to know." He told her he'd seen Ben Jones.

Just like he'd expected, she wigged out.

CHAPTER ELEVEN: PARENT

Laramie, Wyoming
Saturday, March 12, 1977, 2:15 p.m.

Patrick

Patrick tapped his foot on the glossy wooden floorboards. He was sitting courtside next to Coach Lamkin, available in case one of the Buffalo girls sustained an injury, with the game due to start in fifteen minutes. In front of him, the team was running through warm-up drills. He knew his lips were moving. Worry about what Perry had seen was eating him up from the inside out. He felt like if he could just get *outside*—go for a run, a hike, even a drive—it would clear his mind and help him harness his energy and thoughts more productively. But he couldn't. Duty kept him here.

He rubbed his palm against his forehead. Had his son stumbled across a murderer? Worse, had that person seen Perry? If it was someone local, Perry wasn't hard to identify or track down, and they'd had a whole week to do it. God, how he wished Perry had said something about it immediately. The kid dumbfounded him sometimes. He should have put two and two together as soon as he heard about the shooting. But what seemed logical and obvious to Patrick never seemed to occur to Perry. His son viewed the world with less suspicion. It was a good trait, he supposed. They were different in other ways, too. Perry didn't bounce his knee, talk to himself, or drive everyone around him crazy with his high expectations. At least not that Patrick had seen.

A ball bounced off the court right at him. He jerked back and caught it inches from his jaw. A girl bounded after it, and he handed it to her.

"Thanks, Dr. Flint," she said.

He nodded. "No problem."

Trish tapped his shoulder. She was crouched behind him. "Dad, can I go to the concession stand with Brandon?"

"No." They didn't need trouble with Kemecke's sister Donna Lewis.

Coach Lamkin leaned in. "Not to be eavesdropping, but you should let her." She turned and winked at Trish.

Trish beamed. "Thanks, Coach. It will be okay, Dad. There are lots of people around. It's not like we're sneaking off somewhere."

"But Mrs. Lewis is here." Not that he *should* let her go anyway. They had promised to support Donna Lewis's rules, whether she was there or not.

"She left after the boys lost again. With her new boyfriend, or whoever it is she's always hanging out with."

Coach Lamkin talked out of the side of her mouth. "What's it hurt, Pops?"

Pops? He was beginning to get a little irritated with Lamkin's interference.

"Please, Dad?"

Trish's big blue eyes did him. "Okay. Just this once."

"Thank you. And I'm sure Mrs. Lewis won't find out. Even if she does, I'm practically on her good side. She didn't even bawl me out or anything today." Trish stood to go.

"Bawl you out?"

"She does that sometimes. Like last week. I told her she couldn't keep mom and me from testifying at her brother's trial. She said, 'We'll just see about that' in a mean tone of voice."

That sounds like a threat. Patrick worked his jaw. Today he was getting bombarded with one piece of bad news after another. "When was this?"

"Um, after the Sibleys let me ride home with Brandon."

"Why didn't you tell us?"

"I forgot about it." She sighed. "And there's something else I forgot to tell you."

He stood, bracing himself, and saw Brandon standing further down the row. He lifted a hand in greeting. Brandon returned the gesture. "What is it?"

"Uh, she said for me to tell you that our family wasn't able to keep Ben locked up, and they won't let us ruin her brother's life either."

"Ben? Not locked up?"

"Not anymore."

Patrick's jaw literally dropped. The kid was supposed to be in juvie until he aged out.

"I was surprised, too. He's out on early release and living with the Lewises again."

"When did you find out?"

"Last Saturday."

"I'm not happy you didn't tell us about this earlier. Days ago. That boy kidnapped you."

"I'm telling you now, though. That's good, right?"

Coach Lamkin whispered, "That's good, Daddy-o."

Patrick gritted his teeth. He wasn't sure which was worse—Pops or Daddy-o.

"Love you, Dad." Trish kissed him on the cheek.

"Love you, too."

She scampered off with Brandon. Then the coach rose and signaled for the players to join her for the pre-game huddle.

Patrick stayed seated on his chair and fumed.

CHAPTER TWELVE: STRATEGIZE

Susanne

Susanne scooted closer to Patrick on the bench seat, close enough to kiss his furry cheek. It was prickly, even after more than two months of growth. They'd just blown through Kaycee, one of those "blink and you'll miss it" type of towns. Only an hour until they would be home. On either side of the interstate, the landscape was white as far as the eye could see. East, into buttes, and west, all the way up the face of the Bighorns. It was austere and beautiful, but winter in Wyoming lasted a long, long time, and she was ready for a change of season. Green grass, baby animals, and wildflowers.

"Hey, handsome." She rubbed her husband's neck. It was as furry as his cheek. "Let me cut this when we get home. Front and back."

He grinned. "It's not spring until March 21st."

"Just the neck then."

He pretended to think about it. "Just the neck, on March 21st."

"Have it your way, Mountain Man." She ran her index finger over the bunched lines on his forehead. "You've been talking to yourself."

He grimaced. "I've been wishing Billy Kemecke died up on that mountain." He glanced in the rearview mirror and frowned.

Susanne sighed. She looked into the back seat. Both of her not-so-little-anymore kids were sacked out, Perry with his head on Trish's thighs, and Trish with her head on Perry's hip. *Good*. She and Patrick could talk freely, if they kept it down. "Unfortunately, I'm not that accurate a shooter."

"I'm not blaming you. You saved all our lives. And I know it's un-Christian of me to wish for someone's death." Now his eyes cut to the sideview mirror. The lines between them deepened.

"Then I guess I'm guilty of being un-Christian, too, because I've had the same thought." She swiveled her head to get a view of the roadway behind them. From what she could see, it was just a normal evening on a mostly empty Wyoming highway. "What are you looking at back there that has you so agitated?"

"What do you mean?"

"You've been watching your mirrors. And frowning."

He slow-nodded several times. "The same station wagon has been on our tail since we got to the interstate."

"Station wagon? That doesn't sound very sinister." She smiled.

"That's probably what Kemecke would have said if someone told him you were walking up on him and look how that turned out."

"True. But it's probably nothing. Half of Buffalo was in Laramie this weekend, and, with the games over, we're all heading home at the same time."

"It's not a car I recognize."

She'd learned to respect his instincts. If something had him rattled, it was probably worth being rattled over, which ramped up her own tension. She knew him well, though, and she didn't feel like she'd gotten the whole story yet. She snuck another peek at the kids. They were still asleep. "What else is wrong?"

He shook his head. "You're persistent."

"And usually right."

"Well, there's Perry's revelation. And Trish also told me that Ben is out of juvie."

"I'm so glad she did. Perry told me, and I was planning on telling you as soon as we had a moment alone."

His voice held a little bit of an edge. "Dad's always the last to know."

"I only found out this afternoon."

He huffed, but it was a self-aware sound. Almost a sigh. "She also said Donna Lewis is being aggressive." He cut his eyes from the sideview to the rearview mirrors.

"Well, that's nothing new."

"Maybe not, but she threatened Trish about keeping you guys from testifying."

A gold Pontiac station wagon pulled alongside them. There appeared to be only one person in it, but it was so low compared to the Suburban that Susanne couldn't see inside it very well. "What? When?"

"A few days ago. Apparently, Trish 'forgot' to tell us."

"I wish she didn't have to testify in court. We never got a ruling from Sheridan county on whether Trish could testify via affidavit."

He kissed her hand. "It's not just *Trish's* testimony I'm worried about."

She leaned her head against his shoulder. "Thank you."

"With Judge Ellis and Jeannie Renkin dead on the same day, I have a bad feeling about the Kemecke family and this trial."

The station wagon was inching ahead of them. Susanne could see the driver now, a woman of about their age who was keeping her eyes on the road.

Susanne said, "Couldn't that just be a bad coincidence?"

"It could. And the Kemecke family might not have anything to do with either of them."

"But then again, they might."

"Yes."

Susanne followed his train of thought. "And now, Perry's news makes you think the killer might have seen him, and that the killer is with the Kemecke family."

"Yes. I'm a little concerned the Kemeckes may have a reason to wish ill on all of you now."

"Oh, Patrick."

The station wagon's blinker came on. Instead of waiting until it had cleared their vehicle, the driver veered into their lane, cutting them off, and slowed down right in front of them. Patrick stomped on the brakes and threw his right arm out. Susanne caught herself on the dashboard, first with her hands, then with her chest. The impact knocked the wind out of her and snapped her neck forward. She narrowly avoided eating the dash.

As suddenly as the station wagon had slowed down, it sped back up.

The driver either hadn't noticed or didn't care that she'd nearly run them off the road. Patrick resumed normal speed.

"Are you okay?" he said.

Susanne scooted back onto the seat. She rubbed her chest. It hurt, and her heart was pounding a mile a minute. "I'm fine." But if the roads had been icy or the visibility bad—even if the wind had been worse—things might have gone a lot differently, for all of them. Funny, but every time she made this drive, she worried about animals crossing the interstate. Sometimes about sleepy truckers. But never about crazy station wagon drivers.

"Dad?" Trish's head popped up. "What happened?"

"Sorry, honey. A, uh, deer ran across the road. Go back to sleep."

"Okay," Trish mumbled. Her head disappeared behind the seat again.

Susanne and Patrick stayed silent for a minute. She expected to hear Perry's voice, but he didn't stir.

Finally, she whispered, "What the heck was that about?"

"I don't know, but it was the same station wagon I was telling you about."

"I hope she's just a bad driver."

"It's hard to take anything at face value right now."

Susanne nodded. "When you're worried about your kids, everything seems suspicious." She lowered her voice further. "If Perry really saw the killer, do you think he's safe?"

"If he really did, no. Take that car, for instance. For all we know, that driver was the killer."

Susanne's stomach churned at the thought. She nodded. "Yes. It might not even be something with the Kemeckes, though. It could be anyone."

"We have to assume he did see the killer and take precautions."

"Like what?"

"Security, for starters. And, if the court in Johnson county is going to hear this case, we need to renew our request with them to have you guys testify via affidavit. Maybe Judge Renkin will help us out since we helped Jeannie."

"It's worth asking him."

"Also, we've got to get Perry to the sheriff's department ASAP with his information."

Susanne sat up straight again. "We could ask them for protection."

"Funny. I forgot to tell you this, but one of the things that Renkin and his cronies were talking about at the funeral home was security. Sheriff Westbury said he has a plan for keeping the courthouse safe. His department is also going to protect the judge. And Governor Rawlins offered state money for trial security, although he was suggesting it be focused on Renkin."

Susanne felt a glimmer of hope. "Maybe they'll help us, too. It's all related."

"It's *possibly* all related."

"True. I was thinking, and this won't be popular, but we have to crack down on Trish seeing Brandon. Especially if Ben might be tagging along." Susanne knew she would bear the brunt of an angry Trish. Patrick had the refuge of work. Susanne had nowhere to hide from her teenage daughter.

Patrick nodded. "I think we should keep both kids home anytime they aren't in school. And be waiting to pick them up when they get out and stick around to make sure they get in after drop-off."

"Agreed."

"And, if the sheriff won't help us, I want to consider our own protection."

"You mean hire someone?"

The steely-eyed look on her husband's face was one of inspired determination. "I have a better idea."

CHAPTER THIRTEEN: SNOOP

Buffalo, Wyoming
Saturday, March 12, 1977, 8:30 p.m.

Patrick

The walk to Judge Renkin's house felt great after hours cooped up in the Suburban. Patrick had opted to drop in on the judge rather than call first. He wanted to make sure their conversation would be face-to-face. It wasn't a long walk—only a quarter mile or so. But the road was slick with packed snow, so he took it slow. He was looking forward to spring thaw and returning to his running schedule. Spring being the muddy season, jogging wouldn't improve much, but he could at least put on his muck boots for sloppy walks. Then he would train for a half marathon during the glorious summer months. He pinched his waist. He'd gotten a little winter-fat. He'd have to ask Santa for snowshoes next Christmas. Or cross-country skis. Or both.

Patrick rolled his ankle on something in the road. "Ow."

A rock, ice, or even a hunk of wood? Luckily, he wasn't hurt, but he was sorry he'd forgotten to bring a flashlight. On his own property, there was plenty of outdoor lighting. The road to the Renkins' house, though, was dark, with only a quarter moon in the sky. He flipped up his collar, then shoved his hands deep in his pockets. A truck cruised by. As it passed, he saw the light column on the top and the sheriff's department markings on the door. Johnson county was making its presence known. That was good for the judge *and* the Flints. Nearby, coyotes started their evening yipping and howling. They didn't bother him. He was respectful of the mountain lion and cubs that had been making incursions into the area, though. The thought of them made him search the darkness for movement. Lions didn't make noise. They stalked and pounced, something he could confirm after one attacked his horse, Reno, a few months back, while Patrick was riding him. It was something he'd never, ever forget.

He turned into the entrance to the Renkin's place. There were no lights on, inside or out. He tromped the unshoveled walk to their front door and rang the bell anyway. He gave it a full minute, but no one came to the door. Just to be sure, he walked to the garage on the side of the house. It had roll-up doors at three bays. The first bay was open and empty. The others were closed. He glanced around. There was no one there to tattle on him, and he'd always believed it was better to ask forgiveness than permission, so, he poked his head in the open bay. Slowly, his eyes adjusted to the darkness.

The first thing he noticed was movement in the dark recess of the third bay. He yelped and jumped back, his heart in his throat. *Mountain lion.* The second thing he noticed was that an animal was perched on the hood of Jeannie Renkin's Cadillac. Patrick pulled out his pocketknife, just to be on the safe side. He'd had occasion to use it for self-protection before, and it was effective. Sturdy, with a six-inch blade. A real Wyoming knife. Wes had given it to Patrick to replace what he called Patrick's "Minnie Mouse" knife, and he'd had SAWBONES engraved in the handle. Patrick was glad he had it now.

"Go away, kitty."

There was a thump as the animal leapt from the car and landed on the ground. Then footsteps padded toward him at a slow, slinky pace. Patrick tensed. He couldn't outrun a mountain lion. He'd have to stand his ground. Just as he was about to go on the offensive, a large black house cat came into view.

He laughed.

"You scared the squat out of me, cat." It wended its way through his legs, and he reached down to pet it. Its fur was long and thick. A Maine Coon, he figured.

He was about to leave when he realized the vehicle in the center bay was a snowmobile on a metal trailer. Patrick had never seen Renkin riding a snowmobile. He couldn't tell for sure, but this one looked sort of yellow. His curiosity got the better of him again, but this time he decided he needed light. He walked to the door and searched on the wall for a light switch. As he fumbled for it, several items clattered to the ground. He cursed softly. Finally, he found the switch and used it.

The overhead light was brighter than the sun. Patrick shielded his eyes. What kind of bulb did Renkin have in there? His eyes took longer to adjust to the light than the dark. When he was no longer blinded by glare, he went to check out the snow machine. It was a dandy one. A Rupp Yankee—a luxury brand. Patrick would have been happy with a cheaper Ski-Doo. But they were still expensive, and so was gas, so he was holding out. Someday.

The cat jumped onto the seat and tested its claws on the black upholstery. Patrick trailed his hand along the yellow chassis. The judge had treated himself to the 40-horsepower version.

The cat jumped down and scratched its head on Patrick's foot. It purred like a smaller version of the Rupp.

"So, fuzzball, where's your owner?"

The cat didn't answer. Goosebumps rose on Patrick's arms, and he suddenly had the sensation someone was watching him. He needed to get out of there. He was trespassing after all. He hung up everything he'd knocked to the ground earlier—a flashlight, a fly swatter, and an ice scraper—then turned off the light and skedaddled. As he walked away, he scanned in all directions, looking for movement, light, or a human shape, but he saw nothing.

He turned toward his own house at the road, but got the sensation that he'd glimpsed something out of place. He whirled around. A beat-up van was parked about a hundred feet down the road. Had it been there earlier? He didn't think so, but he couldn't remember for sure. Again, he searched the darkness, but he saw nothing else. He shrugged. He would have been a lot more concerned if it had been a gold station wagon. He hunched his shoulders against the cold and walked back toward his own place.

When he reached the driveway, Reno nickered at him. The shadows of three horses loomed behind the pasture gate. The house flood lights reached to the old two-story wooden barn, but not all the way to the pasture. Even in the dim light he could see how badly the barn needed a new coat of red paint. It would have to wait for summer.

"Hey, boy," he called to his horse. He walked over to give Reno's forehead a brief scratch.

Reno looked awfully good for a horse that had nearly died on a mountaintop in Cloud Peak Wilderness only six months before, when he'd broken the splint bone in one of his hind legs in his mad scramble to get away from a mountain lion. If Reno had been just any other horse in an outfitter's string, he would have gotten a bullet between the eyes and a rock cairn as his resting place. Reno's rescue—a lengthy, difficult, and dangerous procedure—had taken an army. People had been determined to help the Flints and the special horse, especially after what the family had been through on the mountain with Kemecke and his gang. Patrick's gratitude to the people who'd saved him and to Joe Crumpton, the vet who had nursed him to health, was profound. Now the big horse was retired, fat, and happy, with barely a limp.

Reno tolerated the affection for a moment, then, because Patrick hadn't brought him food, he ambled away. The other horses followed him. Patrick chuckled and went his own way, too.

At the house, he stopped at the woodpile. Before he'd walked to the Renkins' house, Susanne had asked him to fill the fireplace bin. Unfortunately, he discovered he was out of split logs. He set a log on his chopping stump and grabbed his splitting ax from a wall hook inside the woodshed. With the blade poised on the wood, he bent his legs and drew in a breath, then hauled the ax around and swung it. The log split cleanly in two. He dropped the pieces into his carrier. There was something strangely satisfying about splitting logs. He blew out a frosty breath and repeated the process. When he had enough split wood for a full load, he was a little bit disappointed. He turned to go in and stopped short.

The mountain lion he'd worried he'd seen at the Renkin's was standing at the front corner of the house, crouched low, completely silent. The animal looked mature, but small enough to be a female. A female in the winter, needing to feed her cubs? If game were plentiful, she wouldn't be a threat. But it had been a long, hard winter.

"Shoo," he said. His voice came out softer than he'd intended. He raised it. "Get on, now."

The lion didn't move. Didn't look away.

A peculiar feeling came over him. This was the second lion he'd seen that week. Once—maybe—up at Meadowlark. Now there was one here at his own house. Both sightings had occurred when he was by himself. In his research about American Indians for a term paper in college, he'd been fascinated by their belief in spirit animals. Some Indians believed that an animal would reveal itself to a person through physical and symbolic encounters, maybe more than once over the course of the person's life, to guide, protect, teach, and provide balance. Was the lion revealing itself to him? And, if so, what was the message it was passing? He would have to worry about that later, though. Right now, there was a live, meat-eating lion staring him down, and he had to figure out how to encourage it to depart.

"Thank you for visiting, Ms. Lion. If you're bringing me a message, I want you to know, I am listening, even though I don't understand what it is yet."

Her tail twitched, and she made a sound that was part growl, part yowl.

He'd never had the occasion to study an uncaged lion up close like this before, not for this long. She was majestic, and truly fearsome. Even in the dark he could see the musculature under her winter coat. He felt blessed, although he would prefer that she go where she wasn't a threat to pets, livestock, and humans—and thus, herself.

"Run along now. Get far away from here. People are no good for you."

She took a step toward him. Her feet didn't make a sound.

He tensed. "Easy, girl."

She moved closer.

"Okay, Mother Nature, I'm going to have to cut this short before she does something she'll regret." He took a log from his hauler and threw it at the cougar.

She snarled and ducked her head, but she didn't run away.

"Yah, girl! Yah, yah!" He chunked two more in quick succession.

That finally did the trick. In a blink, she disappeared into the inky dark. Patrick released a shaky breath. That had been something else. He decided to leave the wood he'd thrown until he could pick it up in daylight. Just because he couldn't see her didn't mean she'd gone far.

He hauled the carrier into the house and emptied it in the bin by the massive stone fireplace that was the centerpiece of a living room, which was noisy with the sound of the television. During daylight hours, the room had a great view of the banks of Clear Creek and the mountains in the distance. It opened onto an eating area adjacent to their kitchen. A hall to his left went to the master suite, and a staircase near the front door led up to the kids' bedrooms on the second floor and down to a basement with a playroom and indoor shop. They'd moved into the house two months before, and he hadn't found a thing he didn't like about it except the monthly mortgage payment. Susanne professed to love the house just as it was, but she was systematically changing every-thing about it. New curtains. New furniture. And, when it warmed up outside, new paint.

Their clumsy Irish wolfhound, Ferdinand, galloped down the stairs. He charged through the living room furniture like an obstacle course, running into nearly everything he passed. Then he slid to a stop on the wood floors. His big body rammed Patrick in the knees. Patrick laughed and gave his ears a good rubbing.

"Where were you when I needed you a second ago, Ferdie?" But he was actually glad the dog hadn't been outside. If he had, the lion might never have showed herself.

Susanne walked in from the master suite. She was carrying an over-full hamper of laundry. Ferdinand trotted over to inspect the trail of socks and underwear Susanne was leaving behind.

He told her about the lion, omitting his secret belief that it might be a spirit animal with a message for him. Susanne didn't put much stock in mysticism.

When he finished, she looked a little flustered. "Should we do some-thing about it?"

"Nah. She left. She won't bother us." *I hope.* He changed the subject. "I'm thinking about taking Perry in to give a statement at the sheriff's department now," he said.

"You're just trying to keep your beard away from me and my razor."

He laughed.

"Do you think anyone is there this late on a Saturday night?"

He stoked the fire, then added a log. Susanne insisted they keep the living room fireplace lit at all times, and the one in their bedroom almost as often. She had a few conditions for living full-time in Wyoming. A lit living room fireplace was one of them, as was the house it was in. She also required a generous long-distance budget so she could chat with her mother and sister. "I'll call Ronnie and see what she thinks." Ronnie—Veronica at birth—Harcourt, their friend and former neighbor, was a deputy for Johnson county.

He stood, noticing a coffee mug on the mantel of the fireplace. He picked it up. It was cold. There was a film of mold over the old coffee.

He held it out. "One of yours," he said to his wife. She had a propensity for leaving multiple cups a day around the house, then not being able to find them. The moldy surface in the mug was a common sight, too.

She shook her head. "Finders keepers. And I agree about Ronnie. But, before you go anywhere, we have to talk to Trish."

On the TV, a male announcer intoned, "Tonight at ten, tune in for an update on the capital murder trial of convicted murderer Billy Kemecke, scheduled to begin this week in Johnson county." Beside the pomaded head of the newscaster, a picture of Billy Kemecke appeared. Dark hair and eyes. Wearing a jumpsuit and shackles. Medium build, but radiating strength and menace. Patrick glanced at his wife. Her face had lost all its color.

He hurried over to the TV and turned it off. "Tonight?"

Susanne drew in a deep breath, then seemed to re-center. "She asked to take the Suburban to pick up Marcy and see a movie. I stalled her by saying we'd wait for you."

"She wants to go out this late?"

Susanne shifted the laundry to her other hip and winked at him over her shoulder. "They do run second shows at the theater. You were young once, too."

Patrick harrumphed. Other than his thinning hair, he didn't think he looked a day over thirty. He was as physically fit as a twenty-five-year old. And he was young at heart—that's what counted most. He lifted the mustard-colored phone receiver from its wall base in the eating area, dialing Ronnie's number from the list of important contacts taped to the side of the cabinet near the phone. Then he walked into the kitchen and leaned against the big butcher block island, holding the curled cord away from him with one hand.

Ronnie picked up after the second ring. "Hello?"

"Hello, neighbor. It's Patrick Flint."

"Once a neighbor, always a neighbor, hey?" She sounded out of breath.

"Am I interrupting you?"

"No. I was doing stairs and wall sits."

That's what Patrick should have been doing all winter when he couldn't run. Ronnie was a better man than he was, and she was a woman. "I'll make it quick. Perry went off by himself last Saturday up at Meadowlark. It turns out he may have seen Jeannie Renkin's shooter.

He just told us this today, while we were at the basketball tournament in Laramie."

"Jesus H. Christ, Patrick. Do you Flints wear trouble magnets on your backs?"

He chuckled, even though the trouble wasn't a laughing matter. "I want to get him in to give a statement as soon as possible, while it's still fresh in his mind. And this person might have seen him, too. We're a little concerned about his safety."

"With good reason."

"I know it's a Saturday night, but do you think I should go ahead and take him in?"

Ronnie's voice was firm. "Let me just shower and grab my things. I'll meet you there in an hour."

It was a relief she was taking the situation seriously. "I'll take that as a yes?"

"That's a hell yes, buddy."

CHAPTER FOURTEEN: SNIT

BUFFALO, WYOMING
SATURDAY, MARCH 12, 1977, 9:00 P.M.

Trish

Trish slipped her feet into cowboy boots and grabbed her slate-blue down coat. Brandon was meeting her outside the movie theater in fifteen minutes. If she didn't hurry, she'd be late. She took a second to check her reflection in the full-length mirror on the back of her door. Behind her in the glass she could see her room. She and her mom had worked together to duplicate her old one, down to copying the blue and tan floral wallpaper and moving her hanging basket chair and burlap-covered, ruffle-edged bulletin board.

Adjusting the bottom edge of her high-necked white Laura Ashley top, she gave herself a smile. The blouse was edged with lace around the neck and wrists, as well as around the tiny buttons, and it had pleats and poofs in the shoulders. She loved it. And she loved the gloss on her lips. Lip Smackers Strawberry. Hopefully Brandon would think she looked pretty.

"Trish, we're waiting on you," her mom called from downstairs.

She slung a thin-strapped leather purse over her shoulder. "Keep your pants on," she muttered. Her parents thought everything was about them.

As she walked down the hallway, she glanced into the bathroom she shared with Perry. He was doing curls with barbells, shirtless, watching himself in the mirror. She burst out laughing. Perry's face crumpled, but anger quickly replaced embarrassment.

He slammed the door. "Stop spying on me."

"Like I care what you do, squirt."

She trotted down the wooden stairs to the living room. She liked the stairs in their old house better. They'd been covered with carpet and were much quieter. On these floors, everyone always knew when she was on the move. Her parents were sitting side by side in front of the fire on the cruddy old couch that they'd had ever since Trish could remember. Some kind of knubby woven material with different colors of tan and brown threads.

She stood between them and the hallway to the garage, hand on her hip. Her strategy was to say as little as she could and get out of there as fast as possible. "Well?"

Her mom said, "Your dad needs to talk to you."

Patrick scowled at Susanne. It didn't look like he'd gotten that memo. Her mom had never been afraid to yell at or spank Perry and her, but she saved the very worst of their supposed transgressions for their dad to handle. *This isn't going to be good.*

Her dad cleared his throat. "What you told me earlier today, about the threat Mrs. Lewis made to you, and about Ben being out of juvie—it has your mother and me concerned."

Trish stared at him, willing him to hurry up and get to the point.

"Combined with some of the frightening things going on with the trial, we think—"

Trish couldn't let that go—she had to know what he meant. "What frightening things?"

"Judge Ellis in Sheridan died, which means the Kemecke trial is moving to Buffalo. But someone shot and killed Mrs. Renkin, the wife of the judge here, on the same day the Sheridan judge died."

"I know that, Dad. I was there."

"There's reason to believe that someone opposed to the trial is killing people involved."

"Mrs. Renkin wasn't involved."

Her dad sighed. Trish felt a sense of accomplishment. She was getting under his skin without even trying. "Not directly. But who's to say the shooter wasn't aiming for Judge Renkin?"

Trish stared at him. What did any of this have to do with her plans tonight? "Dad, I understand. But Marcy is waiting on me. I've got to go."

Her parents shared an apprehensive look. Her mom took her dad's hands. Trish's stomach knotted up.

Her dad said, "Because of all of this, we're not going to be able to let you go out without us, except to school, until the trial is over. I'm sorry, but that means you're not going tonight."

Blood rushed to Trish's neck and face, making them hot and tingly. "What? For how long?"

"No more than a few weeks. Probably less."

"A few weeks?" Her voice rose to a shriek. "I'm on house arrest for a month?"

"Not house arrest. House protection."

She put her hands on her hips. "This is about Brandon's family again, isn't it? You think they want to hurt me."

Susanne raised her eyebrows. "Don't tell me the thought hasn't crossed your mind."

Trish shook her head rapidly. "Brandon will protect me. He's not like his family."

"But he trusts them. And we don't. So, until this is over, those are the rules."

Trish stomped her foot and shouted. "Unbelievable. I knew you'd find some way to mess things up with me and Brandon again."

Susanne got to her feet. "We didn't mess things up with you and Brandon before, and we're not now. Time will pass before you know it. Besides, wasn't it *Marcy* you were going to the movies with tonight?"

"It was," Trish sputtered. "I'm just talking about, like, in general."

"Nothing is more important to us than your safety." Her dad stayed seated, looking sick to his stomach.

He hated disciplining or disappointing them, Trish knew. Once she'd ridden off on Goldie and left Perry behind. When Trish got home, her mom had demanded her dad spank Trish with his belt. He took her into her bedroom and whispered, "Yell really loud." Then he'd smacked the belt across his own knees, and told her, "Don't make me regret this." She hadn't left Perry ever again, as much as she'd wanted to.

But she wasn't going to make it easy for him this time. Not when it was too late to call Brandon and tell him she wasn't coming. Brandon would just be sitting there in the dark, thinking she'd stood him up. How long would he wait around for a girlfriend who wasn't allowed out of her house before he got bored? And what would happen if he ran into Charla then?

"You're ruining my life." She turned and fled up the stairs to her room.

CHAPTER FIFTEEN: LISTEN

Perry

Perry traipsed after his dad from the parking lot into the courthouse, where they were making a quick stop on their way to meet Ronnie. It was dark and dreary there at night, and there were no welcoming lights on inside. He could barely see his own feet as they came down the sidewalk. It was a little spooky.

The door opened when his dad pulled it. "Someone must still be at work." His dad smiled, like that was a good thing.

They scurried inside. The building was chilly and dark.

"Dad, I was thinking. If we went skiing tomorrow as a family, you would be with me the whole time and keep me safe." His parents had given him the same "safety" and "new rules" speech Trish had gone nuclear about—he'd listened from the top of the stairs—adding that the person he saw at the ski mountain could have been the murderer. Unlike Trish, he'd said, "Yes, sir," and "Yes, ma'am," to them, then asked if that meant he could watch a few more television shows a week. Just *Shazam* and *Happy Days*. They'd okayed the first and torpedoed the latter as, "inappropriate." Whatever that meant.

Patrick chuckled. "Says the same kid who skied off and left his old man last weekend." His dad had on cowboy boots. His footsteps echoed in the empty corridor, firm and manly. Perry's tennis shoes squeaked like a little mouse.

But his dad had a point. "I wouldn't do that again. I'm pretty good at skiing. Maybe I can give everyone a lesson."

"I doubt your mom would let you skip church, buddy."

"Then after."

"We can talk to her when we get home. Here are the stairs. Watch your step. We're going to the second floor."

Perry grabbed the smooth wooden handrail and put his foot on the first tread. The stair well was like a black hole. "So that means you vote yes?"

"It means we talk to your mother."

Perry knew better than to push it any further.

When they reached the second floor, his dad turned left down the hallway. Perry followed him, holding his nose. It smelled like cigarettes up here. John had pulled out a pack at recess the week before. They were gross. Perry was never going to smoke.

"Do you know where we're going, Dad?"

"I've been here once before."

They stopped in front of a big wooden door that was hanging ajar. Perry heard a man's gruff voice.

"I told you last week already. I won't pay you another goldarned cent."

Patrick put his hand out across Perry's chest. He made a soft *shh* sound.

After a pause, the man hollered, "We had a deal!"

Perry sucked in a breath. The man was so angry. Perry felt a little scared, even though his dad was right there with him.

Something thunked against wood in time with the man's words. "Powder River Production Company didn't pay me nearly as much for that ruling as you think they did." The thunking stopped. "And nobody was hurt by it." Then, after only a few seconds pause, the man said, "Whether I run for Senate or not is none of your business. Go to Mr. Ochoa or Governor Rawlins for all I care."

Perry wasn't sure what any of it meant, but it sounded like this guy had done something bad, and somebody else knew about it and was blackmailing him. Whatever the man did, blackmailing was still wrong.

The man—Perry decided it was probably the judge, since that's who his dad had come to talk to—sighed. Perry heard a whump, like the sound of someone sitting down heavily in a soft chair. "How much to make you go away forever?"

Patrick turned and gave Perry's shoulder a soft push. He whispered, "Let's go." They started walking as quietly as they could down the hall. Perry was careful not to let his shoes squeak.

"I'll give you an answer tomorrow."

There was a clack and ring. *He must have slammed that phone down hard.* Then quick thumps. Footsteps. Coming closer, and fast. Patrick snatched up Perry's hand and wheeled him around. The hallway flooded with flickering light. The fluorescents buzzed overhead. A big man stared at them.

"What are you doing in here?" he boomed. His cheeks were red, and his eyes looked funny. Like they had a wet film over them.

Patrick said, "Just on our way up to see you, Judge Renkin."

His dad's voice sounded so calm. Perry wondered if his dad ever felt scared. He didn't act like it. He was also six feet tall, though. Maybe when Perry was as tall as his dad, he wouldn't be scared anymore either.

The judge glowered. "Were you outside my door just now?"

"We were just coming up the steps."

The judge drilled Patrick with his eyes. "Let me ask you a different way. Were you eavesdropping on my conversation?"

Patrick didn't flinch. "What conversation? We just got here."

Perry struggled to keep his face from giving away the truth. He'd never heard his father tell a bald-faced lie before. He was always going on and on about a man's word being his bond, and that there was no legacy as rich as honesty, and other stuff Perry didn't understand except that it meant his dad really, really didn't like lying. Perry had lied about his report card once, and he'd been grounded from TV for a month. So, he knew that whatever they'd just heard, it was pretty darn important for his dad to lie about it.

The judge took off his glasses and dabbed at the corners of his eyes with his thumb and index finger, then put the glasses back on. "I apologize. It's been a tough week. Jeannie's death. The trial coming. That's why I'm in here working so late."

"It's why we came by, too."

The judge gestured at the door. "Come on in."

Patrick said, "Perry, wait out here, please."

"But I thought you said I couldn't stay by myself until the trial was over."

"I'm right here. You'll be fine."

Perry was bummed. He really wanted to listen in on the conversation. The visit to the courthouse was turning out to be very interesting. But he was also still scared. The hallway was long and wide with lots of doors. Whatever his dad said, Perry didn't like being out there alone. At least the lights were on in the hallway. He shivered. But anyone could have come in the open door downstairs earlier. There were a million places to hide. He leaned against the wall and rotated his head back and forth slowly, keeping an eye out, just in case.

Luckily for him, the judge was a loud talker. "Have a seat," the judge said.

Perry heard the whump of two butts hitting chairs.

"What is it you've come to talk to me about?"

Patrick cleared his throat. "I know you've just gotten the Kemecke case and have a lot of other things going on, but do you know when it will be starting?"

"I expect we'll start Wednesday. Your family will be notified by the court before then."

"Susanne and I talked to the county attorneys in both Big Horn and Sheridan about a trial issue. We never heard back from either of them on it."

"What was it about?"

"Well, let me back up to the beginning. My wife and daughter feel very threatened by Kemecke's extended family."

Perry heard a squeak in the stairwell. It sounded like his tennis shoe. He held his breath and listened as hard as he could, but he didn't hear it again.

"So much so that your daughter dates his nephew?"

Ouch. But the judge had a point. Perry didn't understand why Trish dated Brandon, given who his family was and what they'd done to her. Then again, he didn't understand a lot of the things she did.

His dad's voice sounded tight, like he was pretending he wasn't mad. "We don't judge Brandon for his family."

"You're a better man than I am, Dr. Flint."

"Be that as it may, Kemecke's sister, Donna Lewis, threatened Trish that she and Susanne would never make it to the trial to testify. And now his nephew and accomplice Ben Jones is out of juvie. With that and the deaths of your wife and Judge Ellis, Susanne and I are very concerned that someone is trying to keep key players out of the courtroom. Trish and Susanne, of course, couldn't be more key."

"If you're seeking protection, you need to go talk to the sheriff, not me."

"I'm not. Not from you, anyway. I'm here to ask if there's a chance Trish and Susanne could testify via affidavit. If they weren't going to testify in court, there'd be no reason to harm them to keep them from it."

There was a long pause, then the sound of wheels rolling back, and a crash. Perry flinched.

"This is a death penalty case, Dr. Flint. Do you know what that means?"

"Of course."

The judge went on like Patrick hadn't responded. "It means that if the jury does its job, we'll be sending Billy Kemecke for the first lethal injection since its reinstatement by the U.S. Supreme Court last year. I am the judge presiding over a case of this magnitude. Juries don't rely on affidavits when sending a man to death. The defendant, piece of trash though he may be, has the right to cross examine witnesses about the accusations against him. Do your daughter and wife have accusations against him?"

"Of course they do. You know that."

Perry heard the squeak again. This time it was louder and closer. He turned toward the noise and clapped his hand over his mouth to trap his scream. A mustached man with mutton chops, bell bottom pants, pointy snakeskin shoes, and a maroon shirt with long lapels was standing at the top of the stairs. He locked eyes with Perry for a second, then he did an about face and disappeared the way he'd come. Perry whimpered into his hand.

"Then your request is to be made through the county attorney, not by ambushing me late at night, with your child tagging along no less."

"Time is short. I've already talked to two county attorneys and gotten nowhere."

"And you'll talk to ours, or not talk to anyone at all. Either way, the result will be the same." The judge started to shout. "Because if our county attorney brings me such an idiotic request, he won't have time to cover his butt with his hat before I kick it and him back out the door."

Wheels rolled again. His dad's voice was icy but polite. "Thank you for your time, then, Judge."

The man on the stairs had frightened Perry so bad, he'd nearly peed in his pants. He wanted to run in and cower behind his dad. But he didn't have to. Patrick appeared beside him.

"Dad," Perry whispered. "A man. There was a man on the stairs."

"Let's get out of here." Perry's dad took his arm and pulled him along so fast it hurt.

"Ow. Did you hear me?"

Patrick let go of Perry at the stairs. "I heard you. People work here during the day. And there are other people in here at night, cleaning. It was probably one of them."

"It didn't seem like it." He hadn't been dressed like a janitor. Plus, he hadn't had any cleaning supplies with him. It could have been someone there to see the judge, like them. Maybe.

Or it could have even been the person Perry had seen on the mountain.

At the bottom of the stairs, a man said, "Halt. State your name and your business here."

Perry gasped. Was it the man from the stairs? Had he come back to hurt them? But the man standing between them and the door wasn't the one he'd seen a few minutes before. This one was in uniform, like an officer.

Patrick stopped. He sounded confident and cheerful. "Good evening, Deputy. I'm Dr. Patrick Flint and this is my son Perry. We're Judge Renkin's next door neighbors, and we were just upstairs visiting him."

The deputy frowned, like he was thinking hard. "All right, then. Have a nice evening."

Patrick strode toward the door, nodding at the man. He exited then walked so fast toward their truck that Perry was soon left behind. He ran to catch up, his heart in his throat. No way, no how did he want to run into the man he'd seen in the stairwell again, alone out here in the dark.

CHAPTER SIXTEEN: DETERMINE

Patrick

O nce they were back inside the Suburban, Perry had locked the passenger door and pressed his nose against the window. Patrick felt bad that he hadn't taken the boy's concerns seriously. He'd been too wrapped up in his anger at Judge Renkin. Overhearing him admitting to judicial wrongdoing to a blackmailer wasn't even the worst of it. He'd been no help at all, not even offering empathy, when Patrick had tried to talk to him about Kemecke's trial.

"Dad, that light was red," Perry said. "No one was coming at least. You probably didn't see it since you were talking to yourself."

Patrick shrugged. "Sorry. I'll pay better attention."

He wasn't sure his lips would stop moving, though. Renkin's sarcasm and rudeness toward him, a concerned father and husband, was way out of line. He knew the man was under stress, and possibly grieving, too, although he showed no signs of it. But the behavior was inexcusable. And to have Perry there to witness it—what a horrible influence on his son. What respect could he possibly have for authority figures after this? Plus, the things they'd heard the judge saying on the phone made their predicament worse, not better. He wasn't sure the judge had believed his lie.

He turned into the parking lot at the sheriff's office, then parked. "You heard what the judge said?"

"Before, when he was on the phone, or when you were in there with him?"

"Both, I guess."

"Yeah, I heard him."

"You can't repeat it. Not any of it."

"Why?"

"For starters, because I lied to him and said we didn't hear his call."

Perry nodded, his eyes grave.

"And the other stuff. I don't want the Kemeckes to hear that the judge won't do anything to help your mom and sister. It might make them bolder."

Perry nodded again.

"So, you promise not to say anything?"

"Promise."

"Good. Let's go see Ronnie."

The two of them walked to the sheriff's office, rock salt crunching under their feet. Bright, cheery lights were on in the lobby and in a few other places in the building. The door was unlocked, and Patrick led Perry in. He'd never been in the offices before. He would have expected an old west feel, but this was more like a school principal's office, with particle board bookshelves, low nap industrial carpet, and cheap furniture. There was no one manning the front desk, but he wouldn't have expected it this time of night on a Saturday. It was a small town and less than populous county.

He rapped his knuckles on the surface of a metal-sided desk. "Ronnie? You back there? It's Patrick."

A faint voice replied, "On my way."

Perry sat on a tall wooden bench and swung his legs. Patrick exhaled, trying to offload some of the stress that had been building inside him. Man, it had been some kind of day, and it was far from over. He wished he was on the couch in front of the fire drinking a Coors, hip to hip with Susanne and her thimble-sized glass of white zinfandel, her foot over his ankle, the lights out, and no kids at home. Nothing on the television. Just silence and snow falling outside, with *The Road to Gadolfo* within reach on the side table to read after

Susanne fell asleep. Because she always fell asleep when they snuggled in front of a fire.

"Hi, guys." Ronnie strode in and shook both their hands. She stood eyeball to eyeball with Patrick, her hair in one long braid down her back. While he outweighed her by a good bit, she had grown up as a ranch kid, and she was muscular and capable.

"Hi, Ronnie." Perry's voice cracked, and he sounded like a hungry donkey. Puberty wasn't something Patrick wished on anyone.

"Thanks for meeting us." Patrick put his hand in the center of Perry's back.

"Of course. Come on in." Ronnie led them to a small, windowless room not far from the entry area. She set a pen and pad of paper on the table at one end. "I'd call this a conference room, but that would be giving it too much credit." She sat and waited until they'd each grabbed a chair. "Perry, your dad told me you saw someone suspicious up at Meadowlark."

"Yeah. I mean, yes, ma'am."

Ronnie smiled at him. "Manners. I like it. Okay, can you start from the beginning for me—where you were and when, why you were there, and what you saw. That kind of thing. I'm sure I'll have some more questions, too, but, for now, just tell me the story. Okay?"

Perry took a shaky breath. His pupils were dilated. Patrick was taken aback somewhat that his son seemed so nervous. He hadn't been when he told Susanne and Patrick about it earlier. "Dad took us to Meadowlark to ski because it was free. I was by myself and decided to follow a trail through the trees, down near the lodge. It was nearly lunchtime. I was hungry." His voice was tight.

"What day was this?"

"Last Saturday."

She nodded. "Thanks. Go on."

"I didn't think I'd gone very far, but I must have because it took me half an hour to walk back out of there."

Ronnie chuckled. "That tends to happen when you go off trail."

Perry's face relaxed, and his voice loosened up. Patrick's heart swelled. He was so proud of this kid. "I was sorry I did it. So maybe I'd been skiing a couple of minutes when I heard this really loud noise, like CRACK Crack crack crack crack, you know, with an echo at the end, but softer?"

"It reverberated."

"Yes, ma'am."

"Did you know what it was?"

"I thought maybe it was a tree cracking, you know, like, because of ice?"

"That was a good thought."

He smiled. "I stopped and looked around in case it was falling on me. That's when I saw a person and a snowmobile."

"Man or woman?"

"I don't know. In my mind, it was a man, since why would a woman be out there all alone?"

"You never know."

Perry's brow furrowed. "He had on goggles and a snow cap, and a big snow suit."

"How tall?"

"Like you or dad, maybe? But I was kind of far away."

She leaned toward him. "How far?"

"About a hundred feet, I think."

"Did you see the skin color, like on the face?"

He frowned. "No, because the cap went over his face, too."

"Okay. What color was the suit?"

"White. White camouflage."

"Mittens? Hat? Boots?"

"White, too. Everything was white, I think."

"What else do you remember? Anything in the person's hands?"

"No. But there was a big, long bag."

"Color?"

"Green." His eyebrows peaked. "I just remembered that."

Patrick smiled at him.

Ronnie tapped her pen. "That happens when you talk through it. You'll remember things you didn't even notice at the time. You're doing great. Now, what was the bag made of?"

"Canvas, maybe? He was strapping it on the snowmobile with bungee cords."

"Did you see a gun or a rifle?"

"Uh-uh."

"Could one have been in that bag?"

Perry squinted, like he was looking back through his mind's eye. "Maybe."

"What else do you remember?"

"Um, the snowmobile was yellow."

"What kind?"

"Fancy. Kinda new. It looked like a big, fat bumblebee."

"Any stickers on the back, or anything unusual about it?"

"I don't remember. But the backend was all black."

"What about the skis?"

Perry chewed his bottom lip. "Black, I think?"

Ronnie scribbled some notes. "Did the person see you?"

"Yes. I waved. He was looking right at me, but he didn't wave back."

"Did either of you say anything?"

"No. It was kind of creepy. I decided I should get out of there."

"Then what?"

"I figured out how hard it was to go uphill on skis without poles. A little bit later, I heard the engine start."

"How much later?"

"A minute or two. Not long."

"Did you ever see the person or the snowmobile again?"

"No."

"What did you do next?"

"I tried to eat my sandwich, but I'd lost it. Along with my pocketknife." He snuck a look at Patrick. "Sorry, Dad." Patrick shrugged, but he couldn't help thinking about the cost of the knife. It hadn't been cheap. If Perry wanted another, he was going to have to earn the responsibility. "Then I skied to the lodge, but everybody was leaving. I rode home with the Sibleys."

"Did you tell them about the snowmobiler?"

Perry looked at his lap for a second. "No. They said my mom and dad left to take someone who was hurt to the hospital and that the ski mountain was closed." He looked sheepish. "I forgot about everything else, until I saw someone in white camo in Laramie. That's when I told my mom and dad about it."

"Tell me about the person in Laramie. Was it the same kind of snowsuit?"

"No, it was just a coat. I barely even saw it. There were too many people."

"Do you think it was the same person?"

"I don't know. I wasn't paying very close attention at first. And then it took a second for it to hit me. Like a delayed reaction, you know?"

"I do. So, now that you've had a week to think about it, what do you think about this person at Meadowlark?"

He rolled his bottom lip out and shrugged. "Nothing, other than what I told you." He turned to Patrick. "What if the shooter saw me, Dad? I wasn't wearing a mask. And I had my goggles on my head. If he recognized me, he could come after me."

Patrick put his hand on his son's shoulder and squeezed it. "I think that's unlikely, buddy."

"Then why are you making me come straight home after school and not go anywhere without you?"

"To be extra careful."

"That's always good," Ronnie said.

Patrick turned to her. "What else would you recommend we do now, Ronnie?"

"Let's not tell anyone else what Perry saw, for starters. Did you tell anyone, Perry?"

"No."

"Who else besides the two of you know?" she asked Patrick.

"Trish and Susanne."

Perry's face flushed.

"What is it, son?"

"Nothing."

"Is there something you want to tell us?" Ronnie asked.

Perry shook his head, and Patrick let the subject drop.

Ronnie seemed satisfied, too. She pushed back her chair. "This is important information, given that we don't have any other witnesses, no weapon, and no suspect or motive. So have your family keep it quiet, which we'll do here as well. Johnson and Big Horn counties." Patrick knew it was a multi-jurisdictional effort, since the murder had occurred in Big Horn county, but involved residents of and potentially a trial occurring in Johnson.

Patrick didn't move from the table. "I know there's suspicion Jeannie Renkin's murder might be linked to the Kemecke trial. I've heard extra security will be on hand at the courthouse and for Judge Renkin—at least that's what the sheriff and the governor told the judge a few days ago. I was hoping maybe our family could be included in that, too?"

Ronnie's eyes flitted to the side, but then she brought them back and held his gaze while she answered. "I can certainly ask."

"I'd consider it an important personal favor. After Donna Lewis made a threatening comment about Trish and her mother, that they would never get to testify—"

Ronnie's face darkened. "When?"

"Last Saturday. To Trish."

"I don't like hearing that. Did she get any more specific about what she meant? Like what would happen to keep them from testifying or who would do it?"

"No. It was pretty general, according to Trish."

She shook her head. "Well, even though Donna may be nasty, she's not stupid. But go on. I interrupted you."

"I was just saying that with what Perry saw, Donna's threatening comment, and what happened to Judge Ellis and Mrs. Renkin, we're all pretty nervous. Plus, Kemecke's nephew Ben Jones was released from juvie and is living with the Lewises."

"Damn." Ronnie eyes clouded with concern. Then she shook her head, stood, and put her notepad under her arm and her pen in her front pocket. "Please take care of yourself and your family. Be extra vigilant. Call if you see anything suspicious."

"Of course."

"You've given me a lot of information to talk to Sheriff Westbury about. I'll get back with you ASAP with his answer on the protection issue."

Patrick nodded grimly. Ronnie's heart was in the right place, but he already knew how this was going to go—his family's welfare would be entirely up to him.

CHAPTER SEVENTEEN: ENLIST

Patrick

B eside his kitchen table, Patrick stood like a captain at the helm of a ship surveying his crew. Henry and Vangie Sibley. Wes Braten. His boss, Dr. John. The vet, Joe Crumpton. Good people, all of them. They'd come running when he'd put out the call to form a posse. If his family's security was going to be on his shoulders, Patrick would take all the help he could get. He'd explained everything that was going on to them, except what Perry had seen at Meadowlark, and the reason they needed a home-grown security team. With them here, the pressure in his chest was already easing up. This faceless threat against his family—maybe more than one—had been triggering his worst fears of losing his wife and kids. He knew what a blessed man he was. Contemplating losing them, even for an instant, was more than he could bear. A lump formed in his throat and moisture built in his eyes.

Susanne walked from person to person, pouring fresh coffee in mugs.

"Thanks, Susanne." Patrick lifted his, a souvenir from Yellowstone National Park with a picture of a big horn ram on it, to hide his struggle.

"Of course." She put the electric percolator back on the counter and started another pot.

When he'd regained his composure, he blew on his coffee. "So that's where we are. In a perfect world, I could watch all my family members all the time. And I guess if I cut out from work and took them out of school, I could."

Dr. John grinned. His curly white hair had missed a few trimmings. Watery blue eyes twinkled through his crooked wire-framed glasses. "Forget about that option."

Patrick grinned back. He glanced out the window. It was mild and spring-like outside for the first time this season, on the heels of the bitter cold of the previous few days. Green grass was fighting its way toward the sky out of melting snow. Several deer were nibbling it like they were afraid it would disappear if they didn't hurry. It had been a long winter of pawing through snow to get to sparse, dead stalks. From the garage, Ferdinand let out a mournful howl. He felt bad for the big dog, but with a yard full of hungry deer and a house full of guests, Ferdie was going to have to get used to temporary confinement.

"What are you doing to that animal in there, Doc? Torturing him?" Wes asked.

"Pathetic, isn't he? But to Dr. John's point, I already need more time off than my boss would like, for the trial itself."

"My patients will miss you," Dr. Crumpton said.

"Ha." Patrick enjoyed covering for the veterinarian when he was out of town. The things he had learned by trial and error with the veterinary patients had come in handy with his own animals. "As far as you guys go, our biggest concern is the kids' safety when they're at school. But it wouldn't hurt to have someone watching the house, and someone else following us when we are driving them. I know that sounds like a lot. Maybe it's too much. But I don't just want to keep them safe. If someone comes after them, I want us to have enough information that the police and sheriff can catch the bad guys and put them away for it."

"I take it you mean the Kemecke clan?" Wes said.

"It wouldn't surprise us at all."

Henry leaned a chair back on two legs. Susanne winced visibly. The dining room set was her pride and joy. He pointed at people and mouthed *one, two, three, four.* "I count four of us."

Vangie smacked his shoulder. "Five."

"Four," he said firmly, giving her 38-week pregnant belly a pat. "The trial may go on for a few weeks. We need more manpower. Would it be okay for us to recruit a few trusted friends?"

"I trust you, so if you trust someone who's willing to help, send them my way."

Heads nodded around the table.

The doorbell rang. Susanne went to answer it.

Patrick kept the discussion going. "Is anyone here friends with the principals at the junior high and high school? We need to let them know what's going on and ask for their cooperation." He'd dropped his voice so that the kids wouldn't hear, although both were upstairs, supposedly in their rooms. But he'd seen the two of them sneak into the hallway when they were younger to try to catch Santa in the act, and he didn't put anything past them. Especially since Trish was angry at them for keeping her home, and they'd disappointed Perry by nixing his idea for a ski day, in favor of this meeting. "We need the teachers to treat it as an emergency if the kids aren't in class, or if a stranger shows up at the schools for them."

Dr. John raised his hand. "Me. I'm on the school board. I'd be happy to make the calls."

Susanne walked in with Martin Ochoa.

He tweaked the end of his waxed mustache then took a seat, resting his hands on his belly. "Sorry I'm late."

A chorus of hellos rang out.

Patrick smiled. "Mayor, I'm just delighted you're here."

"Wouldn't miss it."

"Now I count five," Henry said.

"How are your parents, Martin?" Dr. John asked.

Martin sighed. "Stubborn as two old mules. I've been trying to get them a house in town where I can help them and they'd be closer to the hospital, but they insist on staying on their homestead. I haven't been able to get the state of Wyoming to take away their licenses, either, although neither of them should be driving. If I could, I might have more success in moving them."

Patrick knew Mr. Ochoa's health was failing. But he was very proud of his homestead. Many of the Basque families in the area had become land-wealthy. Martin's parents didn't fall in that category. His father had scrimped and saved while tending sheep and working odd jobs. When he had enough to buy a couple of acres and put his own stock on it, he'd married Martin's mother. They'd raised one child to adulthood and lived poor but happy, with Mr. Ochoa declaring himself the luckiest of men to anyone who would listen, his whole life. Or that was the story Ochoa liked to tell at chamber of commerce pancake breakfasts, anyway.

Dr. John rubbed his chin. "Give them my best. And let me know if I can help."

"Thank you. I will. Now, don't let me interrupt. Carry on, carry on."

Patrick said, "We were just getting to logistics. I can fill you in on everything else we've talked about when we finish up."

"Perfect."

"Okay, everyone. I'll see what kind of schedule I can cobble together if you'll each let me know your time restraints before you leave. I'll call everyone with it later tonight. And, then, hopefully, we'll be able to fill any holes with your recruits. If that's not enough, I'll see about hiring help."

"You mean like pay them with cash money? That doesn't sound like you, Doc," Wes said. His eyes were twinkling.

"I would hate it. Not because of the cost, though." Patrick might be a penny pincher, but he wouldn't hesitate to spend money on his family's safety. "It's more that I don't want to rely on some rent-a-cop who's paid by the hour, checking his watch, and longing for a nap."

The group laughed. What Patrick wanted was to *know* the people watching out for his family. That they cared about the Flints. That they were trustworthy.

Like the people around him. He swallowed down another lump.

After a little more discussion about logistics, the group wrapped up the meeting.

When the visitors had dispersed, Susanne started washing coffee cups in the sink. "Are you going to call Ronnie? Maybe she has an update from Sheriff Westbury about protection."

He picked up a clean mug and started drying it with a plaid dish towel. "I should. But we would have already heard from her by now if they were going to be able to help."

She slipped her arms around his waist, holding her wet hands away from his back and laying her head against his chest. "You're taking great care of us. You're my hero, you know."

He pulled her in tight. "I haven't done anything."

"Oh, but you have. You have."

They rocked back and forth for a few moments.

When Susanne released him, she dried her hands and brought him the phone. "Call Ronnie."

He took a deep breath. Gathered his thoughts. Rehearsed his words. Planned his calm response for when Ronnie told him Sheriff Westbury had turned down their request. Dialed Ronnie's home number.

"Hello."

"Ronnie, it's Patrick."

She sighed.

His stomach tightened like a sheath. Sighs were bad. He didn't like bad. "Did you talk to the sheriff about security for my family?"

"I'm sorry, Patrick. We're stretched really thin."

Patrick counted to ten. "Maybe someone could keep an eye on the school? Or talk to the principals, to help us express the gravity of the situation?"

Her voice changed, like she was reading words from a paper. "Since no concrete threats or actions have been taken against anyone in your family, I'm only authorized to tell you we'll do our best."

"Dammit." He rubbed his forehead and slumped back against the cabinets. "There haven't been any concrete threats or actions against Judge Renkin either."

"I said that to the sheriff myself. But the judge is a public figure whose wife was murdered, and he might have been the intended victim. It's different."

It wasn't. Not in Patrick's mind. But he knew he wasn't going to win. "Fine. I read you loud and clear. We'll handle this on our own."

"I'm so sorry."

He twisted his wedding ring. "It's not your fault."

"The sheriff has us scheduled eighteen hours a day through the trial. I want to help you guys. So badly."

He believed her. She'd bent over backwards for them before. Without Ronnie, Susanne would never have made it up Dome Mountain on a horse in the middle of the night, where she was then at the right place at the right time to shoot Kemecke, saving Patrick's life, and ensuring Trish's rescue. Ronnie had bucked the sheriff to do it, and he'd taken a chunk out of her hide for it. Patrick would never doubt Ronnie's heart.

But that didn't change anything for him and his family. He hung up the phone. He had a schedule to make for his security posse.

CHAPTER EIGHTEEN: ENSNARE

Trish

Trish had never been so happy for school in her whole life as she was that Monday. Sunday had been long and boring. "House protection" was like being grounded, but without the fun of doing something bad to earn it. At her locker, she'd slipped into Brandon's letter jacket and hung his class ring on a long chain around her neck. She waited for him there, but he didn't show up. He was tardy a lot, so this wasn't unusual. It was a bummer to start her day without seeing him, though. She spent most of the first few class periods writing notes to him and Marcy, using a new multicolor pen. She added a few hearts in red to Brandon's, then signed her name in green with WBS for "write back soon," even though he never did.

On her way to basketball, she stopped at the entrance to the gym. She always met Brandon there before she suited up. Peering through the bodies crowding the hallway, she stood on her tiptoes looking for him. Coach Lamkin was giving all of the girls the week off as a reward since varsity had gone to the state tournament. "Varsity's success is all of your success. You drilled together, conditioned together, and played each other all year. Good job," she'd said, the week before. Even though they weren't suiting up, they still had to be on time for attendance. Trish gave up on Brandon and hustled to the locker room. She beat the late bell by a few seconds.

Marcy was sitting in front of rows of painted metal lockers. She patted the bench beside her. She was shorter than Trish by a few inches and played first string point guard on the JV. Her nose was a cute button covered in a thick wash of freckles. She was wearing her dark brown hair in Pippi Longstocking braids. If Trish had her curls, she'd wear it down every day. Trish had tried to set her up with a few of Brandon's friends, since Marcy desperately wanted a boyfriend. It hadn't worked out with any of them.

She hurried into the spot Marcy had saved for her and handed her the note.

"We had a test last period. I couldn't write you one." Marcy rolled her brown eyes. Her lashes were so dark and long they looked fake.

The coach walked in and flipped her red ponytail over her shoulder. She took attendance, her back to the bank of communal showers that Trish hated, then said, "I expect you to use this period as a study hall." She winked. "Keep it to a dull roar, ladies."

Marcy and Trish exchanged a giggle. That meant they'd write notes and gossip the whole time. A shock wave of female voices began chattering at once. Things were about to get rowdy in the locker room.

The coach raised her voice over the din. "Flint, my office."

Flint? *Her?* That was what the coach always called her, but she barely ever talked to Trish. Although she had been nice to her in Laramie.

The coach disappeared down the short hallway toward her office.

"Oh, my God. What do you think she wants with you?" Marcy pushed Trish's shoulder playfully. Marcy was the star of the JV team. The coach talked to her a lot.

"I have no idea."

Marcy raised one eyebrow. It went up into a point in the middle, like the roof of a house. "What'd you do?"

"Nothing."

"Come on."

"I swear!"

"Right." Marcy laughed. "You'd better go before you get in even more trouble."

Trish walked toward the exit of the dressing room like she was heading for the gallows. She stopped at the coach's small office door, where she touched her underarms. She was pitting out. This was ridiculous. She hadn't done anything wrong. Her grades were great, she was never late, much less missed a practice, she always tried hard, and she never got in trouble at school, unlike at home. *Get it together girl.* She squeezed her hands into fists then opened them and stretched her fingers and palms so far that they inverted slightly. It helped, so she did it a few times. The butterflies in her stomach settled.

She raised her chin and shoulders and knocked on the door.

"Come in." The coach's voice was clipped.

Trish took the biggest breath she could fit in her lungs, then swung the door open on the exhale.

Coach Lamkin was sitting behind her desk, scribbling on some paperwork. She didn't look up. "Have a seat."

A large pile of newspapers filled the only other chair in the room. Trish hefted them onto the floor against the wall, wrinkling her nose at the dry, dusty smell, then sat. Loud clicks from the clock on the wall marked the seconds. Click one-thousand. Click two-thousand. Click three-thousand. Click four-thousand.

At thirty-two clicks, the coach raised her head and met Trish's eyes. "Hello, Flint."

"Hi, Coach Lamkin."

"I'll get right to the point. Are you planning on playing basketball again next year?"

Trish loved basketball. The squeak of shoes on the court, the perfect arc of a jump shot, the swish of a ball through a net, the sting in her hands when she caught a chest pass. She didn't even mind the rubbery smell of the ball or the dirt she had to scrub off her hands after every practice. What she loved most, though, was the idea of being good at basketball, and what other people would think about her if she were a good athlete.

Of course she would play again next year, unless she got cut from the team. "I am."

"Good. You've really been improving on your passing and dribbling."

Trish's mouth dropped. "I didn't think you'd noticed."

The coach frowned. "I notice all my players. You have a great work ethic. You're in better shape than anyone I've got, JV or varsity. Conditioning is critical in the final minutes of a game, when everyone else is out of gas."

Hearing the coach praise her felt unreal, like she was watching a movie version of her life. "Thank you."

"How would you feel about moving up to varsity?"

Of every possible thing the coach might have said, this was the last one Trish would have expected. "Really?" she squealed.

The coach smiled. "I'll take that to mean you're interested."

"Yes. Very. Thank you." Trish stumbled over her words and felt like an idiot.

The coach held up her hand. "Varsity is no bed of roses. And I won't be making any final decisions until the fall. But if you keep working hard and improving, you'll be in."

"I will. I promise."

"You should go to basketball camp this summer. The Flying Queens at Wayland Baptist have a great one. Or you could look for something closer."

A thrill ran through Trish, from her center and fluttering up through her chest. "I'll talk to my parents."

The coach's stern expression softened. "How are you and your family?"

She wasn't sure what Coach Lamkin meant. "Um, good, I guess?"

"It must have been hard, helping Jeannie Renkin after she was shot."

"Oh, yeah. It was." Trish wanted to talk about her future as a basketball star. She was already picturing her letter jacket. "But it was mostly my parents. I'm fine."

"You're tough. That's one of the things I like about you as a potential varsity player." Coach Lamkin pursed her lips. "Your poor mother, worrying about all of you. Especially since Perry saw the shooter."

Trish frowned. Her parents had told them not to talk about that. "That's supposed to be a secret."

"Of course. I haven't said a word to anyone since your mother told me last weekend. She was very upset."

"Yes. She is." Trish relaxed. It was nice having someone to talk to. Coach Lamkin was old enough to give good advice, but way cooler than her parents. "She and Dad have us on house arrest."

The coach nodded with sympathetic eyes. "I thought your dad was kind of rough on you at the game."

If Trish's heart had wings, it would have soared into the air and circled above their heads. "Big time. I know they're scared about our safety and all, but they've got this posse of people watching us night and day. We can't go anywhere or do anything."

"I'd do the same thing if I had kids, but maybe I could help—who should I call?"

"That would be very cool." Trish felt a strange sense of pride that her coach not only wanted her to be on varsity but also wanted to help her family. "My mom or dad, probably."

The coach winked. "I'm a little more fun than most of your chaperones, I'll bet."

Trish smiled. She felt giddy.

The bell rang announcing the end of the class period. Time had flown by. Normally she sprinted out to meet Brandon for lunch, but she wasn't sure if he would be there. She could have talked to Coach Lamkin for hours.

The coach pointed at the door. "Don't forget what we talked about. More practicing. More conditioning. And basketball camp."

Trish practically skipped out, beaming. "I promise."

Marcy was waiting for her outside the locker room. "Tell me, tell me."

They walked together toward the building exit.

Before Trish could answer Marcy, a man entered. He stopped when he saw them. "I'm looking for Coach Lamkin's office. Can you give me directions?"

Trish smirked. Only if he wanted to go inside the girl's locker room. He seemed a little shady, with pale skin, dark bags under his eyes, thin blond hair, and a weird accent. Where the heck was he from anyway? He sounded kind of Russian. She pointed back down the hall. "First door on the left. You have to knock real loud."

"Thanks." He walked the way she'd pointed.

"Okay, now tell me," Marcy demanded.

For some reason, Trish held back with her friend. "It was a pep talk. She was encouraging me to go to basketball camp."

"That's cool." Marcy smacked her gum. "Want to go to A&W with me since Brandon's not here?"

Trish could see Marcy's tongue stretching the gum thin. Marcy was terrible at blowing bubbles and always ended up with gum stuck to her face and sometimes her hair. "I don't have a car."

Marcy blew into the gum. It was too thick. Nothing happened, and she started chomping it again, like a cow with a great big cud. "Me either. My mom needed it to run errands. But Ryan and Jeff are going. They said we could tag along."

Trish shook her head. Brandon wouldn't like it if she went with Ryan and Jeff. He would think it was too much like a double date, even though she and Marcy were just friends with them. Marcy would have liked more, with either of them—she wasn't picky. "You go. I'm going to do my homework. I brought a sandwich."

Marcy's voice was sing song as she tickled Trish in the ribs. "I have some gossip you'll want to hear about a certain teacher getting it on with a certain senior."

Trish wriggled away. "What is it?"

"Are you sure you won't go? I'm getting a root beer float."

"I'm sure. But what's the gossip?"

"Later. Gotta run."

Trish groaned. Marcy waved and ran out to the curb. A gold Chevelle with a black rag top pulled up, the bright sun glinting off its hood. She hopped in the back seat, and the car sped off. Trish was dying to know who the rumors were about. She'd have to call Marcy later to get the scoop.

Before Trish turned to go, a tall, dark-haired boy walked up the sidewalk and into the school. She was so surprised, she froze in place.

It was Ben.

"Trish." He blushed and stuck his hands in the pockets of a black windbreaker.

"What are you doing here?"

A trio of senior girls walked by, their mouths open. One of them was Charla. "Hey, Ben," she said. "I'm glad you're back in town." She blew him a kiss. Ben didn't seem to notice them.

"I was wondering . . ." Ben said to Trish.

She waited. He didn't continue. The silence stretched out. She was starting to feel a little awkward.

Finally, he said, "Maybe we could—"

"There's my girl." Brandon bumped through the door and crutched his way down the hall toward them. His short-sleeved t-shirt rode up into his armpits from the action of the crutches. He scowled at Ben. "I can't leave her alone for a second without my own cousin zooming her." Then he socked Ben in the arm. "Just kidding, man. Bring the truck to the curb. I can drop you at my place before I take Trish to the park for some 'lunch'." The way he waggled his brows and emphasized lunch made it clear he was talking about something other than sandwiches and chips.

Trish dropped her eyes. It was embarrassing when Brandon talked like that in front of people. Ben stuck out his hand for Brandon's keys.

Brandon held them out, then pulled them back and lifted them shoulder high. "You wreck it, you buy it."

"I'm cool."

"I know, man."

Brandon relinquished the keys. Ben stuffed them and his hand in his pocket and folded his shoulders forward. Trish caught his glance as he closed the door, and he shook his head. *What was that about?*

"Nice jacket." Brandon closed in on her, easing her back against the cool tiled wall with his crutches on either side of her like a cage. He swooped down for a kiss.

"Let me see some daylight between the two of you," Coach Lamkin said. "None of that in the school, Trish. My players aren't rule breakers."

Blood rushed to Trish's cheeks. She wriggled out from between Brandon and the wall and looked at her coach. Coach Lamkin was with the guy who'd asked for directions earlier. He looked like he was trying not to laugh. "Yes, ma'am."

The coach and the man left.

"Yes, ma'am, Coach Lamkin." Brandon mimicked Trish's voice softly in her ear.

Trish pulled away from him. "I can't make her mad. She's thinking about moving me up to varsity next year."

Brandon's eyebrows shot up. "You?"

"Yes. Don't you think I'm good enough?"

"Yeah, sure. But it's, like, a lot of pressure, you know?"

"I know. But I don't mind." She remembered her note and stuck it in his pocket. "Hey, I have something I need to tell you. It's bad news."

"What?"

"I'm basically grounded until this trial is over. My parents have everyone in town following me and watching me, and I'm not allowed to go anywhere but school. Perry, too."

He scoffed. "Why?"

"They think we're not safe."

"They're such squares. When will I get to see you?"

"School. And after it's over."

"Great. I basically have an imaginary girlfriend."

Charla entered the building. Brandon glanced up. Charla looked straight down the hall, not acknowledging either of them. It made Trish uneasy, especially after she'd been so friendly to Ben. Was something going on between her and Brandon?

To get his attention back, she moved closer to him until their bodies were touching again. If the coach walked back by, she was toast. "I was going to tell you this morning. Where were you?"

"I had to see a doctor about my ankle."

"My dad?"

"Are you kidding me? My mom would never let me go to him. She wasn't happy he was the one who took care of it at the tournament. I went to Dr. John."

That was the truth. Still, her fists balled up. Her dad was a great doctor. The best in the area. But she knew better than to pick a fight with Brandon about his mother. "Is your ankle okay?"

His face grew dark, and his voice was bitter. "It'll be fine. Just enough to mess up the state tournament and my hopes for a scholarship. I'm supposed to use crutches for a few days, but I've about had it with them."

It wasn't like Brandon to be this negative. Something was off about him today. She tried to reassure him. "You'll get a scholarship. I just know it."

"I'd better. Not all of us have rich parents who can buy our way into whatever school and team we want."

Trish winced. Her parents weren't rich. And she was going to get an academic scholarship by working hard. No one was going to buy her way into anything.

He put his crutches under one arm and limped toward the exit, then turned his head over his shoulder. "Are you coming or not? Ben's waiting. We need to book."

Trish thought about what he'd said to Ben earlier, about lunch at the park. She knew she wasn't supposed to leave the school. Brandon was going to pressure her to go farther than she wanted, she knew it, and, in the mood he was in, he wasn't going to be happy when she said no. She hesitated for a moment, wrestling with her options, but the worst one was if she didn't go and he got upset. He might even break up with her.

"Let's split." She trotted after him, the too-large letter jacket flapping against her thighs.

CHAPTER NINETEEN: HARASS

Susanne

Susanne pushed her shopping cart toward the meat department in the grocery store. It was already too full, and a wonky wheel made it hard to push. As it wobbled up to the glass display case, she heard an unwelcome smoker's rasp.

"What's this I hear about you begging everyone in town to protect you from my family?" Donna Lewis sneered. "That's rich, since it's your husband who killed my mama and my brother. Maybe I should get someone to protect my family from yours."

Susanne fixed her eyes on the rows of meat in the display. She had to be strong and stay quiet. She couldn't give Donna the satisfaction of a response—the woman would just use it as more ammunition later. It was hard to ignore Donna's venom and concentrate on her selections, though. Susanne went over her shopping list in her head. Rump roast, hamburger, and a fry chicken. Rump roast, hamburger, chicken. Roast, hamburger, chicken. But there was no one to help her with them. Where was the attendant?

"Excuse me? Is there anyone here?" She dinged the bell on the countertop.

Donna moved in closer and put her hands on one side of Susanne's cart. "Did you think I wouldn't hear about it?" She snorted. "Not everyone on your little security posse thinks you're as special as you do."

Susanne's mouth went dry, and she rang the bell again. She needed to swallow, but her throat muscles seized up and the insides of it felt stuck together. Donna's revelation had rocked her. Someone they trusted had told Donna about the posse. Had she and Patrick put their faith in the wrong people? She couldn't imagine any of their friends violating their confidence. Yet clearly someone had talked. She had to call Patrick and tell him. But right now, she had to keep her chin up, so Donna wouldn't see she'd landed a blow.

The gray-haired attendant appeared, tying a soiled, bloody apron around his waist. "Sorry. I was eating lunch. How can I help you?" Susanne's comprehension was slow with his thick accent. He was clearly of Asian descent.

Donna shook her cart. "Cat got your tongue, Sue?"

Susanne *hated* being called Sue. Her anger finally overcame her good intentions. She turned so fast that her ponytail swung around and hit her in the cheek. Donna's smile was smug. She looked like one of the Hee Haw girls, with a clingy shirt tied too high and cut too low. Her hair was teased up like a beauty queen past her expiration date. Years of smoking had carved lines around her mouth. She was still a stunning woman and definitely the source of Brandon's blond good looks, but in a way Susanne's mother would have called, "rode hard and put up wet."

"My mama taught me that if you don't have something nice to say, you shouldn't say anything at all." She returned her attention to the attendant. She felt guilty that she didn't know enough about people from Asian countries to recognize his nationality. Overcompensating for her guilt and the awkward scene with Donna, she gave him her biggest smile and most perky voice. "Thank you. I'll have a rump roast—the biggest you have—two pounds of lean hamburger, and a large chicken cut for frying."

"I have those for you in just a minute."

Donna laughed. For a moment, Susanne was afraid the woman was gearing up for another verbal assault. But instead, she walked away, heels clacking on the floor. Tension ebbed from Susanne's body, and she sighed. She couldn't wait for this trial to be over.

"Here you go. Will that be all for you?" The attendant's voice shocked her out of her thoughts. He was extending three brown wax paper packages across the countertop toward her.

"Thank you. That's it." She took the meat. Paper crinkled under her hands.

He held on to it. For a moment, four hands clutched the stack of packages. Susanne's heart kicked up a notch.

"She not someone you want to make angry." He nodded at the figure of Donna Lewis, now far away down the back aisle of the store.

Susanne jerked the meat from him. "Thank you."

She tripped over her own feet in her rush to get away and would have fallen if she wasn't leaning on her hard-to-handle cart. It jerked her to-and-fro as she hurried toward checkout. She found herself longing for the familiarity and community of her Texas home. For people she could trust. For her mother and her sister. It had been Patrick's dream to move to Wyoming, not hers, and she'd struggled to fit in here. For a while, she'd begged to move back home. She didn't fit in, not really, with her Southern ways and her aversion to horses, camping, hunting, and the cold. She didn't even like to quilt, which is what the local women did all winter. That, and drink, which she wasn't big on either. But Patrick and the kids loved it here so much, she'd relented when he offered her a chance to buy her dream house. Lately, she'd finally started making friends, too, which was a miracle.

But now, with this trial and the divided loyalties of people in town, she was feeling a renewed urge to leave. Buffalo had never felt more foreign to her.

Checkout and the walk to the Suburban were a blur, as was helping the bag boy load the groceries. She tipped him on autopilot, not even glancing at his face. Her mind was fifteen hundred miles south. She climbed into the big vehicle—only then noticing her boots were sopping wet from the melt—and pulled out of her parking space.

Just before she exited the lot, a blue Volkswagen bus cut sideways in front of her and stopped. She slammed on her brakes, accustomed to winter conditions and expecting to slide, then grateful for the sun and slushy snow when she didn't.

The other vehicle didn't move.

Susanne peered into it at the other driver. It was a man, pasty, with a stringy dishwater mustache and shoulder-length hair that matched. Like a sickly lookalike for Maurice Gibb of the Bee Gees. What was the matter with him?

He said something. She couldn't hear him, but she was still able to read his lips. "Go home to Texas." His lopsided smile was sinister.

Then he sprayed slush from beneath his tires and cut into traffic heading west. Horns honked, and one truck had to cut sharply away to avoid hitting him.

Susanne gripped her steering wheel, hands trembling and her breathing shallow. This couldn't have been random, could it? It had to have been one of Kemecke's people. Forcing herself to breath deeper and more slowly, she calmed herself down. Behind her, a horn blared. She had planned to turn west toward home, but that was the same direction the van was headed. She would go east instead, toward downtown.

She accelerated and turned left. The honking stopped. She had no idea where she was headed, but she turned onto Main and saw an open space in front of the Big Horn Café, the only coffee shop and bakery in town. Coffee always helped. She parallel parked. After turning off the engine, she did a visual search around the Suburban, looking for signs of more trouble. There was no one around, so she got out and darted inside the shop, closing the door behind her and leaning against it.

The shop was small and poorly lit, holding only three round tables in front of the pastry display and cash register. Brightly colored community event posters covered one wall, and a collection of paintings on sections of tree trunk covered another. The paintings were whimsical—homages to coffee in loopy cursive strokes over bow-lipped women holding steaming mugs. Behind the counter, a tea pot whistled. The scents of coffee, cinnamon, and fresh-baked cookies wrapped her in a comforting embrace. Susanne exhaled. Coming here was the right decision.

"Susanne Flint?" The female voice addressing her was friendly.

Once bitten, twice shy, though. Susanne raised her eyes warily. At the pastry display stood a sturdy woman with a low bun, twenty years Susanne's senior. She recognized her. The woman worked as a nurse at the hospital. Susanne didn't know her very well, but Patrick spoke highly of her, which wasn't the case with all of his co-workers. In fact, the bad blood between the Flints and Donna Lewis hadn't started with her brothers or even the death of her mother. It had arisen when Donna had been fired from the hospital. Patrick had caught her stealing painkillers and turned her in. She'd never forgiven him for it.

Susanne wracked her brain for a name. Katie. No. Cora. No. Dang it. It was on the tip of her tongue. She was going to think Susanne was nuts, though, standing unspeaking at the door like she was barricading it from a horde of marauders.

Susanne roused herself and walked toward her. "Hello. How are you?"

"Can't complain. Just treating myself to a sugary late lunch on my afternoon off. Isn't this weather beautiful?"

"It is. I'm so ready for winter to be over."

The woman winked. "I think we can enjoy a short break from it, anyway. I was just about to sit down. Would you care to join me after you order?"

Susanne didn't usually socialize with women from the hospital, but she didn't want to leave the sanctuary of the shop. It was too small to stay if she rebuffed the offer. "Thank you. That would be lovely."

The woman walked to a table. Susanne eyed the selections. Streusel muffins, chocolate chip cookies, lemon scones. Cinnamon rolls. Pound cake. She smiled. She could never resist pound cake.

"May I help you, dear?" A flour-smudged face smiled over the case at her. Apple cheeks, pink lips, and pearly white pin curls under a jaunty black beret. "I just brewed Earl Grey if you'd care for some."

"Coffee and pound cake for me."

"Cream and sugar?"

"Yes, please."

"Plain or chocolate marbled?"

"Chocolate marbled."

"Will that be all?"

Patrick and the kids would enjoy cinnamon rolls for breakfast tomorrow. She ordered a dozen. "How much?"

The woman mouthed figures as she calculated in her head. She named a total, then wiped her hands on a dirty white apron and adjusted her hat. After she'd taken Susanne's money, she brought a teacup and saucer to the counter along with a bear claw on a bright green Fiesta Ware plate. "Kim, your order's ready."

Kim! That was it. Susanne stuffed a dollar in the tip jar. Kim ferried her drink and pastry to the table, and Susanne joined her a few minutes later with her own.

"Wes told me he's helping you guys with security." Kim ripped off a hunk of bear claw and popped it in her mouth.

Susanne cut a bite of cake. Did everyone know about their posse? There was no point in denying it. Besides, Patrick thought of Kim as one of the good guys. "Um, yes."

Kim chewed, swallowed, then sipped her coffee. "I figured that was why he was parked outside."

Susanne looked out the window, which was hard to do through floofy white curtains and lettering painted on the glass. Sure enough, Wes was parked in front of the Suburban in the big green International Harvester Travelall that he called "Gussie." Gussie was the closest thing Wes had to a long-term relationship with a female. He saw her looking at him and waved.

Seeing him there restored a little of her peace, and she waved back. "Yes. He's good people." She ate her bite of cake. The texture was perfect—moist and dense—and the butter flavor layered with dark chocolate was so delicious she had to stifle a moan.

"He's been so kind to me ever since Jeannie died."

Susanne covered her mouth. "Jeannie Renkin?"

"Yes. She and I have been best friends since Sheridan College. She was a nurse, before she married the judge, although he wasn't a judge yet back then."

"I didn't know. I'm so sorry for your loss."

"Thank you." Kim leaned in. "I know you have to testify in his court-room, and I'm sorry." She wrinkled her nose like she smelled a polecat. "I tried for Jeannie's sake, but I can't say I like him much."

Susanne thought about the way the judge had treated Patrick, the blackmailer conversation Patrick had overheard, and her own impression of Renkin. She wasn't going to talk out of school, but she didn't think much of him either. "Oh?" She sipped coffee, ate more cake, and gave Kim a chance to elaborate.

"He wasn't a good husband. He cheated on Jeannie, over and over."

"Really?" Susanne was honestly surprised. "With whom?"

Kim lowered her voice. "Well, last year it was Donna Lewis, but you didn't hear that from me."

Donna Lewis. Susanne already knew the woman had low moral standards, so she wasn't shocked, although she was a little scandalized. She couldn't stand cheaters. A nurse in Fort Washakie had made a play for Patrick a few months before, and Susanne had been tempted toward violence. Luckily for her, Patrick was ten times the man Harold Renkin was. "While Donna was still working at the hospital?"

"Yes. And it was hard for me to keep my thoughts about it to myself around Donna, let me tell you."

"I can imagine."

"Jeannie knew about Donna. Recently, she told me Harold had some new floozie. But maybe it was still Donna, for all I know. Then, just a week before she died, Jeannie said Harold swore to her it was over. But Jeannie didn't trust him. She told him she was leaving him, and he said—" she whispered loudly "—'over my dead body.'" She nodded. "Well, it wasn't his body that ended up dead now, was it? But it makes you wonder."

Susanne felt her mouth hanging open. She closed it. "You're kidding me?"

"I'm not. And believe me, that man had plenty of reasons not to want a divorce."

"Why not, if he'd taken up with another woman?" *Maybe he was in love,* Susanne thought. Although it seemed a stretch that anyone could love Donna. The woman was awful. And capable of awful things, too. *Was she capable of murder, like her brother Billy?* Jeannie was Donna's rival for the judge's affection, after all. Susanne struggled to pay attention to Kim as her thoughts pinballed all over the place.

"This campaign of his, for starters. For the U.S. Senate. He told Jeanne that politicians don't get divorced. But it's not just that. Jeannie knew about all the dirty things he's done. As long as they remained married, she'd never have to testify against him. But if they got divorced, she could be forced to the witness stand. The stories she could tell there would ruin him."

Susanne had suspected as much. Nobody got blackmailed unless they'd done things they wanted to keep quiet. Bad things.

"That's just *horrible.*" Which was understating it, if anything.

But then Susanne had another thought, and it was a doozie. Was it even appropriate for the judge to preside over a death penalty case involving the brother of his former lover? Wasn't that a conflict of interest because it would make him biased? Or susceptible to pressure from Donna? She could threaten him with revealing the details of their relationship if things didn't go the way she wanted. A small gasp burbled out of her.

Donna could even be the one blackmailing the judge.

CHAPTER TWENTY: SHOCK

Patrick

Patrick looked at his wristwatch again. Three-forty-five. He'd been parked outside the high school for fifteen minutes, per the plan he and Susanne had agreed on that morning: she'd pick up Perry, and he'd fetch Trish home. At first, there'd been quite an exodus of kids and vehicles. Then there'd been a wave of adults—teachers and staff. Now the flow had tapered off, with no sign of Trish.

At first, he'd assumed she'd been held up for basketball, until he remembered the season was over. Next, he'd thought maybe she'd stayed after a class to talk to a teacher or for detention. But he knew he couldn't afford to make assumptions. Not with all that was going on in their lives. He found himself scanning the open fields and creek frontage and realized he was looking for a mountain lion. He wasn't sure why, but regardless, he didn't see one.

Maybe he'd gotten his wires crossed with Susanne. She'd left a phone message with the operator at the hospital for him that afternoon. He'd been taking care of a guy who'd fallen headfirst through a window. Lots of stitches. Lots and lots of little bitty, teeny tiny stitches. By the time he was done, it was too late to call her back before he had to leave. Now, he regretted not taking the time. Had Susanne picked up Trish, and was Perry now standing on a curb waiting for him?

It was possible. But even if it were the case, he had to make sure Trish wasn't at the school. If she wasn't, he would borrow a phone in the office and call home to see what was up before he made a knee-jerk decision about his next move.

He got out of his truck—normally white, but currently looking more Dalmatian-colored because of all the mud—and walked to the building. His boots were waders by the time he made it to the front door. He paused inside to clean them on a mat, getting his bearings as he did. He'd been at the main building once for open house, but, other than that, he'd always visited the gymnasium. Luckily, the administrative offices were visible from the vestibule. He headed for them, wincing at the squelching sound of his sopping footwear.

The admin area was separated from the rest of the school behind glass, like a fishbowl. He poked his head through the main door. The overhead lights were off, and the front desk wasn't manned.

"Hello? Is anyone here?" he called.

A meager beam of light from one small window highlighted a warped floor tile. Devoid of color and decorations save a few personal photos on desks crowded close to each other, his mind conjured a crier greeting kids at the door with the admonition to "abandon hope, all ye who enter here." A narrow hallway led into a warren of offices that reeked of chemical cleaning supplies.

A few beats later, a man's voice answered. "Back here. May I help you?"

Patrick walked toward the voice. It came from inside an office marked "Principal" over the door.

He peered in. The office was more spacious than he would've imagined it, given the sparse reception area and premium on square footage. It was also warmer, in a way that suggested the principal had access to a personal decorating budget beyond whatever was provided by the school district. A chair in front of a scarred-but-handsome wooden desk anchored a multi-colored hook rug. A free-standing wooden bookcase covered most of one wall. Volumes of different sizes and colors were stuffed on the shelves, their spines creased from use. A series of paintings of big-bodied horses with tiny heads and hooves decorated the wall behind the principal. Prancing in front of a manor house. Drinking from a stream. Leaping over a hedgerow.

The man that rose from behind the desk had remarkable dandelion hair. He offered Patrick a smile that displayed coffee-stained teeth with a wide gap between the top center ones. "What can I do for you, sir?"

"Hello. I've been waiting outside for my daughter. I realized I'd better come in and find her or I'd be there until the cows came home."

The man shook his head. "Teenagers. I'm Ted Olsen, the principal here."

Patrick shook his hand. "Patrick Flint. My daughter is Trish Flint. She's a sophomore."

"It's Dr. Flint, isn't it?"

Patrick raised a hand. "Guilty."

"Trish is an exceptional student. She's got a bright future ahead of her."

"Thank you. We're proud of her."

"Strong-willed, too."

"Which is what brings me here today, I suspect."

"Well, let's see if we can find her."

The outer door to the admin area opened. A tremulous female voice shouted down the hall. "Help! One of my students is choking!"

"I'll call 911," Olsen shouted back.

Patrick reacted before Olsen reached for the phone. *He* was 911. But how he wished he had his doctor's bag, which he'd left in the truck. He didn't need the bag to deliver the Heimlich maneuver, though. "Make the call, Olsen. I'm going to see what I can do to help." He ran out the door of the office.

A very young-looking woman was running toward it. They both stopped. The woman was flushed and breathing hard. Her pinned-up hair was escaping its bindings.

"I'm a doctor," he said. "Can you take me to your student?"

"She's right this way."

Patrick nearly choked. "My daughter is here." He sounded panicked even to his own ears. *God, don't let it be Trish, please.*

The woman took a step back. "The girl's name is Marcy."

Marcy. Not Trish. The name rang a bell, but in his relief, he didn't place it. "Lead me to her."

The woman took off at a run that would have earned her a spot in the girl's 100-yard dash for the track team. Patrick pounded after her. Their loud steps echoed in the empty corridor.

As they flew past water fountains, rows of metal lockers, and one closed door after another, he raised his voice over the noise of their feet. "What happened?"

"I'm monitoring detention." Huff. "She was sitting in the back, talking to a boy." Huff. "He started screaming that she was choking." Huff. "And couldn't breathe. I tried to give her the Heimlich." Huff. "It wasn't working, so I ran for help."

Most people didn't know how to administer the Heimlich correctly, so Patrick was still hopeful the maneuver would work. He was worried about the time that had elapsed, though. Without oxygen, humans lose consciousness after about three minutes and can only survive seven to nine total.

"How long ago did it happen?"

The woman turned into a classroom going too fast and rammed against the open door. She shot him a stricken look over her shoulder. "A few minutes." Then she pointed to the back of the room. "There she is."

He hurried in that direction. A cluster of students were bending over someone on the floor. It had to be Marcy.

A pudgy boy with cowlicked hair stepped away from her. His eyes were enormous behind black-framed glasses. "Help her. Please. She can't breathe." His voice sounded young and scared.

Trying to sound calming and in command, Patrick said, "I'm Dr. Flint. Can you give me some room around Marcy, please?"

Eyes flitted to him, then back to the girl. The kids parted but stayed close to their friend.

"Does anyone know what she choked on?" Patrick knelt beside a girl with a familiar face and dark, curly hair in two braids. Marcy. Of course. Trish's best friend. His mouth tightened into a determined line. He couldn't face his daughter if this girl died in his care.

The boy with glasses said, "She, um, she put a rubber ball in her mouth."

That gave Patrick pause. "Hard rubber?"

"Yeah."

Marcy's face had a bluish cast, and she'd lost consciousness. He swept her mouth with his fingers. He could just feel the edge of the ball lodged deep in her throat. There was very little chance he could get it out before she died. He calculated the time until the EMTs would get there. From Olsen's call to mobilization, arrival, and entry into the school, they were four minutes away, at best.

Marcy didn't have four more minutes. It wasn't preferable, but he'd have to do an emergency cricothyrotomy.

"I need a ball point pen casing or a drinking straw, ASAP. I prefer the straw." He hoisted Marcy up with his arms under hers. First, he laid her across a desk and slapped her back five times, attempting to dislodge the ball. It didn't work. He picked her back up under the arms again and made a fist with one hand, locked the other around it just above her belly button, and started abdominal thrusts. By the time a student brought him a straw from a lunch box, he'd performed five thrusts with increasing pressure, enough that he might have broken one of her ribs but hadn't dislodged the ball. The Heimlich maneuver wasn't going to work.

Gently, he placed Marcy back on the floor on her back. He tore off his jacket and positioned it under her shoulders to elevate her neck, with the straw laying on her chest. He pulled out his pocketknife.

"Get the kids out of here, please," he said, without looking away from Marcy's throat.

As if far away down a tunnel, he heard the woman's voice calling to the students. There were footsteps and protesting kids' voices. But his world winnowed down to Marcy. Using the tip of the knife, he made a vertical incision just below her Adam's apple. Then he made a deeper transverse incision in the cricothyroid membrane. Quickly, he inserted the straw into the opening, adjusting its position until he heard air moving through it. He rocked back and watched her chest. It began to rise and fall. Sweat rolled down the side of his cheek. He breathed along with her.

Her eyes popped open. She gave him a look of abject confusion. Then she tried to speak. When it didn't work like she expected, pure terror froze her features.

"It's okay, Marcy. I'm Dr. Flint, Trish's dad." He squeezed her hand. "Don't try to talk. Just nod if you can hear me."

She nodded and squeezed back.

"You have a ball stuck in your throat. You couldn't breathe, and you'd passed out. So, I put in a hole for you to breathe through. You won't be able to talk until we get you fixed up at the hospital. Everything is going to be just fine though. All you need to do is stay relaxed and trust me. Can you do that?"

She nodded again, but scared confusion remained in her eyes.

He became aware of the other people in the room again. Kids were pushing their way back to Marcy, over the admonishments of the woman. He understood. Impromptu surgery in their classroom had to be morbidly fascinating.

The woman gave up trying to control them. Standing beside Marcy with her eyes averted from the girl's throat, she clasped her hands at chest-level. "That was amazing. Thank you so much, Doctor."

"Of course."

"What can I do?"

"Could you direct the EMTs to your room? They should be here by now."

But there was no need. The team was wheeling a stretcher through the door by that time. Two EMTs started loading Marcy onto it. Patrick recognized them. The woman with the funny walk and her tattooed partner. Patrick updated them on her condition.

The woman said, "The straw is holding. We'll fix her up with a better tube in the ambulance."

"Sounds good."

When the stretcher started moving, Patrick walked beside it, keeping a tight grip on Marcy's hand. "This is probably the most exciting detention you've ever had."

Something close to a smile crossed her face, but tears streamed down her cheeks. He continued speaking to her in a soothing tone, banal little nothings to distract her from the pain and fear. By the time they reached the ambulance, the stretcher had acquired an entourage, including the detention monitor, the principal, the students, and, to Patrick's surprise, Wes Braten.

Patrick leaned down to Marcy. "Dr. John will take good care of you at the hospital. You're going to be just fine."

The EMTs loaded the stretcher and left with their patient. Life was full of hard choices. He hated not being able to ride with Marcy, but she was in good hands. And he had a missing daughter to track down.

The detention monitor approached him. Running, she'd been fast and efficient. Walking, her short steps and waddling motion reminded him of a duck. He took a good look at her for the first time. She looked tired and old-fashioned in a high-necked blouse with lace at the collar, but pretty. "I'm Tara Coker. And you're Dr. Flint, Trish's dad?"

"I am."

"I'm her trigonometry teacher."

"I hope she's not trouble."

"No trouble. She's a smart girl." She licked her lips. Her eyes gleamed. "I've never seen someone do a tracheotomy before."

"Crike," he said. "Cricothyrotomy."

Before he could ask her if Trish had been in class that day, Wes interrupted. "Nice to see that knife put to good use, Doc. In fact, I think it lived up to its name."

"Name?" Tara Coker asked.

Wes winked. "Sawbones. I had it engraved for him."

Patrick chuckled. It had, at that.

Wes threw a chin in the direction of his big green Travelall. "Guess who I've got over there in Gussie, afraid to come see you?"

Patrick groaned. "Where did you find her?"

Olsen joined Coker. Both were listening intently to the interchange between Wes and Patrick.

"Stranded. Her boyfriend had a flat tire and no spare. I was just coming off my shift watching Susanne and was on my way home when I saw them."

More to himself than Wes, Patrick muttered, "But she knew I was coming to get her. Why would she leave?"

"Well, I don't think she'd *left* the school, Doc."

"What do you mean?"

"I think she was trying to get *back* to the school. They were at City Park. As in 'parking.' Filling in the gaps in the sketchy details of her story, I'd say they'd been there since lunch."

All of his worry morphed into red, hot anger. "Skipping school." Gritting his teeth, Patrick turned to Olsen. "This is the first I've heard of her doing that. Do you know if she's done it before?"

Olsen shook his head without hesitation. "If she had, word would have gotten to me. This is the first I've heard of it."

"My family has some security issues right now, due to a trial we're testifying in."

"The Kemecke capital murder trial?" Olsen asked.

"Yes. It's a long story." Patrick gestured at Wes. "Wes is on a team, helping watch our six."

Wes put his hands on his hips and thrust out his chest. He was too tall and gangly to look very imposing, though.

"Dr. John is helping us out as well. He was supposed to contact my kids' principals and ask that Susanne and I be notified immediately of any issues with the kids. Like them not being in class or people from outside the school looking for them."

The principal looked away, staring at the purple silhouette of the mountains. "Yes, Dr. John did call."

Patrick's voice vibrated with the tension of a taut piano wire. "Not showing up for class on the day you're told about our safety concerns seems like it warrants a phone call."

Olsen's gaze returned to Patrick. "I apologize for the misunderstanding. I hadn't heard about her absence."

Patrick turned to Trish's teacher. "Was she in trig today, Miss Coker?"

The woman folded her arms across her chest and hunched into them. "No. Not this afternoon. I'm sorry. I didn't realize there was an issue."

Patrick got a bad feeling. "Mr. Olsen, did you even talk to the teachers about the problem?"

Olsen cleared his throat and pulled at a fat, striped necktie. "Dr. John didn't get hold of me until mid-day. I was going to talk to the staff and faculty at our Tuesday morning meeting."

Patrick's fists balled.

Wes put a hand on his arm. "Brandon and Trish are waiting. Given their track record, I'd recommend we get out of here before they disappear again."

Patrick nodded curtly at the teacher, then the principal. "Good day."

Olsen stood. "Thanks for helping Marcy, Dr. Flint. And I'm glad that no one took your daughter. She played hooky. I wouldn't worry too much. Kids do that sometimes. I'll talk to her teachers tomorrow."

Patrick turned on his heel. Over his shoulder, he said, "She won't be coming back to school tomorrow. Or until this Kemecke trial is over."

CHAPTER TWENTY-ONE: DISCOVER

Perry

The Suburban hit a pothole and Perry's math book fell to the floorboard. He was still embarrassed about his mom waiting on him while he worked with his math tutor, parked right out in front of the school where anybody could have seen her and guessed why she was there. Other kids thought only dummies had tutors. He wasn't dumb. His mom had taken him in for an IQ test. When his parents had read him the results, they'd sounded relieved. He was smart. Really smart. Numbers just didn't get along with his brain, that was all. Or letters either. Somehow, what he saw on a page was just *different* from what his teachers told him it was. Letters, numbers—they all swam around and switched places with each other. No one believed him when he tried to explain it, which is why he had to stay after school for help and to finish his work. Again. The tutor was nice, but Perry could tell she was getting frustrated with him. Why did his weird brain have to make everything so hard?

His mom had taken him to A&W for an ice cream float and told him she was proud of him, but that didn't make it all better. He wasn't a little kid anymore.

He bent over to pick up the book before it got soaked from the water that had dripped from his shoes onto the floorboard. Stupid snow. The dirt road to their house was like ice skating in the morning and water skiing in the afternoon. The snow melt was digging some pretty big trenches and potholes, too. The Suburban hit another one, and he banged his head on the dashboard. Then, as he sat up, rubbing it, he saw something yellow whizz past. It was on the side of the road, where the snow was still drifted deep. A police car passed going the other way and splashed mud up the side of the Suburban and onto the windows.

"Hey! That's the snowmobile I saw at Meadowlark!" He was so excited that he shouted, even though his mom was only two feet away from him.

She braked. He caught himself on the dash, then leaned forward to get a look at the back of the snow machine as it zipped along a split rail fence. It was just like the one he'd seen on the mountain. Big. New. Yellow. Fancy. Black in the back. Was the same person riding it? He couldn't see the driver. Not that he knew much about the person anyway. Not really. Other than size—medium—and clothing—a white camo snow-suit. This person wasn't in white camo, but people could change clothes. It might be the killer, or it might not. There was no way to be sure. But that meant it *could* be. Here in his neighborhood. That wasn't good. A stomachache jabbed him so sharply that he bent over at the waist.

He waved his hand forward, over and over. "Go, Mom. We've got to get away. It could be the killer. Go, go."

She floored it, spinning the steering wheel as she did. The Suburban fishtailed and more mud splattered the windows, like soap suds in a drive-through car wash on opposites day.

"Is it still there?" His mom sounded out of breath. "Is it following us?"

The Suburban completed the sliding turn and straightened. Its wheels dug into the sloppy road and it jounced forward. He pressed his nose and forehead against the window to get a better look. His face bounced against the glass, but he didn't care. The snowmobile slowed to a stop in front of their neighbor's mailbox beside a cluster of the tallest pine trees on the road. At first, Perry thought it was turning around to come after them, but it didn't. The person climbed off. He was a big guy in a Stetson and a bulky brown jacket. He opened the box and retrieved a stack of mail, mounted the snowmobile, and tucked the mail under his blue jeans-clad thigh.

As they sped away, Perry said, "I don't think it's him."

His mom started chanting to herself. "Where's Wes, where's Wes, where's Wes?"

"What?"

"We shouldn't be alone. Your dad or someone else was supposed to be here."

His mom was kind of losing it. "It's okay, Mom. Everything will be fine."

She drew in a deep breath. "I know." She pressed her temple with the pads of her fingers.

The snowmobile grew smaller behind them. He could still see it well enough to tell that it went to their neighbor's house, though. "Whoever it was just pulled into the driveway next door to us. I think we can go home now."

His mom pressed the accelerator harder, still driving away from their house.

"Where are you going?"

"I don't want to get cornered. A deputy drove by a minute ago. We could catch up and ask for help."

Perry looked behind them again. "I don't think the snowmobile's coming. We're okay, Mom."

She didn't look like she believed him. "Could you see the person?"

"Yeah. He was big and tall and wearing a cowboy hat and blue jeans."

"It wasn't the person you saw on the mountain?"

"No."

His mom pulled the Suburban over to the side of the road just past Clear Creek. "Was it Judge Renkin?" Her voice was shaky.

"No. It was the guy who lives next door."

She sighed. "Perry, Judge Renkin lives next door to us"

Perry's voice squeaked. "The one whose wife was shot?"

"Yes."

"Huh." He hated it that maybe the shooter had double the reason to visit their neighborhood—Judge Renkin *and* Perry.

His mom bit her lip. "You're *sure* it wasn't the killer?"

"Yes, Mom. I already said so. That person wasn't big like this neighbor guy. Like Judge Renkin, I mean."

"Well, that's good." She drew in a deep breath and let it out slow and quivery. Then she reversed the Suburban. The vehicle yawned and whined as it backed up. When they were past their driveway, she put it in drive, turned in, and pulled it into the garage. On one side of them, bicycles hung from hooks along the wall. On the other hung long-handled tools and sleds. His dad's workbench was in front of the Suburban's bumper, everything in its place like he always kept it.

Perry got out and was just about to shut the garage door, when his dad and Trish drove in beside them in the truck. His mom stood at the door to the house, keys jangling in her hand, waiting.

Trish got out and walked slowly from the truck to the door. She kept her face down, but Perry could see her eyes were red and swollen and her cheeks were wet with tears.

When his dad was close to him, Perry whispered, "What's the matter with her?"

His mom threw her arms around his dad before he could answer.

"I have so much to tell you." Her voice sounded shaky again.

His dad put his chin on his mom's head and closed his eyes. "That makes two of us."

Perry hoped like crazy that she told his dad one thing in particular, the thing that had been bothering him ever since Laramie and especially bad last night at the sheriff's office with Ronnie. His mom had told people that Perry had seen the killer at Meadowlark. His dad needed to know, because he had let Ronnie believe no one knew about it except their family, and that wasn't true.

But it wasn't his secret to tell, and Perry couldn't rat his mom out. He just had to hope she did the right thing and fessed up.

CHAPTER TWENTY-TWO: BOMBARD

Susanne

Susanne whisked the gravy simmering on the stove. She wasn't sure how much more stress she could take. As it was, she'd been like the little teapot, all steamed up. She'd poured some of it out talking to Patrick while she'd hurriedly prepared a dinner of chicken fried venison cubes, canned corn, and mashed potatoes. The trial. Jeannie Renkin's murder. Donna's threats and harassment. Perry's predicament. Trish and the complications her love life were causing for all of them. Their neighbor, the judge. His suspicious behavior. The blackmailer. Kim's revelations about the Renkins' marriage and the judge's infidelity. His ties to Donna. Add to all of that Perry seeing Judge Renkin driving the killer's snowmobile, and she was about to blow her lid.

The potatoes were still boiling, the corn was ready, and the venison was in the oven, warming. She turned the heat to low under the gravy, then poured herself another cup of coffee. She definitely didn't need it. She was jumpy and jittery already. But she couldn't stop herself.

She rejoined Patrick at the table, which was already set for dinner.

His lips were moving, his foot was bouncing, and he was twisting his wedding ring. It appeared her stress level was contagious.

"I think we need to call Ronnie again," she said. "Someone in the sheriff's office needs to know about all of this."

Ferdinand put his head on the table and sniffed her cup, then sat and placed his chin on her leg. She scratched his neck.

Patrick nodded. "Are we in agreement about holding Trish out of school until after she testifies?"

Even though the brunt of dealing with her daughter's anger would fall on her, Susanne knew they couldn't trust Trish's judgment. To keep her safe, they had to keep her home. "Unfortunately, yes."

The phone rang. Both of them startled. Susanne's coffee sloshed onto the table. Ferdinand jumped back, then slunk to his bed with his head down and his tail tucked. Now the dog was anxious, too.

"I'll get the phone," Patrick said.

Susanne poured herself a fresh cup of coffee and grabbed a rag from a hook beside the sink.

"Hello," Patrick said. He held the curly cord in one hand and started pacing the kitchen and eating area. It was a big kitchen, but his long strides ate it up. Soon he was on his tenth lap.

Susanne sopped up the spilled coffee and listened in, but Patrick didn't say anything for several long seconds. In the state she was in, it felt like hours. She threw away a ruined paper napkin, re-hung the rag, and went to stand at the picture window. The creek volume had increased with the melt underway at the lower elevations. The water was churning, like her insides. Every day, it built toward its spring crescendo. The creek didn't give her the peace she was hoping for, so she turned around and put her hands on the smooth, cool table. Her eyes fell on a family portrait hanging on the wall on the far end of the dining area. The kids had been little—five and two, if she remembered correctly. Her mother had taken it in south Texas during the wildflower bloom. The four Flints were sitting in a field of bluebonnets and vivid red Indian paintbrush. At the time, she'd thought their lives were hectic. Kindergarten for Trish. Potty training for Perry. Patrick about to graduate from medical school. If only she'd known how much crazier things would get, she would have relished the simplicity. She certainly longed for it now.

Patrick picked up the volunteer schedule from the hutch and traced down it with his finger. "I appreciate it. We'll take all the help we can get. How about Tuesday from four to nine p.m.?" He paused, then scribbled something. Knowing his doctor's scrawl as she did, Susanne would be willing to wager it was illegible. He hung up the phone.

Trish ducked into the kitchen and retrieved a glass from the cabinet.

"Dinner's almost ready," Susanne told her.

As Trish filled her glass with tap water, she said, "Not that anybody cares, but Coach Lamkin told me she's thinking of moving me up to varsity next year."

Susanne and Patrick shared a look. His wide eyes mirrored the surprise she felt.

"That's great, sweetie. We do care, very much." Susanne walked over to Trish, who'd turned to face them, and tucked a blonde wisp behind her daughter's ear. "I'm very proud of you."

"Not proud enough to trust me."

"You've been making bad choices." Patrick laid the schedule back on the hutch.

Trish's voice rose. "I just went to lunch. I can't help it that we got a flat tire."

Patrick crossed his arms. "Lunch was three hours before school was out. Or more. You'd cut class, with the boy you'd promised not to see outside of school, when we'd asked you not to leave school except with your mom and me. Don't make this worse by twisting things and lying."

She kept going like he hadn't said a word. "And now you won't even let me go see my best friend in the hospital." Trish scowled. "It's like you hate me."

It wasn't technically true that they wouldn't let her go to the hospital. They'd offered to take her to see Marcy, but Trish had balked when they wouldn't let her drive herself there alone. Yes, the girl was definitely twisting the story to suit her own purposes.

Susanne joined Patrick and put her hand on his shoulder. "We don't hate you. We love you. But we're not here to be your friends. We're your parents, and we have to do what we think is best for you. Right now, that means we'll do whatever is necessary to keep you safe."

Trish looked away from Susanne. "So, locking me up in this house with *Mom* will protect me?" Her voice was scoffing. "If someone was trying to get me, Mom couldn't scare off a fly."

Patrick stood. His eyes flashed. "I won't tolerate disrespect in this house, especially not toward your mother. Don't forget she's the one who saved you and me both when she came after us and shot Billy Kemecke."

Trish set her glass down too hard on the counter. "Fine. Whatever you say." She stomped out, turning for one last salvo from the foot of the stairs. "I can't even practice basketball, and I'm out of library books." Then she stomped up the treads like an angry toddler. Ferdinand ran after her, shooting a sheepish glance back at them.

When her bedroom door slammed, Patrick shook his head. "That went well."

"She's impossible."

"Maybe you could take her to the library tomorrow."

"I will. After she does her schoolwork and spends some time with her horse. Goldie has gotten the worst of Trish being in love."

"Good idea. Maybe she could give all three horses some attention."

Susanne felt a pang at his words. Her own horse, Cindy, was a crime that Kemecke wouldn't answer for, but the mare had been one of the victims of his gang nonetheless. They'd slit her throat, for no reason. A lump rose in Susanne's own throat, and she swiped at tears. How could she still be so sad about a horse she'd been afraid of and didn't like to ride? Patrick had offered to find her another horse, but she didn't want one. She hadn't been a horse person in the first place. And a new one wouldn't fix her guilt and sadness about Cindy anyway.

She checked the potatoes. They were ready. She turned off the burner and went to the phone and lifted the receiver. "Ronnie next?"

Patrick nodded. She'd whip the potatoes and serve dinner when the call was done. She dialed Ronnie's home number by heart. When there was no answer, she looked up the number for the sheriff's office in the phone book and tried again.

"Johnson County Sheriff. May I help you?" The woman's voice sounded harried. It also sounded like it wasn't from around there. Boston, maybe?

"Deputy Harcourt, please."

"May I ask who's calling?"

"Susanne Flint."

The line went silent for a few seconds.

When Ronnie's voice came on, she sounded even more harried than the receptionist. "Susanne?"

"Hi, Ronnie. Do you have a moment?"

"Just. I was about to run home for a shower, food, and a nap before my next shift, which is going to be in your neighborhood. I've got judge-sitting duty."

Susanne quickly told Ronnie about Donna's harassment, the threatening man in the grocery store parking lot, and their suspicions about the judge. When she'd finished laying out everything she and Patrick had learned or suspected, Ronnie's silence was ominous.

"Hello? Ronnie?"

"I'm here. Just digesting." She made a hmm sound. "So, you guys think Judge Renkin killed Jeannie?"

"We hope not, but we're worried he might have."

"But wasn't he standing right next to her when she was shot?"

Patrick sidled up to Susanne. She tilted the receiver toward him, and he leaned his head in so he could hear, too.

Susanne said, "We're not saying he was the shooter, obviously. But he had motive to want Jeannie dead, and I'm sure he has the money to hire a gunman. And he should know enough bad guys from his years as a judge and lawyer to be able to find someone willing."

"His motive being the supposed girlfriend?"

"What do you mean by *supposed*?"

"Well, at this point, we don't have Jeannie, or the judge, or the girlfriend confirming the relationship. It's only gossip until we do."

"Kim was best friends with Jeannie. She said Renkin was having an affair with Donna. Donna could confirm it."

"Maybe. But her cooperation is highly unlikely."

Susanne's frustration was climbing fast. She tried another tack. "Isn't it a conflict of interest for the judge to hear the Kemecke case if he's involved with Kemecke's sister?"

"That's a question for the courts, not law enforcement. And it still doesn't help much with motive. Why do you think his girlfriend was a motive?"

Patrick whispered, "We need to talk to the county attorney."

Susanne nodded at him. "Fine. We'll talk to Max." When they talked to Max about the conflict of interest, they could raise the issue of testimony by affidavit one more time. If Judge Renkin was dirty—and she knew he was—then what he'd told Patrick couldn't be taken as gospel. Then she answered Ronnie's question. "Renkin's motive could be to clear the way to be with the girlfriend. Or maybe it wasn't the girlfriend. He could have had it done to keep Jeannie from divorcing him and ever talking about the things she knew that could hurt his senatorial campaign."

Patrick added, "Or even to collect life insurance so he could pay off the blackmailer I heard him talking to."

"I assume that's Patrick, unless you have a new husband or boyfriend you want to tell me about?"

"You got it on the first guess."

"Patrick, you're absolutely sure it was a blackmailer you heard him talking to?"

"Yes." Then Patrick grimaced. "Ninety-nine point nine percent, anyway."

Susanne could hear Ronnie's raised eyebrows in her voice. "Okay. Assuming it was a blackmailer, isn't it just as possible, if not more likely, that the blackmailer was the killer?"

Susanne nodded. She could see the blackmailer threatening the judge's wife, then showing the judge he meant business by following through on it. "Possibly. But then how do you explain the judge's snowmobile being up on Meadowlark with the shooter?"

"I don't, because I'm not sure that it was. There are a lot of snowmobiles around. Even big fancy new yellow ones."

"It would be an incredible coincidence—the judge having a snowmobile just like the person who killed his wife."

"And yet it could be just that. I'm not buying that the judge trusted anyone enough to have Jeannie killed with a long range shot when he was standing right next to her. He could have just as easily taken that bullet himself."

Patrick shook his head. "He wasn't right next to her. He was near her, but far enough away to be safe if the shooter was any good. And his proximity draws suspicion away from him."

"Still, it's a big risk. Listen, I'm not saying you guys are wrong. I'm glad you called. All of this that you've told me is important. I've written it all down, and I'll brief the team investigating Jeannie's murder. But the most likely scenarios are that the killer was someone trying to prevent the judge from hearing the Kemecke case, given the timing, or the blackmailer sending a message to Renkin."

Susanne's voice broke. "Please, Ronnie. He lives next door to us. He's going to find out Perry was a witness—the only witness—if he hasn't already. Perry. Our son. If there's even a chance that the judge is behind Jeannie's death, we need to find out. You said you're his next babysitter. Can you look into it for us—just a little bit?"

"I can try to ask him a few questions, but I can't torture a confession out of him. Honestly, we don't even have enough to get a judge to issue a subpoena for his records."

Patrick spoke through gritted teeth. "But you don't have anything else either. No other witness. No weapon. No nothing."

"I'm not disputing that."

If Ronnie had been in their kitchen, Susanne would have grabbed her by the hands. "Just find out whether Jeannie had life insurance, please. And maybe who the girlfriend is. And the blackmailer."

"You're dreaming. I'll try for the life insurance."

Susanne exhaled. "Thank you, Ronnie."

"Now, I gotta go. You guys be careful."

"We will."

Ronnie hung up. Susanne put the receiver back on the hook, and she and Patrick exchanged a worried glance.

She said, "Trying for the life insurance is better than nothing."

But not much. Not much at all when the safety of their kids was at stake.

CHAPTER TWENTY-THREE: CHOOSE

Buffalo, Wyoming
Tuesday, March 15, 1977, 6:00 a.m.

Patrick

Rubbing his eyes with one hand, Patrick downed the last of his fourth cup of lounge coffee. This time of the morning it was still fresh, although not as good as what Susanne made at home. By mid-day, the contents of the pot would be burned and bitter. He stretched his arms over his head, sitting forward on the plush couch. The lounge was small but comfortable, with two velour recliners in addition to the sofa. All great for catnapping. Like the rest of the hospital, the decoration stopped with furniture. What money the hospital had went to function, not form.

He slapped his cheeks, trying to shock himself into alertness. He'd been on-shift since five a.m. and he was hurting for certain after a mostly sleepless night. Until his alarm went off at four-fifteen, he'd paced the house, his eyes drilling into the darkness, looking for threats. Never mind that Henry was on patrol and that he knew he could trust him with his and his family's lives. His brain wouldn't let him rest. It conjured up worst case scenario after worst case scenario, each ending in a bloodbath with no survivors. He'd kept his shotgun at the ready, in hand more often than not. Leaving his family to come to work was one of the hardest things he had ever done.

If this trial went on for a month, how would he possibly hold up? The worry was eating him alive.

Dear God, I know I don't visit your house of worship as often as I should, but I'd sure appreciate an easy day, where I first do no harm. Today the bar might go no higher than that. And if it did, it would still be a good day as a doctor. He'd been lucky this morning, so far. Or maybe it was the patients who'd been lucky. He'd had no cases that taxed his abilities. Strep throat. A flare-up of gout. Five simple stitches in an arm. He'd even had time to check on Marcy, where he found her well, other than her very sore throat and the stitches in her neck.

He straightened his monogrammed white doctor's coat and hurried back from the lounge to the duty nurse's station, where Kim looked wide awake and unruffled in pink scrubs. A teetering stack of files was perched in front of her, and she was riffling through them.

He smiled at her. "What do you have for me next?"

"Live it up while you can. Your slate is clear."

"I'd try for a nap, but that would guarantee a rush."

She laughed. "Don't you dare, then. I'm almost due for a coffee break."

"I'll grab one for you. Two sugars and a cream, right?"

"You don't have to do that."

"It's no problem. Back in two shakes."

True to his word, Patrick returned quickly with the milky, sugary coffee. Kim was just hanging up the phone. He handed it to her without spilling, even though his hands were trembling from sleep deprivation. "Here you go."

"Thanks, Dr. Flint." She sipped it. "Perfect."

For a moment, he considered asking her about Judge Renkin and Donna Lewis. But that felt too much like prying into the private conversation Kim had with Susanne. Besides, Susanne had already asked her about it at the time. "I'll be in my office catching up on some reading." *With my eyes resting.* He turned to leave.

Kim stalled him. "I just got a call from my daughter."

"Isn't she getting ready for school?" Casey was a year behind Trish. She had been a late-in-life baby for Kim and her husband.

"She is. She got a call from a friend with some news so juicy that she called me right away. It will be of interest to your family, too."

Patrick's heart lodged in his throat. The trial? The judge? The Kemeckes? Jeannie's murder? He forced himself to remain calm and choked out a normal-sounding reply. "What is it?"

She put a hand next to her mouth, like she was sharing a secret. "The high school is looking for a new girls' basketball coach."

His brow furrowed. The information was so completely out of left field that he was speechless.

She laughed. "Your expression is priceless."

He recovered. "Since when? And why?" Trish would be dying to know, if she didn't already. He bet someone had already called her. He wondered how breakfast was going for Susanne with their churlish and uncooperative teen. Not good, if Trish had gotten that news, he'd bet.

"Casey's friend overheard her English teacher talking to her math teacher in the hall yesterday, and they said that Lamkin won't be available next school year."

The telephone rang. Kim answered, listened, said, "Just one moment," then held it out to him. She whispered, "Well la-di-da. It's the governor's office. For you."

Patrick's eyebrows shot up, stretching his tight, tense forehead. The governor? He'd only met the man once, at Jeannie's viewing. He took the phone, cleared his throat, and said, "This is Dr. Patrick Flint speaking."

He turned away from Kim, wishing he could take the call without an audience, but he was limited to the privacy he could find between where he was standing and the end of the cord. He stretched it to its max.

"Dr. Flint, this is Shep Rawlins."

"Governor. You're an early riser."

"There are some things I like to take care of outside normal business hours. I'm glad I caught you."

Patrick's radar went up. He was something the governor needed to take care of outside normal hours, as in "without any witnesses?" That was ominous. "To what do I owe the honor of a call from you?"

The governor's voice sounded amused. "I'm not sure I'd call it an honor. More like a chance to do me a favor, Patrick. May I call you Patrick?"

Patrick flinched. Something about the request made him want to say no, even though he didn't usually stand on ceremony. "That would be fine. What's the favor, sir?"

"I've been told you've asked for police protection for your family. Because of the Kemecke trial."

That was simplifying things, but it wasn't incorrect. "Yes, sir. I have."

"I also heard you've made . . . we'll just call them *inquiries* about Harold Renkin. To the authorities."

Patrick got really uncomfortable, really fast. From Susanne's lips to Ronnie's ears last night, and, by six a.m., on to *the governor*? He and Susanne had wanted the information to go to the sheriff's staff, but he hadn't dreamed it would get to Cheyenne overnight. If the governor knew, who else did? A cold dread seeped over him. Did *Renkin* know? He forced his attention back to the call. "Uh, yes I have."

"I'm not sure if you're aware, but Harold is a good friend of mine. He's also running for the U.S. Senate. I think he's going to do a lot of great things for the people of Wyoming, in addition to the bang-up job he's doing for us as a judge. This *historic* capital murder trial is just one example of that." He paused, as if to let Patrick speak, if he chose to.

Patrick didn't choose to.

The governor didn't miss a beat. "I'd consider it a personal favor if you could give the old boy a chance. He didn't have anything to do with his wife's death, and he sure doesn't mean any harm to your family. I give you my personal assurance on that."

Unless Rawlins had killed Jeannie himself, his assurance meant nothing to Patrick. Evidence. As a doctor, he was trained to collect evidence—information—and let it lead him to a conclusion—a diagnosis and a course of treatment. Nowhere in his education was he taught to let personal assurances guide him, no matter how many times a patient showed up at the hospital with a spouse who assured him that his wife hadn't been drinking before she wrecked her car. Or a wife who assured him that her husband had never laid a hand on her before and wouldn't ever do it again. Or with a mother who assured him that her son would never get into a bar fight. Assurances weren't evidence. They were more like what attorneys used—arguments. Arguments, which were motivated by personal interest. In the case of attorneys, that interest was more professional, but still personal in the sense that it was put forth to advocate for a client's position.

Rawlins' assurance was nothing but advocacy for Renkin.

Patrick waited for the governor to finish.

"Could you do that for me, Patrick? And, in return, I'd like to do something for you."

The quid pro quo. Patrick fought to keep the sardonic edge in his head out of his spoken words. "What's that?"

"I'd like to send one of the best members of my security team to Buffalo in the morning to ensure the safety of your family during this trial."

Patrick felt like he'd just taken a big bite of boiled okra. He needed to answer the governor, but his mouth felt slimy even thinking about it. His family's safety came before anything. But his ethics were important, too. If he refused the governor, which felt like the honorable thing to do, he had the posse. And he knew that Ronnie was always in the background, ready to help in case of emergency.

"Patrick?"

But if he said yes to the governor, he'd get the security guard, who would protect his family from any and every source of danger, even if it turned out to be the judge. The Flints had already made their concerns about Renkin known to the sheriff's department. It wasn't like Patrick would be turning a blind eye on Renkin by taking the governor's offer.

Dang it. He'd be a fool not to take the protection, even if it felt slimy.

"All right," he choked out.

"Wonderful. Shall I have Juan Morales report to you at the hospital tomorrow?"

"The trial starts tomorrow."

"All right. Let's say the courthouse then."

"The courthouse. Yes."

"This call has been a real pleasure, Patrick. If you'd ever consider a move to Cheyenne, let me know. I'll be looking for someone to head up the Board of Health for my next term." He chuckled self-deprecatingly. "Assuming the people choose to re-elect me." But his tone of voice didn't sound like he doubted they would.

The bull pucky was getting so deep, Patrick felt like he needed to clean his boots.

The young receptionist poked her head around the corner. "Got a possible heart attack in the waiting room. Fifty-five-year-old male with chest pains."

Patrick and Kim exchanged a look. He nodded and said, "I'm sorry, Governor. We have an emergency. I have to hang up now."

"Duty calls here, too."

The governor was just starting to say goodbye as Patrick hung up the phone.

Kim touched the stethoscope hanging from her neck as she stood. "Put him in a wheelchair and get him into exam room one."

The receptionist nodded and disappeared back around the corner.

"I'll meet you there," Patrick told Kim. He needed a minute to recover from the unsettling call.

Two minutes later, Patrick went to join Kim and the patient. He looked up as he entered the exam room and stopped short. A pale, broad-shouldered man with a starter belly reclined on the exam table. It was the man who may have killed his own wife. The judge who had dismissed Patrick's concerns about the welfare of his wife and daughter. The neighbor who might be on the hunt for Patrick's son. And the subject of the smarmy call he'd just had with the governor of Wyoming.

Harold Renkin.

The judge's first words were, "You've got to help me, Dr. Flint. I think I've been poisoned."

CHAPTER TWENTY-FOUR: DOCTOR

Patrick

Hours later, Patrick knocked on the door of the room where Judge Renkin was resting, as was his regular practice. Patients deserved respect for privacy, even when the expectation of it was very low. It was these little things, in his opinion, that made people feel human. Feeling human was important to their mental status and overall well-being. To healing. So, he waited for Renkin to re-invite him, even though he'd been in and out of the door ten times already.

Renkin grunted. That was good enough, and Patrick slipped inside, shutting the door behind him. Renkin had color back in his cheeks and was sitting up straight on the bed, a white sheet washed repeatedly to a dingy color pulled up to his waist, and wearing a frayed blue gown open to the back. The room was small, with white walls, sheet vinyl flooring, and no furniture except for a plastic chair with metal legs for visitors, although he'd had none, and a black-seated rolling stool for the doctor. Along one wall was a countertop with medical supplies and equipment in cannisters—cotton balls, swabs, and bandages. Below it was cabinets and drawers.

Under Patrick's *first, do no harm* mantra for the day, it seemed he'd succeeded with the judge. It hadn't been easy, given his reservations about the man, as well as the odd timing. He couldn't help wondering if Renkin's ER visit and Rawlins' call were related. It was too big a coincidence not to question it. He had to shake it off, though, and focus on his patient. This patient. No matter who he was.

He held up a stack of papers. "I have your repeat electrocardiogram and your second round of blood work back. It shows no change from your initial EKG and blood work—no evidence of a heart attack or heart damage."

Renkin had exhibited increasing displeasure with the staff while resting under observation between the initial round of tests and the second round four hours later. But now he lifted his face heavenward. In a throaty voice, he whispered, "Thank you, God." Then he locked eyes with Patrick. "What about signs of poison?"

Patrick pulled the stool toward the table and sat. Although Renkin had been worried about poisoning when he'd arrived, the symptoms he'd described had sounded more like intestinal upset, an episode of anxiety, or a potential heart attack. Patrick hadn't ruled out poisoning, but he'd proceeded with that hypothesis in parallel to the more likely causes of Renkin's distress. "We won't get a tox screen back for a week to ten days. But if you'd ingested a type of poison capable of causing a heart attack, you'd have already had one by now. And you haven't. I don't see any other symptoms that point to poison, either. How's your chest pain?"

Renkin palpated his chest and shoulder. "It's still sore, but mostly better."

Patrick slow nodded several times. "You're under a lot of pressure. Your wife's death. The capital murder trial. And . . . other things." The judge shot Patrick a glare, but Patrick didn't give him a chance to interject. "I think it's most likely that this was an episode of acute anxiety."

Renkin pushed himself upright in the bed. His face turned red, which made Patrick even more confident of his diagnosis. The man was under the grips of extreme stress and emotions. "Anxiety? Like a mental disorder? Impossible. It felt like I was having a heart attack, not like I was going crazy."

Patrick had expected his reaction. Most people wanted to be told they had something that could be fixed with a pill or a knife. And they equated anything mental with "crazy." Crazy couldn't be fixed, and it changed how people were regarded by others. It was difficult to get patients, or the public, to understand that mental issues were a normal part of the human condition.

"Not a disorder. An episode. And I'm not saying you're crazy."

"Sounded like it to me. People have labeled Judge Ellis as loony tunes since the story came out that he killed himself. I can't let that happen to me, too."

"I didn't say you were crazy, Judge. And, for the record, I don't have any reason to think Ellis was either."

He harrumphed. "Mental disorder."

"Anxiety episode."

"Preposterous. I don't know how you could even reach that conclusion."

"From the evidence—your symptoms. The ones you had as well as the ones you didn't have." Patrick ticked a list off on his fingers. "You had an accelerated heart rate and rapid breathing. You were pale, sweaty, and tired. You had chest pain down into your arm, but you didn't have some of the other symptoms I usually see with a heart attack. Like neck or jaw pain. Nausea or indigestion. And, as I said already, your EKG and blood work were good."

The judge shook his head. "You can't ignore the coincidence. Judge Ellis died under suspicious circumstances on the eve of the Kemecke trial. Now, on the eve of the same trial in my courtroom, I have this attack. Ellis was no more suicidal than I am, and I can assure you that I'm not. Our sheriff thinks the tox screen will show Ellis was drugged. And I think that's what my tox screen will show, too. My money says Kemecke's supporters are behind my . . . episode."

"If they tried to kill you, they didn't succeed this time. But I don't think you were poisoned or drugged. I've consulted with the cardiologist in Casper. In an abundance of caution, I'd like you to stay overnight so I can repeat the blood work in twelve hours."

The judge's voice was a shocked roar. "Impossible. The trial starts in the morning."

Patrick wasn't a skeptic by nature, but it was possible the judge had been faking since he'd walked into the ER that morning, to throw suspicion off himself and create sympathy. If he had, he was even more dangerous to the Flints now. Patrick didn't mind at all that by keeping the judge overnight he would keep him away from Susanne and the kids. It would bridge more of the gap until the governor's security guard arrived, too.

He stood his ground.

"Exactly. You're an important man to this state and county. We need to take good care of you."

"Good care of me? I won't sleep a wink here. I have to be at my best. I have a duty to the people."

If Patrick couldn't convince Renkin to stay, he couldn't legally hold him against his will either. He could be stubborn and require him to sign out against medical advice, but it was a stretch. Renkin just didn't have the risk factors to support that decision. He wasn't obese, didn't have diabetes, and claimed no personal or family history of hypertension or heart disease.

Patrick decided he had to let him go without the signature. "All right. It will be your choice. But if you're leaving, you're doing it against medical advice."

Renkin sneered. "Dr. John wouldn't be such a hard ass about this."

"I'm not being a . . . I'm not being hard. I'm standing behind my medical opinion. I can't guarantee this won't happen to you again. You might even be in the beginning of an incident that will escalate tonight."

"Duly noted."

Patrick grabbed his stethoscope. "Let me listen to your chest one more time." He rubbed his stethoscope on his own shirt to warm it, then slid it under Renkin's gown, moving it several times as he listened closely. When he didn't hear anything out of the ordinary, he took Renkin's blood pressure. Then he counted his pulse.

Finally, he nodded. "I'm going to need you to schedule a follow-up appointment about your blood pressure. It's 160 over 110. That's not immediately dangerous, but it's too high. For the sake of your health, I'd like to see you do something to control the stress in your life. It wouldn't hurt you to lose some weight and drink less, too."

"You're kidding, right?"

"I can assure you, I'm not."

"Fine. I'll make an appointment for after the trial."

Patrick never ceased to be amazed at how quickly patients could go from prioritizing a health situation to rationalizing why it was no longer important. Nothing short of an emergency deserved attention. But that is just what the situation would become if they put off care too long.

"Will you at least come in for daily blood pressure checks? The staff can handle them in just a few minutes. No appointment necessary. That way we can put you on a diuretic if your blood pressure doesn't come down."

"Fine."

Patrick thought Renkin coming in every day for BP checks was about as likely as Susanne asking him to get her another horse. "We can release you now, and you can make your follow-up appointment before you head home."

"Is my deputy here?"

"Your protection detail?"

"Yes."

"I'll check while we get your paperwork ready." Patrick stood.

Renkin cleared his throat. "By the way, Dr. Flint. I appreciate you volunteering this year as the team doctor for the basketball season. That kind of community spirit says something about a man."

Patrick nodded. "Thank you. I enjoyed it, and it made my daughter happy, too. She's crazy about basketball." He shook his head. "She's going to be devastated that her coach won't be back next year. Lamkin has been so successful with the program, too. It's going to be a big loss for the school."

"Yes. Yes, she has. But I trust the school district to find an appropriate replacement." The judge frowned, then stood and held his gown closed. "I think you're aware I'm running for a U.S. Senate seat?"

"I'd heard that." As recently as his call with Rawlins, but he didn't tell Renkin that.

Renkin waved his hand in front of his chest. "We've got to keep this quiet. My condition."

Patrick chafed internally at the use of the word we. He always protected patient confidentiality to the best of his ability. The barking dog was normally the patient, although the medical provider was usually blamed. He knew his voice was a little stiff when he said, "We don't disclose confidential patient information."

"Still, just in case, I would prefer this be classified as an inconclusive diagnosis instead of acute anxiety. Even indigestion would be better than anxiety."

"You didn't have any symptoms of a gut ailment."

"Work with me, Dr. Flint."

Patrick walked to the door, opened it, and exited, then leaned his head back in. "You can call it whatever you'd like. I won't contradict you."

Then he shut the door firmly and took a few calming breaths. After the day—the week—Patrick was having, Renkin wasn't the only one whose blood pressure was elevated.

CHAPTER TWENTY-FIVE: EXULT

Susanne

Susanne stood in a shaft of warm sunlight just outside the open front door to the house. A police car drove past on the dirt road. The beefed-up security presence of the Flints' own posse combined with the officers protecting the judge was comforting. Henry had arrived an hour before. He'd parked his truck in front of their house, turned off the engine, and put his hands behind his head and his feet on the dash and hadn't moved since. *Asleep?* She waved, and he waved back. *Nope. Just relaxing.*

Relaxing sounded good. Their situation was wearing on her, and she could have used a nap in a hammock with warm sun on her face. She loved this time of year. Longer days. The end of the harsh winter so tantalizingly close that she could probably convince Patrick to let her shave his beard. A smile crossed her lips. Maybe she was fooling herself, but she thought it was even starting to smell like spring. Loamy and fresh, like new beginnings. She'd just put out her hummingbird feeder an hour before, and already she had seven of the little terrorists fighting each other for the four perches. Their wings were a whirring chorus that varied only in intensity when they dove or accelerated, and their feathers were like robes of emerald green and ruby red against the backdrop of the remaining snow.

From the front porch stoop, she had a good view of Trish but was far enough away that she didn't absorb any of her daughter's lingering wrath. The girl was brushing Goldie's flaxen mane. The palomino mare was tied to the hitching post in front of the barn, blonde and petite beside the hulking blackness of Reno. Trish had agreed to care for Reno today but had balked at working with Perry's chunky little paint, Duke.

Reno. Their miracle horse. Symbolic of their family, possibly? That they didn't give up. That with the help of friends and family, they could survive anything? That there was a life of peace and tranquility out there for them? She certainly hoped so. Trish lifted one of Reno's giant hooves and cleaned the muck from it with a hoof pick. Ferdinand padded over and scarfed it up the second it hit the ground. It was mostly manure, and Susanne cringed. That dog was going to try to kiss her face later, she just knew it.

Poor Duke stood watching them with his head over the gate and his eyes downcast. If ever a horse could be hang dog, he was. Trish must have noticed, too, because she set Reno's hoof down and went to the paint. His head popped up, and he nickered. She reached into her pocket for a cookie and slipped it in his mouth. He bobbed his head as he chewed, and Susanne heard Trish laugh as she walked back to Reno.

Inside the house, the phone rang. Susanne shouted, "Trish, I have to run get the phone. I'll be right back. Henry's here."

Trish ignored her. Or maybe she didn't hear her. *Nah*, Susanne decided. Her daughter was ignoring her. Susanne ran for the phone, snatching it off the hook on its sixth ring.

"Hello?"

"May I speak to Susanne Flint?" It was a woman's voice. Familiar, but not someone she immediately recognized.

"Speaking."

"Hi, Susanne. This is Barb Lamkin."

Why would Trish's basketball coach be calling her? She hoped they hadn't gotten Trish in trouble by keeping her out of school. "Hello, Coach Lamkin. I have Trish home with me today. I hope she didn't miss a practice?"

"Call me Barb. Oh, no, no. She's good. I'm giving them the week off before we start our spring practice schedule. That's not why I'm calling."

Now Susanne was really confounded. "Oh?"

"I had a great time talking to you at the tournament in Laramie, and you've been so nice to me at church. I wanted to see if you'd like to meet me for lunch today."

"Don't you have school?" Susanne regretted the blurt as soon as it was out of her mouth. She should have just said thank you. Coach Lamkin—Barb—was a grownup and could manage her own schedule.

But Barb just laughed. "I don't have a long lunch break, but I do eat offsite some days. It's easier for me to do it when the girls are on hiatus. If you're busy, or if you're not a lady who lunches, maybe we could go to the shooting range some time."

Susanne felt a stirring of pleasure. She was doing better and better in the friend department, although she wasn't about to choose the shooting range over lunch. Or anything. She'd never been asked to socialize over gunpowder and lead before moving to Wyoming. But Barb was a Wyoming native, and she fell in the tough and capable category of women that Susanne hadn't fit in with her first few years in Buffalo. But she was fitting in with Barb now.

A female voice spoke behind her. "Susanne, what are you up to?"

Susanne turned into the cord, wrapping herself. It was Vangie. Of course, she fit in with Vangie, too, but that didn't really count since Vangie was from Tennessee. Susanne smiled and twirled three-hundred and sixty degrees in the opposite direction, freeing herself.

"Hold on a second, Barb." Putting her hand over the phone, she pointed to the receiver and whispered to Vangie, "It's Barb. Inviting me to lunch."

Vangie made O's with her mouth and eyes. Her tiny body and enormous belly made her look like a lollipop in her red maternity dress and white snow boots. "Are you going?"

"I can't. Trish."

"You can leave her with Henry and me."

Susanne cocked her head, thinking. "In that case, would you want to go, and we could just leave her with Henry?"

Vangie patted her belly. "The baby does need food."

Susanne uncovered the mouthpiece. "Sorry. Vangie Sibley is here with me right now." She paused, giving Barb a chance to invite her.

Barb took it. "Why don't you bring her? I'll bring another teacher with me, and we'll make it a foursome. Do you know Tara Coker?"

"I've heard the name."

"She's new in town. She took over after the Christmas break for the upper level math teacher."

"I'll look forward to meeting her."

"You'll like her. She's plucky like you."

Plucky. Susanne had been called perky and spunky before, even feisty, but never plucky. She mused on it for a moment. She wasn't one hundred percent sure what it meant, but she liked it. "Where and when?"

"Could you be at the Busy Bee in ten minutes?"

"See you there."

She hung up the phone, turning to her friend. "You're so adorable it hurts me."

"Stop. I'm about to pop." She offered her elbow, and Susanne put a hand through it. "Let's go break the news to Henry that he gets a chance to redeem his teenager-watching reputation."

CHAPTER TWENTY-SIX: DUCK

Patrick

At the nurse's station, Patrick saluted Kim, who was tapping a pen against her cheek. "I'm running home for a quick lunch. Dr. John will be covering for me until I get back."

She waved but barely looked up from her paperwork. "See you in a few."

As he walked, Patrick stuck one arm through a sleeve of his quilted jacket, then repeated the process on the other side. He reached the vestibule at the same time as Judge Renkin. Renkin averted his eyes and didn't speak.

Patrick pushed the door open for the older man. *Keep your friends close but your enemies closer.* The door squeaked, which reminded Patrick he needed to let the maintenance staff know it needed to be greased. "I hope you have an uneventful night. Don't hesitate to come back if anything seems out of the ordinary."

The judge nodded. His behavior was so markedly different from earlier, that Patrick wondered if he'd spoken with the sheriff or the governor. Did he know about the Flints' suspicions? About the deal Patrick had struck with Rawlins? Patrick hoped not.

The two men walked into the parking lot, down the same aisle. The lot was close to empty. Not a busy day at the hospital. And still Patrick and Renkin had managed to park near each other. With Renkin spending so much energy ignoring Patrick, the proximity made Patrick self-conscious.

The judge paused behind a shiny black Dodge Ram truck, digging in his pocket for keys. A recent model. It didn't appear the man suffered used vehicles. He stepped around his truck bed to the driver's side. Patrick walked faster to put some distance between them.

CRACK. PFFFT.

For a moment, the sound didn't trigger recognition in Patrick. But only for a very short moment. It was clearly a rifle shot. After another fraction of a second, Patrick realized the bullet had passed somewhere between him and the judge. The shot hit the asphalt a few yards behind them, sending up a spray of debris.

"Get down!" Patrick shouted. He dove behind a parked woody station wagon. "Are you okay, Judge?"

CRACK. PING.

A bullet hit the metal exterior of a vehicle, although which one, Patrick couldn't tell, other than it was close.

"I'm fine. I wasn't hit." CRACK. Glass shattered. "That one was close. It got my side window."

"It seems like you might be better off behind your truck."

There was a short pause, then Patrick heard a rustling noise.

"On my way now."

Patrick's mind raced like the trained emergency responder he was. What if other people were in the parking lot, under fire like Renkin and him? No one had cried out, but that didn't mean someone hadn't been hit. If someone was injured, he had to help.

He shouted, "Is anyone else out there?"

No voices answered.

The judge gave a horse's laugh. "Just the shooter."

Patrick glanced over at him. He was hunched behind his truck's bumper. "Did you see him?" *Or her.* But odds favored the shooter being male, in his ER experience with gunshot victims.

"No."

Patrick thought about the security posse watching his wife and kids. Maybe he should have scheduled someone to keep an eye out for him as well. But why would anyone want him dead? Possibilities whirled through his brain like images in a kaleidoscope. He was testifying against Kemecke, but not as a witness to murder, or as the victim of kidnapping. Maybe the shooter was trying to scare him for some reason. That didn't make sense to him though. If someone wanted to scare him, they'd go after his family. And what would they be trying to scare him away from? With a jolt, he thought about his call with Rawlins. The governor had made a deal with him to back off Renkin. If Renkin wasn't here under fire, the scare-tactic theory might have worked in relation to him. Or maybe it did. The shooter might not realize Renkin was here, too. Or was the judge avoiding suspicion by putting himself near the line of fire, knowing he wasn't the target? If he'd done it at Meadowlark, he could be doing it again here.

He shook his head. He needed to focus on the immediate danger of his situation. And he knew his ideas were a stretch. It was more likely that whoever was out there, they were aiming at Harold Renkin. He'd save the deep thoughts on what that meant for his family for later, when he was out of this mess.

CRACK. PING.

Another bullet buried itself in the body of a nearby vehicle. He had to figure out how to get the shooter to stop. He couldn't make it happen from his crouch. Someone would have to advance on him. Or loud sirens might do the trick.

"Where's your security?" he asked the judge.

"Damned if I know. Doughnut break, maybe? But when I find them, I'm going to kill them."

A horrible thought crept into Patrick's mind. Had the officer abandoned his post, possibly on purpose? Or maybe he was even in on the attack? If so, that meant Patrick couldn't trust law enforcement. But how to know? "How trustworthy is your detail?"

CRACK. PING.

"I was just asking myself the same question."

"We're sitting ducks out here."

In the midday, small town quiet, he heard the emergency room doors squeak open. Heels clicked. Women's voices chattered and laughed.

"Stop!" he shouted. "Someone's shooting into the parking lot. Don't come out here. And call 911. Please!"

"Oh, my goodness," one of the women said. Her voice was nearly as high-pitched as the squeak of the door.

A second woman shouted to him in a deeper tone. "Are you okay?"

"Yes, but we won't be much longer. There are two of us pinned down out here."

"Okay, we're on it," she said.

There was a clicking of retreating heels, then the door squeaked again. Outside it grew deathly quiet. Long seconds passed. A minute. One of Patrick's calves spasmed with a charley-horse. He grimaced and stuck it out to the side, trying to stretch it out with no luck. He clenched his teeth and tried not to think about it. Patrick's thoughts recycled on who the shooter might be. Someone hired by Renkin or Rawlins? Kemecke's gang? The person blackmailing Renkin? One of his disgruntled ex-lovers? A cuckolded husband? An angry defendant from his court? The list was long.

Two minutes. The pain from his cramp was making Patrick lightheaded.

He pulled his leg back in and rocked back to front to back on his toes to stretch his Achilles, while his mind raced. He dug his thumbs into the knot in his muscle. Assuming for a moment that the shooter was trying to kill the judge, Patrick wasn't sure that would change anything for the Flints. It didn't mean Renkin hadn't hired someone to kill his wife or that he wouldn't come after Perry. In the heat of danger, Patrick's slimy feelings about saying yes to Rawlins were gone. He couldn't wait for Morales to arrive. If the extra security had been here today, Patrick might not still be hunched behind this car listening for the whistle of an approaching bullet that would lodge itself in his flesh.

At three minutes, Patrick's cramp started to ease up. There'd still been no more shots. The quiet felt charged and unstable, and he didn't like it.

"You still there, Judge?"

"I am."

"How's the ticker?"

"No change."

"That's good news at least."

Patrick paused, listening for the slightest of sounds. He heard birds. Distant traffic. A dog barking. But nothing else.

After another half a minute, he said, "I think the shooter left."

"Probably heard you sending for help."

Patrick's truck was two vehicles down from where the judge was hiding. He wasn't about to move from his cover until the cops came. The good cops, he amended, again wondering where Renkin's security was.

Sirens approached.

Patrick closed his eyes. *Thank you, God.* With anticipation of the end of their situation, his emotions moved quickly from relief to joy, even humor. A picture formed in his mind of the judge earlier that day, insisting that someone had tried to kill him with poison. "Hey, Judge, you know how you were wondering whether someone had tried to kill you?"

"Yeah?"

"I don't think you have to wonder anymore."

CHAPTER TWENTY-SEVEN: JUDGE

Susanne

B arb and her friend were being seated at a heavy, round table on an elevated section of the dining room in the Busy Bee. Susanne realized she had seen the friend before. *At church, with Barb,* she thought.

As usual, Barb was eye-grabbing, today in a lime green wraparound dress and gogo boots. A scarf held her wavy red hair off her face. The ends hung with her hair over her shoulders. She outshone and towered over the other woman, who looked average in height and everything else. Barb as Ginger to her friend's Mary Ann, a la *Gilligan's Island.* The friend was wearing round tortoise glasses, low-heeled pumps, a mid-calf skirt, and a long-sleeved shirt with a blousy tie at the neck. Her light brown locks were in a loose, low bun. Pretty, but prim. A schoolmarm.

Susanne let Vangie climb the steps to their table first.

"Look at you. Any day now?" Barb hugged Vangie.

"The good Lord willing."

Barb laughed. "This is Tara. Tara, these are my friends. Vangie is the pregnant one. The other is Susanne."

Tara shook their hands. Hers were silky soft and long-fingered, fluttering through Susanne's like a little bird.

"Nice to meet you, Tara," Susanne said. "I'm Susanne Flint."

Tara's voice was as soft as her hands. "Flint? One of my trig students is named Trish Flint."

"She's my daughter."

"I met your husband, too, up at the school. Dr. Flint. He was quite the hero."

Susanne smiled. She loved hearing people say good things about Patrick. "So I heard. I'm just glad Marcy is okay. As is Trish. The girls are inseparable."

The four women took their seats.

Tara said, "Trish missed trig today. Is she sick?"

"No," Susanne admitted. "We've pulled her out of school until she's done testifying in a trial that starts tomorrow."

Tara put a hand to her mouth for a moment. Her nails were bitten to the quick. "That's right. I heard Dr. Flint say that yesterday. I've read about the trial, too. And what happened to her." She shook her head. "To all of your family."

Some of Barb's flowing locks fell in front of her shoulder. She flipped it to the back. "I've volunteered for your security posse. Yee haw."

Susanne said, "Thank you. Both of you. And, Tara, Trish will get the assignments from a fellow student."

"I'll bring them to your house."

"You don't have to do that."

"It would be my pleasure. Trish is very conscientious. One of my best students. I know she'll want to keep up."

"Well, then, that would be lovely."

Tara reached toward two purses on the floor. One was black vinyl. The other brown leather. She choose the brown shoulder bag, then dug out a pen and a store receipt. "What's your address?"

Susanne recited it to her.

Tara dipped her head to write. Her glasses slid down her nose. "I'll stop by after school."

"If you're sure. I could go to the school and pick them up."

Tara pushed her glasses up. "It's no problem. Will Trish and Dr. Flint be there?"

Susanne paused, a little put off by the question. Her tone was stiff. "Trish will be. With my son Perry and me. My husband will be at work."

"Oh. Okay."

Susanne exchanged a glance with Vangie. Her friend raised an eyebrow. One by one, the women picked up their menus and perused them, then all ended up ordering chef salads.

"We're watching our girlish figures," Barb told the waitress.

"But I'm having dessert," Vangie declared.

They all laughed, except for the waitress, whose facial expressions were so stony she could have posed for Mount Rushmore. She was wearing wooden-sole clogs. Susanne would have looked stony if she were wearing shoes like that, too. Those dang things were painful. It reminded her that her own feet hurt. She'd worn cute boots with high wooden heels. A mistake.

"They're usually pretty fast," Barb said, when the waitress had clomped off.

Tara nibbled a fingernail. "I hope so. I can't be late. I really need this job."

"You just moved here?" Vangie asked her.

"A few months ago. I substituted last fall until this opening became available."

"Where are you from?"

Tara looked down. "All over the state, really. A few places in Montana."

Barb flashed a toothy smile. "She moved here for a boy."

Tara glared at Barb.

The waitress interrupted with four iced teas and a caddy of sugars. Vangie quizzed the poor young woman about how her tea had been prepared. As a Tennessean, she liked her sugar stirred into hot tea, and it was an ongoing source of angst for her that people in Wyoming didn't embrace this concept. Still stone-faced even after that, the waitress left them again.

Susanne and Vangie stirred sugar into their tea. Tara and Barb did not.

Barb patted Tara's hand. "Tara is shy, so we don't make her talk about her beau. I, on the other hand, am most definitely not. And I have an announcement." She paused.

Susanne leaned forward, all ears.

A bell on the entrance door jingled. A gust of wind followed Johnson County Attorney Max Alexandrov into the small restaurant. Shouting and chanting could be heard from the sidewalk outside, and

Susanne saw a line of people walking and waving poster board signs mounted on pickets. DEATH PENALTY IS MURDER. EXECUTE JUSTICE NOT PEOPLE. CAPITAL PUNISHMENT IS THE COWARD'S WAY. The stream of people was diverse. Young and old. Country and even a citified man in a slick gray suit who looked familiar to her. Susanne dreaded the gauntlet she'd have to walk to the courtroom.

Max's eyes lit on their table a few feet away, and he tipped his cowboy hat at them before removing it. Susanne waved. Max had looked tired and sad for months now, ever since his wife left. Today he seemed rejuvenated. He looked confident in ostrich skin boots and a blue western suit with wide lapels and brown stitching. She'd hoped he would do some trial prep with Trish and her, but she'd gotten the call that morning that the trial was on for tomorrow. It appeared they were out of time. They'd practiced their testimony with the Sheridan county attorney, and, before him, they'd met to go over their statements with the county attorney in Big Horn. Maybe Max had everything he required in his files. Susanne needed to talk to him, though, about Judge Renkin's conflict of interest with Donna Lewis. Patrick had left him a message about it the night before, but Max hadn't called them back. Or not at home anyway. Maybe he'd reached Patrick up at the hospital.

She realized he hadn't looked away from her group. She glanced back and forth between the women, trying to figure out which of them had him looking like a hungry man in a room full of ribeyes. Tara hadn't reacted to him. Vangie was more interested in perfecting the sugar in her iced tea. But Barb flicked her eyes to Max and then back to her nails. *Bingo*, Susanne thought.

Susanne lifted her hand to get his attention, but, right before she did, he moved off toward the counter seating. She decided to waylay him as he was leaving. "You can't keep us in suspense any longer, Barb. What's your announcement?"

Barb lifted her glass. "I've given my notice to Buffalo High School."

"What?" Susanne said. She set her glass down with a thump. Trish was going to be crushed.

Tara didn't look surprised.

Vangie said, "Whatever for? You've been so successful here."

Barb put one hand on her tummy and glanced down at it, then back up at each of them in turn. Her eyes sparkled. "My fiancé and I will have an announcement soon. But I wanted to give the school plenty of time to find a replacement. The girls deserve that."

Susanne put both her hands around her tea glass. Surely Barb wasn't telling them she was pregnant out of wedlock? They were budding friends, but not close. Down south, women went to great lengths to ensure no one ever found out when a baby was conceived, if it was before there was a ring on the mother's finger. Were things that different in Wyoming? And, if so, how was Susanne going to explain it to Trish?

Under the table, Vangie's fingers dug into Susanne's knee. She'd obviously drawn the same conclusion. As much as Susanne had adjusted to Wyoming, there were just some things about Texas and the south she would always be more comfortable with. The beginnings of a headache hit her like a ton of bricks at the base of her skull, and she moved a cold hand from her tea glass to the back of her neck.

She latched on to the element she felt she could safely address in polite lunchtime conversation. "Fiancé? You're engaged? Congratulations. When are you going to tell us who he is?"

"It won't be long, now that I've given notice at the school."

Vangie let go of Susanne's knee and put her hand over her chest. "You simply must let us throw you a shower." Susanne couldn't help but notice she didn't specify whether it would be a wedding shower or a baby shower. "When's the big day?" Again, ambiguous. Vangie was deep-fried southern perfection.

"We haven't set a date, but soon. It's something of a shotgun wedding." Barb winked.

Susanne smiled at her so brightly her cheeks ached. She wasn't looking forward to breaking this news to her already surly daughter.

Maybe things had been easier before Susanne started fitting in with the locals.

CHAPTER TWENTY-EIGHT: MISTAKE

BUFFALO, WYOMING
TUESDAY, MARCH 15, 1977, NOON

Trish

After putting Goldie and Reno back out to pasture with Duke—where Goldie immediately rolled in the mud and ruined the grooming Trish had worked so hard on—Trish and Henry went inside for lunch. She put leftover beef stew on the stove to warm, while Henry built a roaring fire in the living room. When Trish dished up bowls of piping hot stew and set them on the table, she went to get Henry, but found him asleep on the couch with his boots off and his hat over his face, Ferdinand on the floor beside him.

So much for a bodyguard.

Outside, she heard a vehicle engine. It was too soon to be her mom, so it was probably her dad coming home for lunch. There was enough stew for him, too. She decided to meet him outside so she could warn him Henry was napping. When she quietly opened the door, she got a surprise, though. It wasn't her dad's old white pickup. For a split second, she panicked, her parents' paranoia finally getting through to her. She was alone out here, vulnerable.

But she recognized a distinctive thump noise and gasoline smell. It was Brandon's truck. Her heart leapt. He'd even brought his new snow-mobile in the truck bed. She was dying to ride it. He'd saved up and bought the big yellow monster in January, then hadn't been able to take it out because of basketball season. Maybe he was going to ask her to ride up in the mountains. Surely her parents would say yes—what trouble could she get into up there? Besides, she really needed to spend quality time with him.

Things had ended badly the day before. She hadn't wanted to skip class, but he'd refused to take her back to school after lunch. He'd laughed at her and called her a goody two shoes. She thought he'd change his mind, and she didn't want to walk, so she'd stayed in the truck with him.

It had been secluded in the park. A wintertime weekday. One thing had led to another, as she'd been afraid it would. She wouldn't let him past second base. Not then, or ever, except for one time a few months before. It had scared her. He was so intense. So strong. So, so, so . . . bull-ish. Literally, like the bull in the pasture near their old house. Once she'd seen a cow unable to get up off the ground for days after the bull was done with her. That old bull had one thing on his mind and one thing only, and, from the look in Brandon's eyes, it was all he thought about, too.

Trish wasn't ready. So, ever since then, she'd made up excuses. But a girl could only be on her "time" just so often. She'd tried to use that excuse again yesterday, but he didn't buy it.

Then she'd just told him no.

They'd had an argument. A mean one. He'd accused her of being a tease. Said she was too much of a little girl for him. Then he tried to pull a wild U-turn in the parking lot, hit a curb, and flattened his tire. Thank goodness Wes had shown up. She'd torn off Brandon's letter jacket and class ring and left them in the truck, then Wes had driven them back to the school. Trish had left with her dad, and Wes had given Brandon a ride home.

Brandon hadn't called at all the night before.

Trish was sick about it, certain he was going to break up with her. By that morning, she'd decided that maybe she was ready for sex after all. He was her soulmate, and they were going to get married someday anyway. It would be fine. Just not in City Park in the middle of the day. Somewhere private and romantic—they could make it special.

What a relief he's here now. Even though he knew her parents would disapprove, he came anyway. She ran toward the truck, coatless, smiling so wide it stretched her mouth. The truck was muddy and dirty all the way up the windows. Brandon liked to drive it fast, and with the snow melting, that meant slush splashed onto the roof. She grabbed the handle and opened the door, throwing herself up and onto the seat. Brandon's letter jacket wasn't there where she'd left it. The truck reversed and was halfway out of the driveway before she'd even shut the door.

She laughed and turned to her boyfriend. "I'm sorry about yesterday, Br . . ." Her voice trailed off.

It wasn't Brandon driving the truck.

"Hi, Trish."

It was Ben. He gave her a shy smile and accelerated, plowing them through the middle of a mud storm.

If he hadn't helped his horrible father and uncles kidnap her, she would have thought he was good looking. As handsome as Brandon, even, although he wasn't as popular. Of course, he'd only lived in Buffalo a few months before everything happened. She hadn't known why he'd moved in with Brandon and Mrs. Lewis before. She didn't really know him then other than as the shy, quiet new guy who didn't play sports.

Everything else she knew about Ben now was from *that night*. That terrible, terrible night, when he'd driven her up into the mountains, and she'd ridden behind him on Goldie into Cloud Peak Wilderness. When Billy Kemecke had killed his cousin right before her eyes, her mom had shot Billy, and her dad had stuck a knife in Ben's dad's throat to save her. Images flashed through her mind, like it was happening all over again. One after another. Bad men, blood, and dead eyes, wide open and staring at her. She never talked about what had happened, not to anyone. She'd thought if she just went on with her life that she'd get over it. Mind over matter, like her dad always said.

He was wrong. She was wrong. It hadn't worked. Somehow, she had to make herself quit reliving that night. But it had gotten hard with Ben back.

"What are you doing here?" Trish put her hand on the door. She wanted out. Wanted it badly. She looked through the flying mud. They were going too fast for her to jump out.

"I thought you might want to go for a ride, since you've been cooped up in your house. I like to go fast, but I'm a good driver."

He grinned and she saw a round scar under his right eye. A memory surfaced. Near the beginning the school year. Maybe in late August? A dark-haired boy had held his jacket over her head and run her into the school during a thunderstorm. Inside the vestibule, they'd stood under his jacket for a second, so close she could see the little round scar under his right eye. Then the bell had rung, and she'd yelled, "Thanks," and run toward her classroom. "What's your name?" he'd shouted after her. She had turned then and smiled at him, jogging backwards. "My name's Trish." Whatever he'd said in return had been covered up by the loud voices of students hurrying to class around her. *Never mind,* she'd thought. *It's not like we don't go to the same school. I'll see him again.*

But she hadn't. Not until the horrible night.

She chewed the inside of her lip. "On the snowmobile?"

"Maybe."

"I don't have a coat." She wished she had Brandon's letter jacket with her. It was big, thick, warm, and felt safe. "And the snowmobile's Brandon's anyway." A truck passed them going toward Trish's house. At least she thought it was a truck from the sound it made. She couldn't actually see it or whoever was in it, which meant they couldn't see her, and she couldn't flag them down.

"It's his truck, too, and I'm his cousin." His voice was teasing. "I'm just borrowing it."

"Where is he?"

He turned without hitting the brakes, accelerating onto the highway. "I dropped him off at school after lunch. He said you're out of school until the trial is over."

The mud made loud plops on the undercarriage. The tires started humming. Wind streaked the mud on the windows.

Trish had planned to jump out when he slowed down at the intersection. *So much for that.* "Oh. Yeah."

They drove without speaking for a minute. Trish watched him with her peripheral vision while keeping her eyes straight ahead. She felt stiff and nervous, and her heart was beating hard and fast, like hail on a roof. "I'd better just get back home. My parents will be worried about me. I'm not supposed to go anywhere without permission."

"Okay. We don't have to snowmobile. We won't be gone long."

"We shouldn't be going up into the mountains at all."

"We can't go the other way. I don't want anyone to see us."

Now the hail storm of her heartbeat was pounding inside her skull, too. This was déjà vu, riding up into the mountains in a truck with Ben, when she didn't want to. Only this time, she wasn't blindfolded. She could get away, before it was too late. She just had to gather her courage and wait for the truck to slow down on one of the hairpin turns ahead. There were lots of them. Lots of chances to get away. She repeated her dad's mantra, the one he'd used when he was teaching her, Perry, and her mom self-defense. The one she'd used to keep herself sane on the horrible night. "Whatever a bad guy is going to do to you somewhere else is always worse than what he is going to do to you right here. So fight, fight, fight." She'd fight if she had to, because she had to get out before he took her wherever he'd planned.

The truck was climbing. Trees flashed by on either side of them. Seconds, precious seconds, were ticking by. Ben navigated some gentle curves without decelerating. She gripped the door handle, ready for her chance.

"Are you okay?" Ben asked.

She kept her gaze on the road, her mind on their speed. "I'm fine."

"I'm not kidnapping you, you know. I just want to talk to you in private."

Like saying it made it true. Her heartbeat didn't slow down. "Okay."

"I don't want Brandon to hear I was with you. That's all."

His words made a tiny crack in her armor. Was he telling the truth? She knew that even on that horrible night, his crazy uncles and dad forced him into it. They would have killed him and her if he hadn't done what they said. "Uh huh."

He kept driving like he was in the Indianapolis 500. They passed signs posted on a rock cliff. Boring signs that her dad loved, about how the rocks were, like, a bajillion years old. They were rocks—who cared? Thinking about her dad made her feel guilty and sad. She'd jumped into the truck, knowing her parents would have said she couldn't go with Brandon. And they didn't know where she was. No one did. If she never saw them again, it would be her own fault.

Ben put on his blinker and slowed to make the right turn toward Hunter Creek Corrals. She tensed. This was a sharp turn. He'd have to slow almost to a stop. She could jump out here.

He touched her arm. His fingers were warm. "I'm so glad you're here." With his other hand, he spun the steering wheel. The truck slowed and he coasted around the turn.

She didn't jump. What was wrong with her?

He drove another half mile and pulled off the road. He put the truck in park facing Clear Creek. Her house was just a few miles east along the creek, Trish knew. She could follow it all the way back to her house if she had to. There was still a lot of snow up here. It would be hard, but she could do it.

"Walk with me down to the creek," Ben said.

Trish wanted to stay closer to the road. There weren't many people up here this time of year, but there were some. It felt safer. "I don't want to."

"All right. Well, I have something I've been wanting to tell you, so I think it's best if I just get this over with." He swallowed. "Right." He swallowed again. "This isn't easy to say."

"You don't have to say anything. Just take me home. I won't tell Brandon."

He turned toward her. "I like you, Trish."

"Please stop. You're scaring me."

"It's not like that. I really like you. I just want a chance to talk to you without Brandon around. And for you to really listen to me."

"If I listen to you, will you take me home?"

"Of course. Just five minutes. Please."

"Promise?"

"I promise."

She took a deep breath. "Five minutes. I'm listening."

He put both his hands on the steering wheel and drummed his thumbs until he started to talk. "Juvie was bad, Trish. Really bad. Some of those guys were criminals. Like my dad and my Uncle Billy. I know what I did on the mountain was wrong. I was scared, but I never should have let them force me to do those things. To take you. But if I hadn't, I wouldn't have gotten to know you a little. I think about riding up that mountain on your horse. The way you felt against me. With your arms around me. And how you smelled. And you were right. If we'd run off together, everything would be great now."

Trish recoiled against the passenger side door. When she remembered that night, it was with horror. But when he remembered it, it was about how she smelled and felt? And what did he mean that everything would be great now if they'd run off together? Then it hit her. He was thinking she had meant the two of them should have run off *together*.

"No. No, no, no, Ben. I didn't mean we should have run away together. I meant that together we could have escaped your crazy family and gotten back to my parents, who would have helped you. Brandon and I were sort of already going together then."

He shook his head. "Everything is the way it is because I let my dad and Uncle Billy force me into doing those things. If I'd listened to you and we'd made a run for it, you wouldn't be scared of me or hate me." He reached for her hand. She jerked it away from him. He looked sad. "Trish, the things you said at my hearing. The way you stuck up for me. I knew then you felt like I did. It kept me going when things were hard in juvie."

"But I didn't. I don't."

This wasn't going well. Should she make a break for the creek? He was so much bigger and stronger than her. If he wanted to, he could catch her and tackle her and do whatever else he wanted. He'd said he'd take her home in five minutes. Would he keep his promise? She looked down at her wristwatch. He had one minute left.

Ben licked his lips. "Tell me there's not ever a chance for us, and I'll leave you alone. I'll let you date my loser cousin and never say another word about this." His eyes were shining, pleading.

Trish's insides churned like a gopher was digging its way through her guts. If she said no, she wasn't sure what he would do. He'd said he would leave her alone, but would he? Could he? But she couldn't say yes. She couldn't lie.

She gripped her hands in her lap. "I don't know. I'm with Brandon."

Ben slammed his fist on his leg. Trish jumped, and a squeak escaped her mouth. "Trish, his mom is crazy. She had her boyfriend Stamey over yesterday planning something to keep Uncle Billy from going to trial. They asked me if I wanted to help them."

"Help them how?"

"I don't know, but today someone shot at the judge when he was at the hospital."

"My dad was working at the hospital today. Is my dad okay?"

"I think so."

"Think or know?"

"Think."

Trish held her watch face up toward him. "Your five minutes is up. Please take me home. I have to see about my dad."

Without a word, Ben put the truck in reverse and turned around, then shifted and left the parking lot for the highway toward Buffalo and Trish's house. Trish could barely breathe, afraid if she made a sound, he'd change his mind. A few times she stole a glance at him. There was a tear in the corner of his eye. When he saw her looking, he swiped it away with a jerk of his hand.

He pulled up to her house to drop her off.

Henry walked out with a shotgun.

Ben looked sick. "Oh, man. I've got to get out of here. I can't go back to juvie. I haven't done anything wrong."

Suddenly, Trish went from scared of Ben to hurting for him, and she wasn't sure why. "I'll talk to him. It will be okay." She jumped out and ran around to Ben's window, which he'd rolled down. "It's my fault Henry. I thought we'd be back before you woke up."

Henry's face was stormy. "Your mom is out looking for you, and I called the sheriff. Someone's on their way."

"I'm so sorry. Really."

Henry's lips moved like her dad's did, with no sound coming out. Maybe it was a dad thing—Henry's wife *was* about to have a baby. He turned on his heel and headed for his truck. Trish started to go after him, but Ben's voice stopped her.

It was urgent, cracking with emotion. "There's one more thing."

"What?"

"You deserve to know the truth. To be treated better."

"What do you mean?"

His face was splotchy red. "Brandon is seeing someone else behind your back."

Snow crystals pelted Trish's nose. She hadn't noticed the wind pick up or the temperature drop, but clouds had rolled in. The bright spring-time world of earlier had turned winter dim again. Her knees buckled, and she put a hand on the front hood of the truck for support. "Who is it?"

"I shouldn't say."

"It's Charla Newby, isn't it?"

"I can't tell you who it is, Trish."

Hurt and jealousy pummeled Trish senseless. Even in that moment, some rational part of her knew that how she felt wasn't Ben's fault. Brandon was the one cheating on her. If it was anyone's fault it was his. Although maybe it wasn't Brandon's fault either. He barely ever got to see her, and, when he did, she made up excuses to keep him from touching her. She'd read books. She understood that guys had strong urges. That some girls weren't brought up like Trish was, to save sex for marriage. Or even to save it for when they had a boyfriend. So maybe it was also his mother's fault, and her parents', and a whole lot Charla's, and maybe partly Trish's?

But it still hurt. It hurt crazy bad, and it made her lash out at the nearest target. Ben. The messenger. Who she drilled like he was a bullseye in a shooting tournament.

She turned on him. "How dare you?"

"How dare I what?"

Spittle sprayed from her mouth. "How dare you try to ruin my relationship with Brandon? He's not even here to defend himself. I hate you, Ben Jones. I would never, ever, in a million years date someone as disgusting as you. I can't believe I tried to keep you out of juvie. I hope you go back and stay there, where I don't ever have to see you again." She gasped for a breath, then kept going. "You'd better look for another place to stay, because after I tell Brandon everything you said, you'll be out on your tail so fast, you won't know what happened." A frantic energy burned through her, and she pushed away from the truck. She wanted to run, run hard, but she didn't know where, only that she needed away. "Now get out of here, unless you want me to get you thrown in grown-up jail this time."

The shocked, humiliated look on Ben's face as the color drained out of it made her feel better for a few seconds. But only for a few. By the time his look changed to fury, she was regretting her outburst. He hadn't deserved it. But she didn't know how to take it back. All the frenetic energy coursing through her vanished, and, instead of running, she wanted to melt into a puddle right where she was standing.

Ben left, spraying mud, water, and snow from the tires behind him and all over her.

Her mom's Suburban barreled into their driveway. Trish just stood there, tears pouring down her cheeks, covered in mud, stock still as snow fell around her.

CHAPTER TWENTY-NINE: BUTT

Patrick

"Is there anything else I can do for you?" Ronnie walked to the front door, escorted by Ferdinand. She'd been close by, on a shift guarding the judge, when Henry had called in Trish's short-lived disappearance.

"No, but thank you," Susanne said.

"We're just sorry to bother you," Patrick added.

"No bother." Ronnie turned the knob, then stopped. "Oh, by the way, the answer on the life insurance question was yes."

"On Jeannie, paying out to her husband?"

"Yes."

"How much?"

"Enough to settle some fairly large debts. I've told the investigating team."

Patrick knew it. He nodded in grim satisfaction. "Thank you, Ronnie."

She smiled. "I hope you feel better soon, Trish."

Trish was sitting on the couch with her face buried in Susanne's shoulder. She didn't lift her head, and her reply to Ronnie was unintelligible. Patrick was embarrassed, but if Ronnie was bothered, she didn't show it. She slipped out and shut the door. Ferdinand slumped onto the floor just inside the door and whined. When they'd lived next door to Ronnie, she'd been the dog's special friend, often giving him a second breakfast when he went to visit her.

Patrick paced the length of the living room. After he'd passed his daughter three times, he couldn't contain himself any longer. He whirled to face her. "What on God's green earth were you thinking?"

Her back heaved with sobs. Her wail was muffled against her mother. "I don't know. But you don't have to roar at me like some kind of *lion*."

Patrick ground his teeth. He'd spent the last few hours sequestered with the succession of law enforcement officers who had showed up en masse to investigate the shooting. City, county, state, and even some feds, because the feds always showed up in Wyoming. As many people as were on the case, it didn't sound like they had any leads. No one saw a vehicle or a person that roused any suspicion. They'd retrieved the slugs in the parking lot, and he'd seen crime scene investigators tracing back the paths of the bullets, but they'd returned disheartened. Down to the last man—and one woman—they'd opined that the target had been Renkin. If Patrick hadn't been so eager to finish up and get out of there, his feelings would have been hurt that they didn't think he was worth shooting. He'd finally escaped, heading for a very late lunch and the sanctuary of his home, only to walk in on an epic showdown between his wife and the daughter who just wouldn't give them a break.

He still hadn't eaten lunch, either.

"Do you realize someone tried to kill Judge Renkin and me today? And that it was probably about this trial and the family of those boys you insist on running around with?"

She sat up, sniffling. "I know, Dad. But it's not my fault."

"Everyone is just trying to keep you safe, Trish. Yesterday, Wes sacrificed his time off work to help, and you skipped school with Brandon. Today, you ran off with the boy you're supposedly afraid of, the one who kidnapped you, while Henry was here."

Her eyes were impossibly blue behind a layer of tears. Her lower lip quivered. "I didn't ask them to help."

"Whether you realize it or not, we *need* their help. And it's not just our volunteers, either. Your actions have gotten the principal of your school involved. And the sheriff's department. Word is getting out that you're acting like a spoiled brat who doesn't care about anybody but herself. Do you think when people hear that, they'll want to keep dropping everything to help you?"

Trish threw herself back into Susanne's shoulder and started wailing again.

Susanne patted her back. "Patrick."

"What? It's true."

"I think she gets the point. So do people two counties over."

Patrick rubbed his forehead violently. "What can we do differently, Susanne? Do we have to lock her in her room?"

Trish's head came up, and Ferdinand rose, tail tucked. "No!" she shouted. She jumped to her feet.

Ferdinand snuck away toward his bed in the laundry room.

"What would you do if you were us, then?"

"You don't understand *anything*. Even if I told you, you wouldn't understand."

Patrick sighed. Notwithstanding that she hadn't answered his question, she was probably right. He didn't understand what made her do the things she did half the time already, although he loved her anyway. In some ways, she was so much like him. In a few, she favored her mother. But in many, she was her own unique and baffling creature. He rubbed gooseflesh on his arms. The room had grown colder. Outside it was a whiteout. The flakes were big and thick. The roads would get bad quickly. Kim had promised to call if they needed him at the hospital. He was only ten minutes away, except for the rapidly accumulating snow. If he got an emergency call, he'd have to take the Suburban. It had good snow tires and four-wheel drive. He didn't want to leave Susanne and Trish to shovel the truck out to go get Perry, but he wouldn't have to if he weren't called in.

He went over to the fireplace. They were low on logs. He stoked the fire and stacked the remaining logs on top of it. Then he sat down heavily on the hearth. "Try us. How much worse could it get?"

Trish scrubbed at her eyes. "Ben said Brandon is ch-ch-ch-cheating on me. With Charla."

A blinding rage flashed up in Patrick. What was wrong with Brandon? Trish was such a tough girl about so many things, but not when it came to her heart. There, she was tender and critically low on self-esteem. He hated that since she'd started dating him, her world revolved around being Brandon's girlfriend, when she was so much more than that. Hadn't they raised her to believe in herself? She was ten times the person that boy was. And he was treating her like garbage. Patrick was glad Brandon wasn't here, because he wanted to take the kid out behind the barn and whup him good.

Susanne reached for Trish's hand. "I'm so sorry. I know how much you like him—"

"I don't just like him, I *love* him, Mom. We're planning on getting married. He's my soulmate."

Patrick sure hoped they weren't planning on getting married anytime soon. He didn't know whether Trish's feelings were real or not. He'd felt that way about Susanne at Trish's age, and their relationship had stood the test of time. But most teen romances were temporary. Chances were this one was, too. He knew better than to say that, though. He probably shouldn't say they had far bigger problems than one teenage boy's libido and lack of morals either. He managed to hold back, just barely.

Susanne stroked Trish's hand with her thumb. "And I know you and Charla are competitive—"

"Anything I ever want, she tries to take away from me. Well, she can't have Brandon!"

"What has Brandon said about all this?"

"What do you mean?"

"Did he admit to cheating on you? Does he *like* Charla?"

"I don't know. I haven't had a chance to ask him. Because of his mom and because you guys kept me out of school."

Susanne got up and went to sit on the hearth with Patrick. "So, Ben told you? Today when he came over?"

"Yes."

"Are you and Ben becoming . . . friends?"

"Not really. No."

"Why did he come over then? Just to tell you about Brandon?"

"No." Trish's face colored and she backed up a step. "He, um, wants to be my boyfriend."

"Over my dead body," Patrick said, his voice dangerously close to roar-level again. The only thing worse than Trish dating Brandon Lewis would be Trish dating Ben Jones.

"I know, Dad. I'm not an idiot. And you don't have to yell. I'm not deaf either."

He bit the inside of his lip to restrain himself from debating the idiot issue, based on recent behavior.

Susanne held up her hand in a 'hush' gesture. "Is everything okay there? With you and Ben?"

"He's pretty mad at me."

"Why?"

"When he told me about Brandon, I said some mean things. But that's not what's the matter. Brandon and Charla are what's the matter."

"So, yesterday in the park with Brandon—you weren't there talking about Charla?"

"No."

"Everything was fine then?"

"Not really." Trish stuck her hands in her back pockets.

"What happened?" When Trish hesitated, Susanne said, "Trust us, honey."

"He, um, he wanted to have sex and I didn't."

Now the roar was inside Patrick's head. Every muscle in his body tightened.

Susanne squeezed his knee to keep him quiet. "I'm proud of you."

Patrick began to relax. Susanne could handle this topic better than him.

Trish turned away from them. "Well, it's cost me a boyfriend because now he's messing around with other girls."

"Lots of boys want to have sex. That doesn't mean it's true about him and Charla. Ben might have only told you that because he wants you for himself."

"Charla is a slut."

Susanne frowned. "Trish, that's uncalled for." Trish rolled her eyes and Susanne didn't pursue it any further. "You need to talk to him."

"I *can't*."

"Why?"

"For starters, because I'm scared he'll say it's tr-tr-tr-true. But also, I can't tell him Ben told me."

"Are you afraid of getting in between them?"

"No. Because Brandon would be upset that Ben came here, and that I rode off with him alone in the truck."

Patrick balled his fists. "You don't need Brandon telling you what to do."

"He isn't, Dad."

Patrick didn't believe her. "You're the one who wanted to skip class yesterday?" The Trish he knew was much too conscientious a student to do that.

Trish stared at the floor and bit her lip.

Patrick gave a sharp nod. "I didn't think so."

Susanne stood up. "Patrick, could I have a word with you in the kitchen?"

He followed her, checking his watch. He felt bad that he'd run out on Dr. John and the staff at the hospital.

Susanne poured them each a coffee.

"Thanks." He took a sip. It was lukewarm, but it was caffeine.

She set her cup down and slipped her arms around him. He squeezed back with one arm, the other holding his cup aloft so he wouldn't spill coffee on her. "I'm so glad you weren't hurt today. I'm sorry I haven't even had a chance to tell you that, with this newest Trish drama consuming our attention." She shuddered against him. "The thought of someone shooting at you is awful."

"They missed me by a mile. That wasn't even the most interesting part of my day."

"Oh?"

"I got a call from Governor Rawlins."

"You're kidding me."

"It's a long story, and not all of it is good, but he's sending one of his security team members up tomorrow to help us until the trial is over."

Her weight slumped into him. "That's wonderful news." Then she released him and motioned him over by the refrigerator, where their voices wouldn't carry back to Trish. She whispered, "About Trish. I think it would be cruel not to let her try to resolve this with Brandon, Patrick. It could be days or even a week or more before she's back in school."

"She needs to dump him."

"Maybe. But she can't if we don't let them talk."

"Are you forgetting part of the problem is his mother?"

"About that. I was thinking maybe I could take Trish up to the school to see if Brandon wanted to come talk to her here. Or at the library. Somewhere I could be sure she was safe and that his mother wouldn't find out."

The phone rang. Patrick groaned. He let go of his wife and snatched it up. "Hello?" He felt the cold wet nose of his dog on his free hand. Poor Ferdinand didn't like it when his family was upset. Patrick massaged his head.

The caller was Wes. "Doc, we've got a multi-vehicle accident half an hour or less out. This darn spring snow."

"I'm on my way."

He hung up. "I have to go. Emergency. The kind that is going to take hours and hours, I'm afraid, so don't wait dinner for me. Would you mind if I took the Suburban?"

"Go ahead."

"I hate that I don't have time to clear the driveway for you, but you've got Trish to help you."

"It's not a problem."

"And make sure she rides with you to pick up Perry, please. I don't want either of you alone. Not in this weather and with the roads like this, and not after the things that happened to you in town yesterday."

Susanne nodded. "What do you think about what I suggested—letting Trish talk to Brandon?"

"I'm fine as long as it's in public or here. But she messed up, Susanne. There has to be consequences. Make her do the shoveling. Get her to do some chores around the house. We can't let her just lay in her room like this is a vacation."

Susanne drew in a deep breath. "My head is killing me. How about I go take care of things at the hospital and let you supervise Trish's consequences?"

She did look pale. "I definitely drew the longer straw today." He kissed her on the forehead. "My mother swears by a cup of coffee and salty popcorn for a headache."

"I'll try it. I just wish we had more time to talk. It's the story of our life lately. I have so much to tell you."

"Me, too. Quickly, anything important?"

"Oh, just about my lunch with Barb and her friend. I ran into Max, but I didn't get a chance to talk to him about the conflict of interest. We still need to, before the trial, which means today. He didn't call you, did he?"

"No. Do you mind trying him again?"

She nodded and hugged him. "I'll do it as soon as you leave. Drive safe. And don't get in front of any more bullets. You're everything to me, you know." She pressed her face into his chest for a few seconds.

He soaked in her warmth. He got choked up on his response, and only half of what he wanted to say came out, but he thought the rest, with everything he had. "Be careful." *You're everything that's precious to me, too.*

CHAPTER THIRTY: CONQUER

Trish

Trish pushed the shovel under the snow and walked it like a plow toward the barn, then tossed the load as far as she could when it got too big. Their driveway and parking area were just too large to scoop the snow up and carry it one shovelful at a time out of the way. The parking area at their old house had been a lot smaller. After a winter of keeping this big space clear, her dad had promised that next year they'd buy a snow scraper for the front of his truck. He probably wouldn't though. Not while she and Perry were at home and he could make them do the work.

This was like her three thousandth trip. With each one, she was creating deeper and deeper mounds of snow. Now it looked like someone had dumped a bag of extra-large marshmallows on the ground, where they'd partially melted. The snow was heavy. Her shoulders and thighs ached and sweat dripped along her hairline. Her nostrils burned from the cold air, so much that she smelled blood. Her own. She'd had a nosebleed earlier. Little droplets had rained onto the shoveled ground, where they'd looked like pomegranate seeds. She lost her focus for a second, remembering, and the blade of the shovel hit a rock. It jammed the handle into her chest, right at her diaphragm, and knocked the wind out of her.

"Ow."

This sucked. Big time sucked. And her mom hadn't been helping, not one single solitary second. She'd said she had a headache and was going to her room to shut her eyes. But she must not have closed them very long, because she still opened the door and checked up on Trish every five seconds. Maybe a little less, but *still*. Trish knew shoveling was part of her penance, and if she didn't do it, her punishment might last longer. She'd rather do almost anything than shovel snow, though. Cleaning toilets even sounded good right about now.

She gazed out toward the creek as she caught her breath. Not that she could see the water. The snow was coming down so hard it was shortening her sightlines and muffling sounds. By the pasture fence, Goldie clambered to the water trough, wet snow packed in balls so high under her hooves that it was like she was wearing heels. The mare looked pretty with her back blanketed in snow. She sucked down big gulps of water, her nostrils blowing steamy clouds over the tank. She lifted her head. Water streamed back out her mouth like she was a horse fountain statue. Trish smiled, although as bad her mood was, she wasn't sure how it had sneaked out. Goldie ambled back into the pasture, to her little herd, where they ignored their shelter and lined up with their butts to the wind.

It was amazing how well the horses did in the cold. Dad called it the "two out of three" rule. Cold, wet, and wind—the horses could handle any two together, but not all three at once. They were good at staying dry in most weather, so the two out of three rule wasn't usually a problem. Their hair adjusted to temperature, even creating water resistant air pockets between their bodies and the outside world. That's why the snow on Goldie's back wasn't melting, and why her blonde coat wouldn't get very wet.

New snow had already covered the ground she'd cleared. Trish dug her shovel under the snow one last time. The shovel wasn't quite wide enough, and snow spilled off either side, but she didn't care. She was D-O-N-E-done with shoveling after this row. Not only did it suck, but it had given her way too much time to think. She didn't want to think. Everything she thought about made her sad and nervous. After this, she was going inside until it was time to pick up the runt from school and go talk to Brandon. Just thinking about that gave her butterflies. She'd have to shower before they left, so she needed to hurry. She walked her shovel-plow toward the barn, leaning, and pushing with her legs. When she reached the big structure and finished distributing the snow onto the piles, she leaned the shovel handle against the side wall and went into the house.

"Mom?" Just inside the doorway from the garage, she stripped her boots off and set them on a boot stand. She put her gloves, hat, and jacket on hooks. Water started pooling below her footwear.

Her mom didn't answer. Good. That meant she wasn't going to be making her do any more penance before they left. Trish went to the bathroom and turned on the shower. She picked up Perry's dirty underwear and socks with the tips of her fingers and flung them in the middle of the floor in his room. Boys were such pigs, and Perry was the worst. She returned to the bathroom. There were barbells and a coffee cup on her counter. She made a face and peeked in the cup. Sure enough, a thick layer of mold complete with floating round spores covered the coffee. She slid it toward the sink but didn't pour it out.

When the water was hot and the mirror steamy, Trish gathered her hair up into a ponytail and stepped under the spray. The water was amazing. It was the first time she'd felt good all day. Good enough that she could let all the pent-up feelings inside her bubble up and out where the water could wash them away. Within seconds, silent tears were streaming down her face. Everything was so messed up. Brandon, most of all, but Marcy nearly dying, her parents being so hard on her, the trial coming up, and even Ben. Trish wanted to forget Ben had ever told her anything and just go on with things like they were. But part of her knew she could never forget the things he'd said. Any of them. How could she? Her mom had said talking to Brandon about it was the right thing to do. Trish guessed she was right.

Trish soaped herself up, then rinsed. If she talked to Brandon, she had to tell him the things Ben had said. And, no matter what she'd said to Ben earlier, she was worried about what would happen to him. Brandon was his cousin. Ben lived in his house. And Brandon's mom was crazy. Would they kick Ben out? Would they be mean to him? Even hurt him?

She had to call Ben. To warn him. She'd known it, deep down, from the minute her mom had said she'd take Trish to talk to Brandon today, and it had been eating a hole in her stomach ever since.

She turned off the shower and dried off. She put on her favorite Gloria Vanderbilt jeans and a fuzzy blue sweater. Then she stared at the phone. Did she have the courage to make the call? She wanted to dive under the covers and hide instead. But she didn't think she could live with herself if she didn't do it.

She snatched up the phone and dialed the number for Brandon's house.

Mrs. Lewis answered. "Hello?"

Trish made her voice higher pitched, trying to disguise it from the woman. "May I speak to Ben please?"

"Who is this?" Mrs. Lewis's voice sounded suspicious, like it always did.

Trish hadn't thought up a lie ahead of time, so she used the first name that popped into her head. "Goldie. Goldie Reno."

There was a silence on the other end. Finally, Mrs. Lewis said, "Just a minute, Goldie."

Trish felt an inappropriate giggle threatening to burst out. She pressed her hand against her mouth.

"Hello?" It was Ben's voice. She'd never talked to him on the phone, and he sounded different. Younger.

"Don't tell Mrs. Lewis, but this is Trish."

He didn't answer her.

She hurried to get her words out, afraid he would cut her off. "I know you're mad at me, but please don't hang up on me. I need to tell you something important."

"What." He didn't say it as a question, just as one flat-toned word.

"First off, I'm really sorry. I, um, I said mean things that weren't true. I was upset about what you told me about Brandon. I know it wasn't your fault."

"Okay."

No other response? Wow. She'd expected something different. Like forgiveness. It didn't feel great not to get it. She bit her lip. "I told my parents what you said."

"About us?" His voice held a note of panic.

Hmm. Us? More like him. And she had. But that wasn't what she meant, and she didn't want to upset him. She'd already done a good enough job of that earlier, and she was about to again. "About Brandon."

His exhale into the mouthpiece was like a little windstorm. "Oh. Good."

"They think I should talk to him. I'm going to try to, this afternoon. I wanted you to know. Because he's probably going to be pretty mad at you for telling me."

"Can you say someone else told you?"

"Who?"

Ben was quiet for several seconds.

"Ben?"

"You can't. What I know, no one else knows."

"I'm sorry."

"It's the right thing. No matter what happens."

It's the right thing. That's what her mother had said. Most people thought Ben was a criminal. He had participated in a crime, so maybe that made it true. It was funny that someone like him would be concerned about doing the right thing. She didn't know what to think about that. "I hope so."

"When are you going to talk to him?"

"My mom is taking me up to the school to see if I can catch him after last period."

"I'm supposed to pick him up. I can just leave him a note on his locker to take his snowmobile to your place. He was planning on riding it today anyway if it snowed. That way you won't miss him."

"Thank you, Ben."

"Yeah. Well, I'd better get going."

Trish's throat felt tight and funny as she hung up the phone.

CHAPTER THIRTY-ONE: CONFUSE

BUFFALO, WYOMING
TUESDAY, MARCH 15, 1977, 4:00 P.M.

Susanne

The pain in the back of Susanne's skull throbbed rhythmically, as if a prisoner was trying to bust out of her brain with a mallet. Only *she* was the prisoner, standing at the foot of the deck in her own backyard, her vision blurred, snowflakes splatting on her face like little welcome ice packs. When had the headache started—at the surreal lunch? When Trish had disappeared? When she'd learned Patrick had been under fire from a sniper that morning? When she and Patrick had tried to have a conversation with Trish about her terrible choices? If she were answering that as a multiple-choice question, she'd check the box for all of the above.

She'd known the headache was in full force by the time Trish had shoveled the driveway, under protest. Not even the prospect of being allowed to talk to Brandon had improved her daughter's mood. She'd been sullen and uncommunicative when they left to pick up Perry. Susanne had started to turn toward the junior high, and Trish had snapped, "Take me to my school first."

"Why?" Susanne's voice had been weak.

"I'm going to ride home with Brandon."

The headache had sapped her resolve and made her brain foggy. She was so tired. Tired of worrying. Tired of arguing. Tired of her daughter's negativity. Tired of trying to keep her thoughts straight and stay awake. "That wasn't the plan."

"Brandon brought his snowmobile. We'll go straight home."

"You can't drive it through town."

"We can take the back way. Along Klondike."

Susanne hadn't had the strength to argue or the brain power to think through the downsides. Brandon wouldn't let anything happen to Trish. So, she dropped Trish by a big yellow snowmobile that was parked across the street from the school, just as Brandon was walking up to it. He waved.

Trish slipped her hands into her gloves. "Bye."

"Be careful. Go straight home." Susanne's words had slurred.

The door slammed shut. Too late, Susanne's brain fired up enough that she remembered her promise to keep Brandon and Trish at home or in public. Riding a snowmobile wasn't in public. How could she have made that mistake? As the snowmobile churned through the snow away from her, though, she knew there was no way she could follow it. She was going to have to trust Trish and Brandon. She put the truck in gear and a wave of dizziness and nausea swept over her. Trish was probably better off on that snowmobile than she and Perry would be in the truck. Susanne suddenly knew she just needed to get home. She shouldn't be driving in this condition.

She'd driven to the spot where Perry was waiting for her.

"Where's Trish?" he'd asked.

Susanne hadn't thought about what to say to Perry. The truth, she guessed. "Riding home with Brandon."

Perry looked astonished. "I thought she wasn't supposed to."

"She's not. I decided to trust her."

Her son's eyebrows rose. "Won't Dad be mad?"

If Trish and Brandon lived up to her trust, she'd never have to confess this sin to Patrick. "We won't need to tell him."

"What Dad doesn't know won't hurt anyone?"

"Right."

"Mom, I'm not sure that's always true."

Susanne's stomach roiled with building nausea. "What do you mean?"

"Like, what about you telling Coach Lamkin I saw the snowmobile and shooter up at Meadowlark?"

He was right. "I shouldn't have done that."

"Ronnie asked Dad if we'd told anybody about it. He said we hadn't. I didn't say anything, but I knew you'd told the coach. She could have told someone, and they could have told someone, and that's how gossip starts. I hear you tell Trish that all the time."

Susanne winced. "I'll tell him."

Perry gave a crisp nod.

She and Perry had beaten Trish and Brandon to the house. Susanne hurried inside and ate a second helping of the salty popcorn she'd made earlier. Ferdinand curled up at her feet, where he immediately passed gas. The smell was horrible. It wasn't uncommon for him and didn't usually bother her, but now the smell was too much. She started gagging and sprinted for the bathroom.

She barely made it. After the vomiting stopped, Susanne had decided cold air might help her. She'd left Perry in the living room to keep an eye out for Trish and Brandon.

Now, out behind the deck in the backyard, she leaned over and scooped up a handful of snow. Although the temperature was falling, it wasn't frigid out, so the snow was still damp. Perfect for packing in a ball. She made one and slipped it under her hair, where the pain was worst. Pressing it, she closed her eyes. Blocking her vision seemed to supercharge her brain, and it started cycling through its loop of stress. The Kemecke trial started tomorrow. She and Trish would have to sit in the same courtroom as that hideous man and talk about the things he'd done, right in front of him. He'd be convicted, but that wouldn't make the trial any less of a nightmare. And everyone knew what had happened last time—he'd murdered a deputy en route to the state penitentiary and escaped, which is when he ended up at the Flints, with Susanne tied to a chair while he plotted against Patrick.

"Mom." Perry's voice was a paddle to the pinball of her thoughts. "Mom. *Mom.*"

Her voice came out thick and slurred, like she was talking through a mouthful of melted caramel, only it tasted like the coffee, popcorn, and chef salad that had just come back up. "What?"

Perry pulled on her arm. "They're not here yet. Should we go look for them?"

Susanne weaved toward the deck steps. The cute boots she'd worn to lunch and never changed out of weren't a good choice for traction, and she slipped and went down hard, chin first on the lowest step.

"Ow!"

"Mom! Are you okay?" Perry crouched over her. "Your chin is bleeding."

She dabbed her gloved fingers to her face. They came away bloody. Funny, it didn't hurt, but that might be because the back of her head hurt far worse. She tried to stand, pushing up from the ground with her hands. She made it to her knees, but everything seemed wobbly. Her stomach erupted again without warning, and she fell back to the bottom step, right into the disgusting puddle of chin blood and vomit.

"Mom, ew."

She pushed away and twisted her body, landing on her backside in clean snow. "I don't feel so good," she mumbled.

"Should I call Dad? You probably need stitches."

She lifted her head. Droplets of blood plopped on her down jacket. "Maybe. But I have to deal with Trish first."

"Want me to run check and see if they're here?"

Susanne nodded. A mistake. The world tilted sideways. She swallowed down more nausea. "I may need a ride to the hospital." Forget the stitches. Maybe Patrick could do something about her headache.

"From Brandon?"

"Or Trish. Or whoever is on duty watching us."

"How do I find them?"

"We'll cross that bridge when we come to it."

Perry, clad in snow-appropriate moon boots, galloped around the deck and up the slope of the back yard. He disappeared around the side of the house. She let her head drop back into the snow.

CHAPTER THIRTY-TWO: FRIGHTEN

Buffalo, Wyoming
Tuesday, March 15, 1977, 4:00 p.m.

Trish

Brandon stared at Trish. "I got the note from Ben."

She nodded. "My mom is letting me ride home with you, if that's okay?"

He didn't smile. He didn't touch her. The aftershocks of their fight the day before were still quaking, and she hadn't even talked to him about what Ben told her yet.

"It's cool."

He settled onto the seat. She climbed on behind him. He smelled like the cheap soap in the pump dispensers the school kept in the locker room showers. Slipping her arms around his torso, she wondered if this would be the last time she held him. Tears threatened again, but she refused to give in to them. Brandon accelerated, and the power of the machine threw her backwards. She gripped him tighter.

Brandon raced along the unplowed backroads. From time to time, he veered off the side for better snow. Trish had only ridden a snowmobile once before. It was up at Bear Lodge. Her dad had rented two of them, and their family had taken turns at the controls, riding double. She'd been wearing a full snowsuit, snow boots, and a face shield then. They would have been nice to have now, instead of her jeans, imitation Dingo boots, puffy jacket, and dinky little cap and gloves. Brandon was giving off a little heat, at least. She buried her face against his back to protect it from the pelting snow, and to hide her eyes. It was a little scary going this fast.

When they reached Klondike Road, they were about two miles outside of Buffalo, in the middle of foothills ranch country. Brandon turned back toward the western edge of town, then he cut the engine. He didn't get off or look at her.

His voice sounded far away. "What's the deal, Trish?"

"What do you mean?"

"Like, I mean how did Ben know you were coming up to the school, you know?"

She didn't want to have this conversation here. Not out in the bleak, barren cold. But she had to tell him something. "Um, I called him."

"Why?"

"So he'd tell you."

His body was rigid. "You know what I mean."

She took a deep breath. "I heard you cheated on me."

"From who?"

"It doesn't matter."

"It matters to me. Someone is spreading lies about me."

Ben had said he was the only one who knew. That it was okay for Trish to tell Brandon. She still felt like she was betraying him by doing it, but she had to. "Ben."

Brandon rolled his shoulders. A sound like a growl came from his throat. Suddenly, he gunned the engine on the snowmobile. It shot forward before Trish had a chance to grab hold of him again. She tumbled backwards off the seat and landed face-up in the snow. For a moment, she didn't move. Her head rang, and she was dazed. She watched the millions of snowflakes plummeting toward her face, ending in little wet plops on her cheeks and nose. It was mesmerizing. She wasn't sure how much time had passed before she wrested her gaze from the tunnel of sky down to her body. She didn't think she was hurt.

She heard the sound of the snowmobile receding in the distance. Brandon had to realize she'd fallen off. She sat up, shivered, and stared after him. He didn't turn around. He wasn't coming back. She was alone.

Trish stood. Her emotions went to war inside her. Anger, fear, sadness. But giving in to them wouldn't do her any good. She scrambled up the embankment through snow drifted to her knees and back onto Klondike. There was less snow there. She brushed herself off as best she could. Her body heat was melting snow into her clothes and boots. She wasn't freezing cold yet, but she would be soon.

She clenched her fists and started walking.

CHAPTER THIRTY-THREE: STRIKE

Susanne

S usanne groaned. What was wrong with her? The bloody chin was obvious. But she'd never had a headache like this one before, with the blurry vision, the vomiting, and the white-hot pain. She leaned toward the deck railing and clutched it, pulling herself to a dizzy, wobbly standing position. She shielded her eyes against the glare of the light fixture coming through the kitchen window.

"Come on, Susanne. You've got to get moving."

She dragged herself up the steps then shuffled a path through three inches of fresh snow, her eyes on her feet the whole way, her arms out for balance like a ballerina in second position. At the back door, she paused, catching her breath. She eyed her dirty, bloody gloves and then the door handle. For a moment she thought about taking the gloves off, then decided against it. She valued her skin, and she wasn't putting her bare hand on a wet doorknob in below freezing temperatures. She opened the door. The new floor mat was the only absorbent item within reach. She stepped onto it, then skated it across the linoleum to the half bath down the hall.

She flipped on the lights. They hurt her eyes, and she squinted. Then she looked into the mirror and moaned. The woman staring back at her was ghastly. Pale and hollow-eyed, with vomit on the front of her coat and blood dripping down her chin, neck, and chest like a cannibal after a feast.

She shut the lights back off. They hurt her eyes and her head, and she didn't need them. Turning on the hot water and grabbing a hand towel, she sucked in a deep, shuddering breath. She couldn't go to the hospital looking like this. She moistened the towel and added soap.

Then the room started to go black, and she fell in a heap with her cheek pressed against the bathroom floormat.

CHAPTER THIRTY-FOUR: OPPOSE

Trish

Trish's heart leapt at the sound of a vehicle engine headed her way. Her parents had always warned her not to accept rides from strangers, but she wondered if there was an exception for when you were about to freeze to death? She was wet and tired and so far from home. She knew her parents were afraid someone was going to try to hurt her to keep her from testifying. But who would believe she was crazy enough to be out in this weather? They'd never be looking for her out here. Still, she hoped it was someone she knew in the vehicle. Someone nice.

As it drew nearer, she recognized the whine of the motor. Not a car or a truck. A snowmobile. Then a big yellow snow machine materialized out of the whiteness in front of her. Brandon was back. Trish had never been scared of him, despite the plentiful bad seeds in his family tree. She wasn't sure if she should be scared now. He'd never hit her, and he hadn't pushed her off the snowmobile. She'd just fallen because she wasn't holding on.

And maybe he hadn't realized she was gone at first because he was upset?

She snorted. That was wishful thinking. Of course, he knew. He may not have hit her, but he'd left her to freeze to death and without protection. Something tugged at her heart, a physical pull in her chest. He'd come back, though. He'd made a mistake. His emotions had gotten the better of him. He was here now. And she needed a ride home.

Brandon circled around and pulled up beside her. He motioned for her to get on behind him. She bit her lip, but, after a moment of hesitation, she did. This time, she locked her arms around him before her butt hit the seat. Without a word, Brandon gunned the engine like he had before, but this time, she stayed on. If she'd thought he'd driven fast earlier, it was nothing compared to his speed now, like he didn't care what happened to them. She was a goner if she fell—her head would split open like a cantaloupe.

The snowmobile hit a bump, then went airborne. The rotating snow tracks whined in the air. The back end started to sink and gravity pulled Trish backwards, wrenching at her shoulders and locked hands. Her feet lost purchase and her stomach tumbled in a sickening free fall. Then the skis and chassis landed with a crushing impact that snapped Trish's teeth into her lip.

But she hung on.

Brandon didn't let off the gas. A few minutes later, he turned off Klondike and began winding his way along the creek side road toward Trish's house. The wind had teased tears from her eyes, then dried them on her cheeks. Her wet clothes and the cold were an unbearable combination with the gusts. She thought about the "two out of three" rule. Horses could survive any two out of three. Cold, wet, and wind. Trish was facing all three.

Brandon made the last turn, going too fast. The back end of the snowmobile swung out, and for a moment, Trish thought they were going to tump over into the ditch. Then it regained traction, and they were in her driveway. The snowmobile came to a stop in front of the house. Trish was shaking like an aspen leaf, and her teeth were chattering.

Brandon jumped off. His face was red from the wind and rage. "I've delivered the princess home safely. Now I'm outta here."

Snowflakes were melting on her face and pooling on her cheeks. She reached up to brush the wetness away and realized she was crying. It was so humiliating. She climbed off. Everything would be okay if she made it okay. He had brought her home even though he was upset. "Please don't leave. I'm sorry. I shouldn't have listened to Ben."

He shook his head. "This is whacked."

"I know. I said I'm sorry."

"Who do you trust, me or him?"

"You. Of course, you."

"He's a criminal."

"I know." She felt a flicker of guilt. She didn't believe Ben was a criminal. But she'd agree with anything Brandon said if it would make things right between them.

"All criminals lie."

"You're right, Brandon."

Brandon crossed his arms. He was breathing hard, and he made a huffing noise. "Where did he say I supposedly cheated on you?"

"He didn't."

"See? He was just making it up. Totally bogus."

Trish swallowed back a fresh wave of tears. "I just, I love you so much, Brandon. And when we were broken up, you did go out with Charla, and I was afraid that she would, you know, do things I wouldn't."

"Like, she would, if I wanted her to."

"Did you? When we weren't together, I mean."

"Me and Charla?"

"Yeah."

"I don't think you want me to the answer that question." He smirked.

Trish moaned. She had her answer. "When? Where?" She hoped it wasn't in his truck. Or anywhere he took Trish to be alone.

"You're tripping. Why do you want to know?"

"I, uh, I guess I don't." She tried to believe her words. What did it matter what Brandon had done with Charla in his truck, as long as he loved Trish?

"You're going to have to stop being so square if you want us to stay together."

"What do you mean?"

He crossed his arms. "Like, we've been dating a long time now."

"Six months, except for our break-up."

He nodded. "So, when are we going to, you know, do it?"

His words were like a punch in her stomach. "Do it?" She swallowed hard. "I'm not ready."

"Charla is. Other girls are. What's your problem with it?"

Trish put her hand over her mouth. All thoughts of the cold and her humiliation were long gone. She couldn't believe this. She thought he loved her, but he wasn't talking like he did. Brandon was her whole world. Her eyes burned, and she deflated like a leaky balloon.

Perry came barreling toward them from around the corner of the house. He was puffing between words like he'd run ten miles, not across the yard. "Mom fell. She hit her chin. She's bleeding. She needs to go to the hospital."

"Hold up, little man." Brandon frowned. So did Perry. "Trish, where was I when Ben was talking about me behind my back?"

She looked at her feet. "I don't know."

"When was it?"

"Earlier."

Perry's voice interrupted them. "Hey, your snowmobile. It's . . ."

Brandon turned to Perry. "Get back in the house. This is between me and your sister."

"But, my mom."

Brandon glared at him. Perry fled to the front door. He slipped on the steps but caught himself with one hand, then scurried inside.

Brandon leaned against his snowmobile. He had a funny look on his face, like he was really happy about figuring out something that didn't make him happy at all. "Did he come here after he took my truck at lunch? Today?"

"Um . . ." Her voice trailed off. Now wasn't a good time to talk about this part. Not when Brandon was so angry and her mom needed her. She felt torn down the middle between them.

He cupped a hand around his ear. "What's that?"

"Yes. Around lunchtime."

"He talked to you here? Like, where we're standing now?"

"Not exactly."

"Where, then?"

"We drove around."

Brandon stood up and punched the air with his forefinger. "You got in *my* truck with *him*. What else did you do?"

Trish tried to grab his hand, but he snatched it away. "Just talked, Brandon. That's all. I promise."

"About me cheating on you."

"Yeah."

"And what else?"

"Just stuff. He, uh, he told me about juvie."

"Did he make a move on you?"

"No." That was technically true. He hadn't tried to get her to kiss him or anything. Telling her he liked her was different.

Brandon enunciated each word. "Did he touch you?"

She hesitated. Ben had put his hand on her arm. How could she explain that without Brandon going ballistic? But she couldn't lie either. "Brandon, I didn't do anything."

Brandon shouted, "He did. He put his hands on you. And you're sitting here chewing me out for what I've done with other girls when you were with him?"

Trish's face crumpled. "Wait. You said you didn't do anything with Charla."

"Who said anything about Charla?"

Trish's head was reeling. Brandon *had* cheated on her, but not with Charla? She'd been so sure it was her nemesis. "You've been with other girls while we've been dating?"

"Experienced ones."

Trish gasped and put her hand over her mouth. Her knees felt weak. How could he say these things to her? Wasn't he even sorry?

"You deserve whatever you've got coming to you." Brandon snorted. "My mom was right. You're just a phony little goody two shoes." He slammed his body down onto the seat of his snowmobile. "We're done, Trish. Peace out."

He and his new yellow snowmobile slingshotted out of the driveway and Trish's life.

Trish buried her face in her hands and sobbed.

CHAPTER THIRTY-FIVE: SICKEN

Susanne

Susanne woke up to find Ferdinand licking her face. "Ferdie, stop."

The dog sat back on his haunches, towering above her and looking down his long nose and wiry mustache at her with concerned eyes. He whined. Susanne sat up and leaned against the bathroom wall. He moved closer and she stroked his head.

How had she ended up here? Her brain was like a battery with a critically low charge. But then she remembered coming in to clean up her chin. She touched her head. It still hurt, but not quite as much. She pulled herself up by the bathroom countertop. Ferdinand leaned against her thigh. The dizziness and nausea weren't as bad as they'd been. She looked in the mirror. Her cut was barely bleeding anymore. Some of the blood on her chin and neck had dried to a brownish-maroon crust. She re-moistened the rag and started cleaning herself up while Ferdinand kept a watchful eye on her.

The front door burst open. Ferdinand didn't react.

"Mom," Perry shouted. "Where are you?"

"In the bathroom by the kitchen."

His footsteps pounded toward her. He caught himself on the door-frame. His eyes were wild.

"What's the matter?"

"Brandon and Trish are here. They're fighting. He's being a big ... a big ..."

"Don't say it." She put her rag down. "Let me get my jacket."

"You're wearing it."

She looked down, then frowned. "So I am."

"Maybe we should call dad."

"Maybe. Let me see what's going on with Trish first."

Perry put a hand under her elbow. Her heart swelled a little. He was such a sweet boy. Together, they walked to the front door, Ferdinand trailing them. Before they could reach it, though, the door flew open. Trish stumbled in, wet, and in tears.

"Mom," she wailed. She threw herself into Susanne's arms.

Ferdinand shoved his nose between their shins, trying to hug everyone at once.

As bad as she'd been feeling, Susanne wanted nothing more than to help her daughter. She stroked her hair. "Thank God you're okay."

"But I'm not. Brandon *is* seeing someone else. Someone older and more experienced. He dumped me. *He* dumped *me.*"

"Older and more experienced? Who?"

"He didn't say." A horrified look crossed her daughter's face. "Oh, no."

"What?"

"Marcy told me there's a teacher at school involved with a student."

Perry shook his head. "No way. Brandon and a teacher?"

"I don't know." Trish jumped back, then noticed Susanne's face. "What happened to you?"

"I fell and hit my chin on the deck."

"We have to get her to the hospital," Perry said. "You have to drive."

"But I'm sopping wet. Can I change clothes first?"

As the kids were debating the issue, memories were surfacing in Susanne's compromised brain. Snippets of conversations. Images from the last few weeks. And then a thought formed. A bad one. Susanne covered a gasp with her hand. Perry grabbed her elbow again.

Trish cocked her head. "What is it, Mom?"

"Coach Lamkin. She has a boyfriend. Or maybe a fiancé. In

Laramie, she told me there was a big age difference between them. She wouldn't tell me who it was, because of parents' perceptions about her as a coach. She said I'd recognize his name when they went public."

Now it was Trish's turn to gasp.

"I thought she meant he was older. Then today at lunch she said she'd resigned, so she'd be able to tell me who he was soon."

Perry's mouth dropped open. "You think Coach Lamkin's boyfriend is Brandon?"

Trish shook her head violently. "No. It can't be. Coach Lamkin cares about me. She'd never do that to me."

Susanne heard a vehicle pull up outside.

"Brandon's back!" Trish ran to the window with her big dog beside her.

CHAPTER THIRTY-SIX: PREY

Trish

A rush of hopeful feelings coursed through Trish. Brandon had changed his mind. She could ask him about Coach Lamkin. He'd tell her it wasn't true. Everything would be okay. She peered out the window beside the door, hand on the knob.

Devastation rocked her all over again. It wasn't him. It was someone in a brown Chevrolet pickup. A truck that belonged to someone she saw every day.

Coach Lamkin.

"It's her." She swiped tears from her eyes.

"Who?" her mom asked.

"Coach Lamkin." Inside, Trish was fighting off the growing suspicion that her mother was right. The timing of Coach Lamkin showing up as Brandon left was just too big a coincidence not to be *something*. Was she here to gloat? "I'll see what she wants."

Ferdinand whined and pawed at the front door.

"Then we need to get Mom to the hospital," Perry said.

"I'll be fine, Perry," Susanne said. "It's okay."

"Back, Ferdie." Trish slipped through the door without letting the dog out. She stood on the stoop.

The truck parked, and a white cap popped out, then the rest of Coach Lamkin followed, bundled in a belted navy wool coat. "I just saw a snowmobile blow out of here like hell on skids. Is everything okay?"

Trish stood up straight, fighting back a sob that suddenly needed out. Had her coach betrayed her? "I'm fine."

Lamkin put her hand on Trish's elbow. She cocked her head as she studied Trish. "Clearly, you're not. Where are your parents?"

"My mom and Perry are inside. Dad's at work."

"Was that your boyfriend?"

The sob broke through, but Trish caught it against her knuckles. Was her coach playing some kind of sick mind game with her? She regained control. "He used to be. Not anymore."

Coach Lamkin pulled Trish into a hug. "Ah. A break-up."

Trish didn't hug back. "Y-y-y-yes."

Lamkin patted Trish's back. "Those can be bad. I'm sorry. It's that Lewis boy, right? The cute one who plays forward?"

Of course she thinks he's cute. "Yes."

"Let me guess—he wasn't faithful."

Trish pulled away from her. Suspicions were churning inside her. "How did you know?"

"He's a good-looking boy with a reputation. Coaches aren't deaf and blind, you know. But did you really think you were his only one?"

Words stuck in Trish's throat. She struggled to get them out. "I . . . yes. I trusted him. We love—loved—each other."

"Take it from me. With a boy like him, you should just expect to share and not get all worked up about it. I've dated enough boys like Brandon to know."

Trish stiffened. *I'm sure you have. Are.* She couldn't stand the game any longer. "What are you doing here?"

"I'm your security tonight. You know, with the posse your parents put together. That's how I knew about the snowmobile."

"Were you parked on the road?"

"Yes. I wanted to give you some privacy. It looked . . . heated."

Had the coach been watching the Flints or watching Brandon? Trish's fingernails dug into her palms, and she realized her hands were balled into fists.

The door to the house opened and shut. "Trish?"

"Out here, Mom." She hugged herself.

Susanne walked toward them with slow, unsteady steps.

"Susanne! Are you okay?" Coach Lamkin took Trish's mom by both arms.

"Not really. My head hurts, I've been throwing up, and I fell. The kids were about to take me to the emergency room."

Trish said, "Coach Lamkin is our security tonight, Mom. She saw Brandon here and came to check on us." She knew her voice sounded brittle, but she couldn't help it.

"Thank you, Barb."

Coach Lamkin made a sad face. "I'm sorry you're feeling bad. You seemed fine at lunch. Was it something you ate?"

Trish had never been violent before. But she was feeling violent now. Something about the way Lamkin was talking to her mom made Trish want to sock her coach in the nose.

"I wish I knew."

"How about I drive you in?"

"Trish will do it."

Coach Lamkin let go of Susanne and put her arm around Trish's shoulders. Trish wanted to shuck it off but restrained herself. "Trish is too upset to be operating the truck in these road conditions. I'll drive my truck. It's not a problem." She walked toward her truck, her arm still on Trish, pulling her along.

Susanne didn't follow them. "We need to get Perry."

Then the squirt came running out the door.

Susanne waved him over. "There he is. Hurry, Perry. We're leaving for the hospital. Coach Lamkin is driving us."

"Hi, Perry," Coach Lamkin said. She pulled a long green canvas bag off the truck's bench seat and threw it in the bed.

"Uh, hi." He slid to a stop. His eyes cut to the coach, then back to the bed of the truck.

"What's the matter?" Susanne asked.

He squinted and his forehead mashed into wrinkles. "Nothing?"

Trish watched her brother climb into the truck. He had a funny look on his face that sure didn't seem like nothing.

CHAPTER THIRTY-SEVEN: WITNESS

Perry

The inside of the truck smelled like a wet dog. With all four of them—Mom, Trish, Coach Lamkin, and him—crammed into the truck's bench seat, Perry felt like a sardine. Of course, he had to sit in the middle and straddle the gear shift because he was the smallest. Reason number one trillion and two that he couldn't wait for his growth spurt.

The coach pulled off her cap and put it on the dash. He snuck a glance at her. Her long red hair was prettier than Ms. Tavejie's hair, he had to admit, but he still thought Ms. Tavejie was better looking overall. And a lot less intimidating. Coach Lamkin turned the truck in a circle, passing by the floodlight over the driveway. It shone in the passenger side window like a beacon on the white wool cap that the coach had been wearing. She gave the truck some gas, and they careened down the driveway and out onto the road.

And then it hit him.

When he'd walked outside and seen Coach Lamkin, he'd gotten a weird feeling. Like he almost remembered something, but not quite.

Then he'd seen the green canvas bag—a big, long one—and the feeling had gotten worse. Now, his stomach burned. The truck bumped and bucked a little as it crossed the bridge over Clear Creek. He shrunk away from the coach toward Trish.

"Stop it, shrimp," Trish snapped.

He motioned for his mom to lean toward him. She was ghostly pale and looked confused, so he pinched her arm. "Mom."

She shifted toward him. "What?"

The truck turned onto the highway into Buffalo.

He whispered, "I need to tell you something."

Trish said, "Don't mind me, just in the middle here getting squished."

"Tell me, then," his mom said.

"It's a secret." He strained toward her and lowered his voice further, so low he couldn't even hear himself.

"I can't hear you."

He tried again.

She sat back. "I still can't hear you."

Trish snorted. "Don't be so rude, Perry."

His mom sighed. "You can't tell secrets when we're packed in together like this."

Coach Lamkin laughed. "Do you need me to put my fingers in my ears?"

"Mo-om. It's important."

"Okay. I'll give you one more try." His mom squeezed over into Trish.

Trish put her arms across her chest. "You guys, stop!"

Perry whispered his secret one last time.

His mom flopped back in the seat. "I give up. This truck is too noisy, and I'm still feeling pretty bad. If it's that important, tell me when we get to the hospital."

He shut his mouth. Out of his side vision, he saw Coach Lamkin turn to look at him. He wasn't sure, but he thought she smiled.

"Barb, you missed the turn to the hospital," Susanne said. She pressed her hand against the window, then put it on her forehead.

Coach Lamkin didn't answer. She didn't turn around either. Perry's stomach started to hurt worse. This wasn't good.

"What route are you taking?" Susanne asked.

Perry watched in horror as Coach Lamkin slipped her hand into the pocket of her coat. She pulled out a little black revolver. Cocking the hammer, she pressed the end of the barrel into his temple.

The steel was cold and hard against his head. He whimpered and held perfectly still.

"Change of plans."

Susanne wasn't looking at the coach. "What do you mean?"

Trish elbowed their mom. "Mom, she's got a gun."

"What?"

"She's got a gun and she's pointing it at Perry's head."

Susanne frowned. "But that doesn't make sense. Barb, what's going on?" Her voice sounded loopy.

Coach Lamkin laughed. "You might not have been able to hear Perry, but I did. Crystal clear. Perry, repeat it for your mother. Nice and loud so we can all hear you this time."

Perry cleared his throat. He felt like he was going to throw up or wet his pants or both. "I said, 'Coach Lamkin is the one I saw up at Meadowlark. The one who shot the judge's wife.'"

CHAPTER THIRTY-EIGHT: REVEAL

Patrick

Patrick pulled into the driveway to the house. When the hospital staff had been able to help the patients from the pile-up faster than expected, he'd decided to sneak out for a nap and quick dinner after all, even though it had been a short afternoon. He'd have to be back by six-thirty to make up the time Dr. John had covered for him, but that was okay. He parked the Suburban close to the walkway. The area had clearly been shoveled, although the snow was starting to accumulate again. The outside lights were on, and his truck was there. Brandon's wasn't, which he counted as a good thing.

"Hello? Anyone home?" he called out, as he entered the door.

No one answered.

Maybe Susanne and the kids had gone to get burgers with a friend. Their family wasn't usually big on eating out. It was a waste of money, and he and Susanne felt strongly about gathering as a family around the dinner table every night that they could. It was important to share that time with the kids. To hear about their days and to let them know that they were a priority. Things weren't the same at a restaurant. But after the day they'd had, he wouldn't blame Susanne if she hadn't felt much like cooking. Especially since she hadn't known about his last second change of plans to come home to eat with them. He shrugged. The nap he was craving *would* be easier in an empty house.

In the kitchen, he checked the table for a note where he and Susanne always left them for each other. There was none. Just a half-full mug of cold coffee, aging. He dumped it in the sink and rinsed the cup, then he opened the refrigerator and pulled out the last of the leftover beef stew. Eating it cold wasn't optimal, but it was still fuel. He ate to live, he didn't live to eat. He served a bowl, took it and some utensils to the table, and sat down facing the winter wonderland of their backyard.

And there she was, a vision in the falling snow. His mountain lion. This time, the gorgeous, tawny creature had a cub with her. The two of them were perched on the deck not ten feet away, staring into the window at him.

"Hey, girl. You're back." Suddenly, he was surer than ever that these sightings weren't random, and his blood felt icy in his veins. *Where are Susanne and the kids?* "What are you trying to tell me? Are you trying to warn me about something?" Her entrance into his life coincided with the threat to his family, and his gut told them the two were related.

He stood, and his movement scared the lions. As one, they leapt from the deck and disappeared into the trees along the creek. He felt their departure in his core, like they'd physically torn themselves from him. Before he could dwell on it, something else drew his attention. Something reddish brown, on the floor by the door. He squinted. Was it blood? He moved closer, knelt, and touched it. It was moist and more red than brown. He sniffed it. Definitely blood. He stood and examined the door. Bloody fingerprints, where someone had pushed it shut. He opened the door, careful not to smudge the prints. The doorknob outside was caked in dried blood, and blood droplets led across the deck and onto the steps, where he found the source. More dried blood, and, to the side, human vomit.

Had Perry fallen when he was outside playing? He could have a concussion, if the vomit was related. With this much blood, the boy would need stitches. Susanne and the kids could be at the hospital right now.

But how would they have gotten there with his truck parked here? He scanned the ground and deck for other clues, but found none, so he hurried back in the house. Intent on calling the hospital, he was sidetracked by the blood leading to the bathroom. The sink and countertop were a blood bath. A head wound, he thought. Nothing bled worse than the head. Which supported his theory that Perry—or someone—had fallen.

The lion had been telling him his family was in danger. He was as certain of it as he'd ever been about anything. He had to find them. His heart was pounding madly, and he realized he was nearing full-blown panic level. There was a reason doctors didn't treat their own family members. It was too hard to remain calm, cool, and collected when a loved one was ill or injured. Right now, Patrick felt anything but calm. He yelled, venting his frustration and anxiety, and ran from the bathroom to the kitchen phone, banging his thigh against the corner of the table on the way. It felt like getting stabbed. He grabbed his leg and reached for the phone.

Before he could pick it up, it rang. *Susanne!* He answered it.

CHAPTER THIRTY-NINE: BIDE

Buffalo, Wyoming
Tuesday, March 15, 1977, 5:30 p.m.

Susanne

"Good thing I have new snow tires." Barb's voice was casual, like they were just a couple of friends out for a drive.

Susanne's head throbbed. She felt anything but casual. Barb was nuts. She had a gun to Perry's head. How Susanne wished she were at her best. "Why?"

"We're going to need them where we're going. Now, Trish, reach into my purse and pull out the duct tape."

Susanne felt her daughter stiffen.

"Don't make me ask again, Flint. You may be in good shape, but I can assure you, you don't want to be running wind sprints dressed like you are in this weather."

After another few seconds of silent resistance, Trish dug into the purse on the floorboard. She came up with a silver roll of tape.

"Good. Now, Susanne, starting with Trish, secure her wrists and ankles with the tape. Then we'll move on to Perry."

Susanne and Trish locked eyes as they made the tape exchange. Susanne tried to tell her daughter to be brave and that everything would be all right. Trish's pupils were dilated and her nostrils flared, but she held out her exposed wrists, side by side. She'd taken off her gloves when they got in the truck. They all had, except for Perry.

In a cheery voice, Barb said, "Nice and tight, please."

Susanne worked a fingernail under the end of the tape, then pressed it against Trish's sleeve on one wrist. She unrolled the tape as she rotated it around Trish's wrists two times. The tape stuck fast.

"One more go-round, if you don't mind."

Susanne put a third layer of tape around Trish. "I'm sorry," she mouthed at her.

"Now her ankles."

Susanne bent over. The position forced the air from her lungs and sent a wave of nausea cascading through her. She wrapped fast and blindly and sat back up, pressing her fingers against her lips.

"Flint, hold those ankles up where I can see them."

Trish leaned back and slung her ankles onto the dash. Barb glanced over at them and pursed her lips.

"That will do. Now, on to Perry."

Trish swung her feet back to the floorboard. Susanne pushed into Trish to get slightly in front of Perry and reach his wrists. His gloved hands were trembling in his lap. Big tears pooled in his eyes. "It's okay," she mouthed to him. "I love you." His wide eyes said he understood, but he kept his head motionless, with Barb's gun barrel still pressed against his temple. Susanne wrapped his wrists, then laid across Trish's knees to get to his ankles.

Barb kept glancing down at them. Susanne didn't think she could see Perry's ankles, so she only pretended to wrap the tape the second and third times. When she was done, she held her breath, but Barb didn't comment.

"Your own ankles next."

Susanne wiped sweat from her forehead. She put her ankles over Trish's and started wrapping herself. Barb had a clear line of sight and watched her the whole time. Susanne hated immobilizing herself. Hated it even more than she hated doing it to the kids. She was their mother. They were her responsibility. How could she protect them if she was trapped? She was already at a disadvantage because of the headache. Maybe if she had been herself, had been able to *think*, they wouldn't be in this mess now.

"Looks good. As soon as you're done, we'll be making a stop."

Barb must have been driving in a circle around town, because they were back near the turn to the hospital.

Susanne said, "I am done."

"Not quite. Tape Perry's wrists up on the rearview mirror."

Susanne's heart cracked. Her emotions had been numb with shock, but they were catching up to her fast now, and she wanted to cry. All of the blood would drain from his hands. It would be painful, quickly. Plus, leaving his feet loose wouldn't do much good if his hands were taped to the mirror.

"Can't I—"

"No."

Slowly, Perry lifted his arms over his head. Susanne wrapped his wrists twice, sticking them to the mirror.

"Three times."

She added a third layer of tape.

"Now, tape your wrists to Trish's."

"What do you mean?"

"I think you can figure it out."

Susanne started the tape on Trish and got it halfway around their four wrists.

"That's as far as I can go."

Barb pulled the truck into a dark, empty gas station, stopping with the driver's side door next to a pay phone at the corner of the building. "I'll take it from here." She turned off the truck. "No funny business. Even if you get loose, I've got Perry." She opened her coat and tucked her gun in the waistband of her jeans. "Hold your wrists up for me, ladies."

Susanne thought about defying Barb's order and making a break for it, but she knew she would fall face first out of the truck. Running would be impossible. Screaming wouldn't do any good. They were alone, and the station was closed. If Susanne made her mad, Barb might hurt one of the kids. Or leave Susanne and take the kids without her. As long as the three Flints were alive and together, Susanne bought another chance for escape with every moment that passed. She had to believe that and wait for the right time.

She clenched her teeth. She and Trish stretched their wrists toward Barb.

"Good." Barb wrapped them five times, then taped them to the handhold over the glove box. "Now, I still have tape left. Can we agree on no screaming, or do I need to add some tape to your mouths? I don't want to make this anymore unpleasant than I have to. I actually like you guys."

Trish's words exploded in the truck cab. "Are you and Brandon . . . are you . . . are you . . . doing it?"

Barb stared at Trish for a moment, then exploded with laughter. "Oh, you poor thing. You really don't have a clue, do you?"

Trish's voice broke. "You are. I knew it."

"No, Flint, I'm not. Children aren't my thing. But Brandon is seeing someone."

"A teacher?"

"As a matter of fact, yes. But let's keep that between us. We don't want to get Tara fired."

"Who?" Trish croaked. "Who is Tara?"

"Tara Coker?" Susanne said. "The one you brought to lunch today? She's sleeping with my daughter's teenage boyfriend?"

"MY Ms. Coker?" Trish shrieked.

Barb laughed. "I warned you, Trish. With a boy like Brandon, you just have to share and accept it." To Susanne, Barb said, "Tara wasn't very pleased with me for inviting her to lunch with you. I didn't tell her you were coming. It was a fun surprise for me to see her with her boyfriend's girlfriend's mother." Barb winked. "Now, I have a phone call to make, if you'll excuse me."

Barb got out, leaving the door open. She dropped change in the slot, then dialed the phone.

"Mom, what is she going to do with us?" Perry whispered.

"I don't know. Hopefully nothing."

"Right," Trish said. "She's just going to tape us up and hold a gun to Perry's head and do nothing."

Susanne sighed. Now wasn't the time to rebuke her daughter. "Point taken. We have to get away from her."

"How?" Perry's voice broke. Young man to young boy in one syllable.

"I don't know yet. Right now, we have to concentrate on staying alive until someone realizes we're gone. Your dad and Ronnie will figure it out."

"When? Dad won't be home for hours."

Outside, they heard Barb say, "I have your star witnesses, so you'd better not hang up on me."

Susanne frowned. Star witnesses? That sounded like a trial. It had to be the Kemecke trial. Was she talking to Donna Lewis? Susanne dismissed the thought immediately. Trish and Susanne weren't stars for the Kemecke clan. They were stars for the state of Wyoming. That meant it had to be the county prosecutor on the other line. Max Alexandrov.

"There's no trial without them. You have half an hour to meet me at our place." *Their place? Holy smokes. Barb was dating Max. Max was the father of her baby.* "Come alone. If you make me happy, you'll get them back, and your career will be made. If you don't, you won't. It's that simple."

Barb was lying, of course. Susanne knew that from the second Barb realized Perry could identify her, the Flints were history. A thought teased her laboring brain. Susanne had been so focused on *what* Barb was doing, that she hadn't stopped to think about the *why*. As in *why* had Barb shot Jeannie Renkin? Was it for Max, because he wanted the trial in Buffalo for the sake of his career?

Barb listened for a moment, then turned back to the truck and leaned her head around the door. "My friend wants to hear you each say something."

"Who is it?" Susanne said.

"Thank you, Susanne. Now you, Trish."

Trish muttered. "Whatever."

She went back to the phone. "Did you hear them?" After a pause, she said, "No more excuses." Then, "I love you."

If that was love, Barb had a funny way of showing it. It sounded a lot more like extortion to Susanne.

CHAPTER FORTY: DISMISS

Patrick

"Susanne?" Patrick shouted into the receiver. "Where are you? Are you okay?"

The heavy breathing in his ear didn't sound like his wife. It sounded masculine. Anxious. A little like a man in the early stages of congestive heart failure. Whoever it was, a cat had his tongue.

"Who is this?"

The voice was a rasp. "You wanted to talk to me about keeping your wife and daughter out of court. Let's talk."

"Judge Renkin?"

"Yes."

Patrick's brain felt like he'd just stuck his finger in an electrical outlet. "I don't follow you."

"Come to my place. We can talk there."

The blood. The vomit. The truck parked at home but his family gone. "I can't. Someone bled all over the place at our house, and there's no one here. I need to run to the hospital to check on my family."

Patrick heard an odd sound on the other end of the line. Like a groan.

Then the judge said, "Damn her."

"Excuse me?" Patrick's temper flamed. He needed off the phone. He didn't need to listen to Judge Renkin badmouth his wife. "I have to go."

"No. Please. I'll go with you to, um, check on your family. Just come quickly."

This was strange. Very strange. His every interaction with Renkin had been odd lately, including at the ER earlier in the day, but this was baffling. And then he had a terrible thought. What if Renkin had been here? What if the blood was his doing, and he already had Susanne and the kids?

"Do you have my family, Renkin?"

"What? No!"

Patrick didn't believe him. "I'm not comfortable with this situation, Judge. I'm afraid I'm going to have to hang up and call the sheriff now."

"No!" the judge shouted. "You can't hang up. She's got your wife and daughter."

And Patrick knew the mountain lion had been right.

CHAPTER FORTY-ONE: RESIST

Trish

The inside of her dad's truck usually smelled like leather, horses, and sweat. Those were scents Trish mostly liked, especially together. But in Coach Lamkin's truck, full-blast defrost recycled the stink of vomit, blood, and fear right into her face. It wasn't just the stench. She couldn't see anything outside either. Visibility was bad. The eastern side of the mountains always got dark early, because of the sun setting behind the range. With the storm added to that, all she saw was snow coming down through the headlights in a slant, which, in a weird kind of way, made it seem like the truck was being pushed toward the drop-off on the edge of the road. The coach was driving too fast, even faster than Ben had earlier. The stink, the dark, the snow, and the speed —combined with being scared and heartsick that Brandon had cheated on her *with her own teacher*—was making her disoriented and more carsick by the second. The fact that she was being kidnapped by her coach was almost not as bad as the fact that the coach was friends with Ms. Coker. She *had known* about Ms. Coker and Brandon. Been part of the sick secret.

Brandon. Why had she ever begged him to take her back after they broke up at Christmas? It was humiliating to remember how she'd groveled when he'd told her he was sick and tired of her bossing him around and embarrassing him in front of his friends. She'd promised things would be different. And they had been.

It hadn't been enough. She hadn't been enough.

But hadn't that been what she'd just heard Coach Lamkin doing on the phone? Begging and making promises to get some guy back? The coach had lectured Trish on boyfriends, but it sounded like she didn't know any more than Trish did.

Anger pushed Trish's emotions to a tipping point, and words flew out of her mouth like flushed quail. "Hey, Coach. If you have to beg him and trick him to make him come back to you, he's never going to love you." Her tone sounded like a taunt. A little disrespectful. Just like she'd intended. She stared straight ahead.

The coach's head whipped around in surprise, then back to face the road. "Listen to you, little Miss Know-It-All."

Her mom elbowed her. Trish turned toward her with a "what?" look on her face.

"Don't make her mad," her mom mouthed.

"Sorry," Trish mumbled.

Susanne raised her voice. "Is it because of the baby, Barb?"

Trish's mouth fell open. *What baby?*

Coach Lamkin's laugh was like machine gun fire. "He wanted me to get rid of it. He lectured me." She lowered her voice. "'Public figures can't have pregnant girlfriends, Barbara.' Like I got this way all by myself. Can you believe that? He literally told me an abortion was safe and legal after *Roe v. Wade*, and that he'd pay for it. He wouldn't drive me to Cheyenne, mind you, but he'd throw in a little extra so I could spend the night in a hotel."

Trish's head was about to explode. Her coach was pregnant, and the father wanted her to have an abortion? It was too much to comprehend.

"That's horrible. I'm sorry," her mom said. Her voice sounded soft and gentle, like it did whenever Trish's dad had a bad day. "He should have married you."

"That's what I thought, but he refused to leave his little woman. Even after she died. He said we'd have to wait a year to marry, so I'd still need to end the pregnancy. To kill *my baby*. He might not want it, but I do. The bastard."

Susanne's brow furrowed. "I didn't know Max was still married."

"Max? Max Alexandrov?" Coach Lamkin snorted. "Who said anything about him? I've had lunch with him once, but he's not my baby's father."

Trish's head was whipping back and forth between her mom and her coach now, like she was standing too close to the court watching a tennis match. It wasn't doing her carsickness any good, and she didn't know where she'd throw up, with her hands taped to the handle on the dash. All over her lap, probably. She swallowed and tried to look straight ahead.

Her mom said, "At the gas station you told him about us being star witnesses for him at the trial."

Trish sucked in a breath, anxious to hear Coach Lamkin's answer, but it was Perry who spoke.

"Mom, it wasn't him on the phone. Coach Lamkin shot Jeannie Renkin so Judge Renkin could marry her. She was talking to the judge."

Coach Lamkin made a gun with her finger and shot it at Perry, leaning away from him toward her door as she did. "Bullseye, kid. And now I'm going to make him pay for rejecting me and trying to make me kill my baby. You guys are the bait at his cabin on Clear Creek."

Trish had heard the coach make three more calls when they were still at the gas station. She'd listened closely, but they hadn't made sense. They were starting to now. Her voice caught in her throat as she said, "The other people you called . . ."

Lamkin's smile was the scariest thing Trish had seen since the night she watched Billy Kemecke slit his cousin's throat. "If I'm going to get away with this, I need help. Luckily, Harold Renkin has lots of people who want him dead. I'll set the stage at the cabin and scat. Then the Johnson County sheriff's department will arrive about the time Peters and Stamey get there to take the blame for me. By this time tomorrow, I'll be on a beach in Mexico, sipping a pina colada through a straw."

"Who are Peters and Stamey?"

Perry said, "Peters is the guy blackmailing the judge. I heard the judge say his name when Dad and I were at the courthouse."

Lamkin nodded, looking impressed. "Yes. And Harold made the tragic mistake of telling me about him. You're one smart kid, Perry Flint. Forget the skiing. You're going to be a rocket scientist."

Trish realized she'd heard the other name. "Stamey. He's Donna Lewis's boyfriend."

"And the patsy she's using to go after the judges to keep delaying her brother's trial until the fifth of never. Which I know about because Donna used to date Harold. When I told her he'd dumped me, she made me her best friend forever."

"What about us?" To Trish's surprise, Perry's voice didn't waver or even crack. "Are you going to kill us?"

The coach turned to him again. "I thought you were smart, but I take it back. Of course I am, Perry. You can identify me, and you were going to tell your family about me. You're the only thing tying me to Jeannie Renkin. I'm sorry. It's nothing personal."

Just then, while Coach Lamkin's eyes were still on Perry, a mountain lion jumped in the road right in front of the truck. It was enormous in the dusky gloom of the headlights. Trish screamed. Coach Lamkin's head whipped forward. She reacted, her arms jerking to the right. The truck lurched toward the rock face towering above them and one of the signs that said the rocks were old as dirt. She wrenched the wheel away from the rock. The truck smashed into the cougar with a sickening thud, skittered to the left, and kept going. Trish's head snapped forward and she braced herself against the dashboard. Beside her, Perry wasn't as lucky. His body slammed into the gear shift and dashboard. The weight of his body ripped the rearview mirror off the windshield.

For a moment, Trish thought everything was going to be okay, until Coach Lamkin's overcorrection sent the truck careening off the side of the road and into the nothingness over Clear Creek.

CHAPTER FORTY-TWO: ALLY

Patrick

J udge Renkin jumped into the passenger seat of the Suburban before Patrick could even take it out of drive. He didn't meet Patrick's eyes.

"Who took my family?" Patrick hissed, accelerating away from the judge's house. He gripped the steering wheel so tight that his hands hurt. "Where are they?"

"They're just up the mountain. At my cabin. With her."

Up the mountain. "Off 16?"

"Yes."

Patrick spun the steering wheel of the Suburban. They careened out of the judge's driveway and turned onto the dirt road. Three of the wheels spun, and the back end slid sideways. Then the big vehicle found traction and plowed through a section of unpacked snow. "Her *who*?"

"Barbara Lamkin." The judge looked out the window then back ahead at the road. "I guess she's obsessed with me and thought taking my trial witnesses would lure me to her." The judge rubbed his forehead, like he was scrubbing off a scarlet letter.

Patrick recognized his own gesture and vowed never to do it again. "But she knows about your cabin."

"Yes. For a short time, we had a relationship. It was a big mistake and I ended it. I loved my wife. I'd never cheated on her before. I couldn't live with the guilt."

Patrick bit his tongue. He had an urge to give the judge a piece of what was on his mind. That he and Susanne had heard about the judge's infidelities. That after hearing the judge on the phone with a black-mailer he had no faith in his morals or truthfulness, anyway. But he didn't want to sidetrack them from the more important topic of where his family was.

He headed west on 16 and accelerated hard and steady. "Go on."

"A few weeks ago, she told me she was pregnant. It's not mine of course, but she had this fantasy that I would leave Jeannie, marry her, and be a father to her bastard child. I told her no, so she went to my home and told Jeannie."

"Told her about the baby?"

"And her fantasy that I would be divorcing Jeannie and marrying Barbara. Jeannie was . . . distraught. She was threatening to divorce me for infidelity. I tried to convince her it was all lies, but I hadn't succeeded yet. It was the worst possible timing for a divorce, with my senate campaign about to kick off." The judge gripped his armrest. "Could you slow down? You're going to go off the road."

Patrick knew he was going too fast and that he was nearly blind to his surroundings, but he wasn't about to let up on the gas. Everything the judge was saying sickened him. Had he and Susanne been right? Had Judge Renkin hired someone to kill his wife and lent them his own snowmobile for the task, to save his campaign? He spat out the accusa-tion. "You killed Jeannie."

The judge wheeled on him. "What? No!"

"Then who did?"

"I believe it was Barbara."

"Not Donna Lewis? Or your blackmailer?"

"What are you . . ." the judge started to say, then he let his face fall into his hands. A few seconds later, he lifted his head. "No. I think it was Barbara."

"Why?"

"Because I believe she used my rifle to do it."

"What would make you think that?"

"Because when I came home from the hospital after Jeannie died, it was on the coffee table. It was loaded. I don't leave it loaded, and I hadn't left it out."

"Did you give it to the police?"

"No. I, um, got rid of it. Someone had left the gun there to incriminate me. I couldn't have her murder tied to me. That wouldn't bring her back."

Patrick wanted to throttle him. An officer of the court, and he was obstructing justice in his own wife's murder? *Despicable.* But saying that wouldn't get Patrick the information he needed. "And you just assumed it was Barb?"

"Not then. But about a week later, I found a lipstick under the seat of my snowmobile. Barbara had never been on it with me. No woman had. I'd seen her use one that looked like it. I think she left it there on purpose, so I'd know."

It made sense, in a twisted way. That meant it was Barb Lamkin that Perry had seen on the judge's snowmobile, after she shot Jeannie. But it didn't take Judge Renkin off the hook. This man and his choices, before and after Jeannie's murder, had put Patrick's family at risk. His whole family. His whole *world.* He pictured their beloved faces. Susanne. Trish. Perry.

Perry—Renkin said Barb had Susanne and Trish. He frowned. "Is Perry with her now, too?"

"Perry? I don't know. All she said was to meet her at our place and come alone. That my witnesses would stay alive if I 'made her happy.'"

"And you believe her?"

"Absolutely not. That's why I called you. I think she plans to kill them and me, no matter what."

Patrick hated the judge. Hated him with every fiber of his being. But right then, he was the enemy of Patrick's enemy: the woman who had his family. And that made them, if not friends, then uneasy allies, at least for now. He would have to come to very quick terms with that.

He rounded a curve, his brain spinning in a maelstrom of thoughts and emotions. A hulking mass in the road blocked his path and jerked his mind back to reality. He pumped the brakes as gently as he could and braced himself with all his strength on the steering wheel, as momentum threatened to propel him up and over the dash.

The Suburban shuddered to a stop a few feet short of a dead mountain lion. But it wasn't the mountain lion that nearly sent Patrick into cardiac arrest. It was the skid marks heading away from it and over the edge of the canyon.

CHAPTER FORTY-THREE: RISE

Perry

When the truck made impact with the rocky mountainside, it jarred Perry's teeth, and they hurt worse than anything else. Then the truck rolled, and his gut, his butt, his face, and the back of his head started giving his teeth stiff competition. For a few blurry seconds, the view out of the windows was a tumbling snow globe of a forest scene at nightfall. Glass shattered and rained in on him. Metal shrieked. Then there was a sickening skid and crunch. The truck jerked to a stop, driver's side down, front end slanted forward. Perry landed in a sprawl across Coach Lamkin and the steering wheel, with Trish's and his mom's legs dangling in his face.

He tried to draw in a breath, but he couldn't. He tried again, and again. His lungs wouldn't work. It felt like there was a horrible weight on his chest, but when he tried to push whatever it was off of him, there was nothing there.

He was going to die.

Then, with a violent gasp, his lungs started working again. After a few quick pants, he probed around on all of the parts that were hurting, which is when he realized his hands were free of each other and the rearview mirror. The mirror was still taped to one of his wrists. He jerked it and the tape off. Pine needles stuck to his gloves and fell on his jeans. He ripped off his gloves—he needed to be able to use his hands. He shuffled his legs. They were loose, too.

His mind went to his mom and sister. "Trish. Mom. Are you okay?" His voice was hoarse, and something in his throat rattled.

Neither of them answered. Bile burned his mouth. *Are they dead?* "Oh, no, oh, no, oh, no . . ." The words tumbled from his mouth like an echo. Then he got control of himself. He had to figure out what was going on. He couldn't flip out. Not now. "Coach Lamkin?" She didn't answer either. Good. He hoped she was dead.

He became aware of blood. His blood, running down his face and arms. And big, soft snowflakes melting on his skin. *The windows are all broken, so the outside is inside*, he thought. Then he noticed the smells. Pine trees. Something coppery. Gasoline. Gas could catch on fire. He had to get his mom and Trish out of the truck. Even if they were dead. He couldn't leave them here to burn up.

He readjusted his body, squashing Coach Lamkin in the process and fighting through the tangle of his mom's and sister's bodies, until he was able to wedge his feet onto the steering wheel and column. Standing on it, he leaned down. His mom and sister were virtually standing on Coach Lamkin now, side by side. Space was tight with their bodies and his vertical in the overturned truck. He reached for his mom first, touching her face.

She groaned.

Tears sprang into his eyes. *She's alive.* "Mom! Mom, can you hear me?"

Again, though, he got no answer. In the last dim light of dusk, he could see her arms, still taped to Trish's and the handhold on the dash. He wiped his tears and started pulling frantically at the tape, but it was taut with the weight of their bodies. His efforts jostled Trish, who cried out, but didn't wake. *She's alive, too.* A strange energy fired him, like he was supercharged. He would save them. He had to.

He worked his fingers around the tape, looking for the end, trying to get an edge, but he found nothing. Maybe he could cut them loose. But with what? He'd lost his pocketknife. Trish and his mom didn't carry knives, even though he and his dad thought they should. He tried to pry the glove box open, to see if the coach kept one in there, but his mom's and Trish's arms were blocking it. *The coach's purse.* He scrambled around, jostling bodies, searching, almost standing on his own hands, until he found it.

It was empty.

He pawed the glassy ground and what remained of the truck door under the coach's body. He found the gear shift, her wallet, and a hairbrush, but no knife. When he lifted his hand, though, he saw he'd cut it on a piece of glass hanging from the sideview mirror. He jerked his hand to his mouth, sucking at the cut.

Duh. He didn't need a knife. He had mirror glass. Probing gently so he wouldn't cut himself again, he pulled out the biggest piece he could find, stuck it in his pocket, and reversed direction. He wrestled his way back onto the steering assembly until he got a good angle on the tape. He started sawing between their wrists. Nothing happened at first. The tape was thick and rubbery. He kept going, because it had to work. It had to. Long seconds passed. Then minutes. He began to mutter and sob. *Come on, come on, come on.* Sweat rolled down his face. He used his shoulder to wipe it off. Still he didn't give up. He blocked everything else out of his mind except the tape, and he sawed harder.

When the first layer gave way, he shouted. "Yeah!"

Who says you have to be big to be tough and strong? He sawed with renewed strength, until his fingers, shoulder, and arm ached. One after another, he sliced through the first four, heavy layers of tape. As soon as he got a cut started on the fifth layer, the tape tore itself from the handhold. When it did, his mom and Trish crashed down on him, pinning him against Coach Lamkin. His body pressed painfully into shards of glass, and he struggled for breath again. Other than a few moans from his mom, though, no one made a sound. Since their barely taped wrists had landed near his hands, Perry decided to finish the job while still partially buried underneath them. He sawed with vigor, but the work got harder instead of easier without the weight of their bodies aiding in his efforts. Blood dripped from his fingers. He hadn't even realized he was cutting into himself with his grip on the glass. For a second, he thought about searching for his glove.

He imagined Trish taunting him, and said the words aloud, just like she would have. "Is that all you've got, runt?"

He clutched the glass, bore down on the tape, and sawed through it. He wouldn't waste any more time.

His breaths were coming in heaving gasps now. He stopped for a breather, but only a short one, then he ripped away the last of the tape binding his mom and sister together. He levered himself around to face their ankles and repeated the process until his hands were so slick from his own blood that he couldn't see the tape. It didn't matter. His shoulder was numb. That didn't matter either. He just kept going.

When he'd finished the last strand, he dug his way out from under them and crawled out the gaping hole where the back window used to be, trying his hardest not to step on them too badly in the process, and kept crawling through the opening between the truck bed and rock. He surveyed the situation. The truck bed had skidded across and gotten lodged on a slanted boulder just above the creek. The world was spinning around him, and every breath was agony. He bent over his knees and tried to think. He had to drag his mom and Trish out. But how?

He peered back through the window. Glass teeth still protruded from its edges. If he pulled Trish and his mom over them, they'd be cut to ribbons. He kicked the glass out the best he could, then he ripped off his coat and shirt and threw them over the jagged shards. Snowflakes pelted his bare torso, but the cold was nothing to him.

He leaned in the window, his belly on his shed clothing. His mom was on top of Trish. Reaching under his mom's arms, he tried to hoist her up. Her weight pulled him back in the truck, and he tumbled on top of the pile of people. As he caught his breath and righted himself, he noticed a funny sound. A WOOMPH noise. Then a smell.

Something burning.

"No!" he cried. "No!"

He jammed a foot once more against the steering column and braced the other on the dash. With strength he didn't know he had, he hefted his mom up. All the curls he had done in front of the bathroom mirror and in weight training for football, all the rows, all the front extensions. They may not have made him into the Incredible Hulk, but every rep had made a difference. He strained. Something in his back hurt bad, but he ignored it. Andy Mill had ignored his injury and gone on to ski the race of his life. If he could do it, Perry could, too. He had to. And then, he realized, he had. His mom was high enough that he leaned forward, squatted down, and jammed his shoulder under her bottom.

"Argh!" he yelled.

With a mighty shove and push from his legs, he sent her toppling through the back window. THUD. He hated the sound. Hated that she might have—probably did—hit her head on the rock or the truck. But that was better than burning to death.

The smell of the fire was growing stronger. *Hurry up, runt.* He grabbed his sister. His back screamed in pain as he heaved. She had crumpled in the floorboard. He couldn't lift her. He stepped off his perch on the dash and column and worked his feet past Coach Lamkin's shoulder until they were firmly against the rock the truck was resting on. He squatted low in the cramped quarters. For once, being small was an asset, but he had always shirked on leg work until his ankle weights lately. He regretted it. Forcing his shoulder under Trish's bottom like he had with his mom's, he braced himself with his hands out to either side, with his own bottom almost at his heels, then pushed up with everything his skinny legs had in them. He roared like an Olympic weightlifter. His thighs were in agony, like they were going to tear in half, but he didn't stop. He couldn't stop.

Slowly, miraculously, her body rose, until she was balanced above him like they were pairs ice skaters in a bloody, macabre lift. But his angle was bad, and he couldn't push her through the window. He had to get her higher.

He put his hands against the ceiling. Carefully, he stepped on the inside of the steering wheel with one foot, his body bent over and climbing like it was a stair, until he was standing on one leg. Trish's body rose, then wobbled, and only the close confines of the seat and ceiling kept her from falling off of him. He brought his other foot into the steering wheel. He squatted again and pushed her toward the window opening, but she wouldn't budge. Why couldn't he get her out? The smell of smoke mingled with fire now. A slide show raced through his mind, pictures of exploding trucks, burning trucks, incinerated trucks. He eased a foot up and around the steering wheel, back to the thick column. Then he hollered and stepped up. Her body rose higher still. He slipped his other foot onto the steering column. Standing on his tiptoes, he finally found the leverage he needed.

THUD. Trish followed their mom out.

Perry started to cry. Big cries, with heaving sobs, snot bubbles, and gobs of tears. But he didn't let it slow him down. He scrambled out the window after his mom and Trish, careful to jump clear of their bodies. Then he dragged them away from the truck, over rocks, snow, and pine cones, all the way to the edge of the stream under a canopy of branches.

First his mom, then his sister, lying side by side, still with their wrists and ankles taped.

But alive.

Only when he was done did he allow himself to look back at the truck. He couldn't see the front end, but he saw the flickering light of fire on the snow. Then he heard a voice from the cab. It was weak, almost buried under the sounds of creek water and crackling flame.

"Help me. Is anyone out there? Help me, please. I'm trapped."

It was Coach Lamkin.

CHAPTER FORTY-FOUR: HACK

Patrick

"No!" Patrick screamed.

He was out the door of the Suburban the second he ground it into park. *Dear God, please let my family be all right,* he prayed. He scrambled across the snowy road, past the mangled cougar to the edge of the drop off and peered over. He smelled the smoke and fire before he could identify their source. Then he saw it. Hulking dark metal and an orange and yellow glow twenty-feet below. A rush of hope spurted through him. The truck had gone over at the best possible spot, the upper end of this stretch of canyon, nearest the creek level. Twenty-feet. Only twenty-feet. *That's survivable, right?*

"Susanne!" he roared.

But it wasn't her voice that answered. It was one that was younger, squeakier, and equally loved. "Dad!"

"Are you okay?" Patrick shouted.

"I'm all right. Mom and Trish are unconscious. But I got them out."

Patrick felt giddy. His family was alive. "Good job, son. I'll be down to get you all in a second." He ran back to the Suburban and opened the back end. The judge joined him there.

"What's going on?" the judge asked.

Before Patrick could answer, a vehicle bore down on them with another in its wake. A virtual rush hour for the mountains. Patrick motioned them around to the right of the Suburban. He grabbed his unwieldy container of emergency supplies, shut the doors, and ran to the shoulder of the road.

He turned to the judge. "Perry said Trish and Susanne are down there. I'm going after them."

But as he spoke, the two vehicles pulled to a stop behind the Suburban. Driver's side doors opened. A man climbed out of each. Closest to them by a sedan, a man in a shiny dark suit slipped and held himself up by the open door.

He shouted, "Renkin, your time is up."

The judge hollered back. "Leave me alone, Peters. Your threats won't work on me."

The second vehicle was a Volkswagen van. There weren't many of them in the area, and Patrick thought it looked like the one he'd seen parked outside Renkin's house a few nights before. At its driver's door, a man with shoulder length hair, bell bottom pants, and a droopy mustache lifted a rifle and sighted it. Before Patrick could process what was happening, the man fired.

The judge's body slammed into the Suburban's back doors, his hand gripping his thigh. "I'm hit!"

Another shot rang out. Patrick flinched and closed his eyes, expecting a bullet. When he opened them, he realized he hadn't been shot.

The judge was crawling on the ground toward the driver's door of the Suburban, clutching his leg. "Help me. Help me."

A new set of headlights illuminated the rock cliffs. Silhouetted in the beams, Patrick saw the suited man—Peters?—pistol at his side, and, twenty feet behind him, the crumpled body of the bell-bottomed rifleman.

Peters yelled, "You're welcome, Renkin. I just shot the lowlife that Kemecke sent to kill you."

He ran toward Renkin. Renkin moaned. Patrick wasn't sure if Peter's plan was to kill the judge, take him hostage, or escape alone, but whatever it was, it didn't happen fast enough. A sheriff's department truck screeched to a halt behind the van, and Ronnie Harcourt jumped out.

She drew her gun on Peters. "Drop your weapons. Everyone."

Peters froze. His gun fell to the snowy pavement, and he put his hands in the air.

Renkin didn't get up. "I've been shot."

Patrick shouted, "Ronnie, it's Patrick. I'm unarmed. Susanne and the kids went off the side. I have to get down there and help them. There's a vehicle on fire."

"Go," she shouted.

He raced down the slope with his awkward, heavy load. The terrain was steep and uneven. Smoke from the fire floated into his eyes. It burned, and they watered, obscuring his vision. He tripped over a rock and landed gut first on his equipment box. It was like a mule kick to the diaphragm. He struggled back to his feet and ran on, stumbling twice more but somehow staying upright. When he reached more level ground near the truck, he saw Perry standing beside two supine figures. A strangled sob wrenched free of his throat, and he ran to them with his box. Perry was so bloody, he looked like he'd lost a fight with a wolverine.

"Perry!" Patrick dropped the equipment box and wrapped his son in a fierce hug.

Perry's body was as tight and strained as a high-tension cable. "Dad, Coach Lamkin is trapped."

Turning back toward the truck, Patrick saw the glow of the flames. But he also heard a voice.

"Help. I'm trapped. Please, help."

"She keeps saying that." Perry wrung his hands. "I was scared to go back and get her. She's a bad person. She killed Jeannie Renkin."

Patrick stared at the truck. The woman inside kidnapped his family, had probably planned to kill them, and *had* killed his neighbor. The truck might explode at any second. Or burn up completely in a few more minutes. If he tried to save her, he could be killed himself. If he didn't try, she might survive anyway. Or she might not.

What the husband and father in him wanted to do was take care of his family and let events run their course.

But, as a doctor, he was in the business of saving lives, not taking them. And letting Lamkin burn to death while doing nothing was almost the same thing. Right about then, it was like he was fighting to keep his head above water in a bottomless icy lake, with his chosen profession a lead weight around his neck.

He ripped the lid off the emergency container and pulled out his ax. "I'll be right back. Stay with your mom and Trish." He stuck the ax through a belt loop.

Perry's voice was anguished. "But the truck's on fire."

He ruffled the hair he was no longer allowed to touch. "It'll be all right, son." Then he ran to the bed of the burning truck and peered in the gaping hole where the back window used to be.

Lamkin was crumpled behind the steering wheel. She saw him. "Thank God," she said, though violent coughs.

"Where are you trapped?"

She lifted her right hand and pointed down. "My hand is pinned. Underneath the door frame."

Patrick tried to wrap his head around the magnitude of the problem. It was worse than he could have feared. There was no way he could get the truck off of her, not without special equipment that would take far too long to arrive from town and get into position, if such a thing was even possible. He needed a closer look. He stepped into the truck and carefully worked himself into position beside her. He waved away smoke, then tugged at her wrist. She screamed, but it didn't budge. The hand was jammed in tight. A clock was ticking in his head, loudly, ominously. He was on borrowed time. Every second that passed was closer to an end that might take both of their lives. That might leave his wife and children without him. He had to act.

He pulled his belt off and started threading it around her torso. "I'm going to try to pull you out. It's going to hurt."

She nodded.

When he had the tongue of the belt through the buckle, he wedged his feet against the dash and seat back and pulled upward with all his strength. Lamkin's screams were ear-splitting, but her body didn't budge. He released the pressure and glanced at the hood of the truck. Was it his imagination, or was the fire growing bigger and louder?

WHOOMP. Something exploded inside the engine.

Not his imagination.

"Get me out of here!" Lamkin cried.

He was out of time and options. He could only think of one, and it wasn't pretty.

"I have an ax. If I'm going to get you out of here before the whole truck explodes, I'm going to have to use it."

"Just do it," she screamed. "Do it, please."

Patrick pulled the ax from his belt loop and unsnapped the blade cover. Quarters were tight for an ax, even a small one like his, but he had to try. He jumped to the ground by Lamkin's shoulder, crouched to get the right angle, and, before he could second guess himself, lifted the ax to his chest, slamming it into the joint between her wrist and hand with all the force he could muster.

CHAPTER FORTY-FIVE: SHAVE

Patrick

Patrick held up two brown paper lunch bags. "One PB&J, cut on the diagonal. One ham and cheese with mustard, cut in rectangles."

Perry snatched the PB&J. His face looked like the winner in tryouts for a job as a punching bag.

"There's my tough guy," Susanne said. She was loading the dishwasher, and she didn't look much better than their son. She had stitches in her chin from her fall on the deck, and one of her pretty brown eyes was surrounded by ugly black and blue swelling.

"I *am* a tough guy." Perry swaggered toward the front door. He turned back. "Can we go skiing this weekend? The slopes are only going to be open for a week or two more."

Susanne rinsed a coffee mug and put in on the top rack. "Possibly. We can discuss it after school."

Trish collected her lunch bag from Patrick's outstretched hand. She was a little less beaten up than her mom or brother. "Thanks, Dad." She kissed his cheek. "Since you're staying home today, I can give Perry a ride to school in the Suburban, if you want. That way you and mom can have a nice quiet morning without having to run around town."

Patrick clasped his hands over his heart. "Thank you so much for your sacrifice."

Trish simpered, eyes sparkling. "I'm all about helping my family."

"How is your head? And your other aches and pains?"

She rotated her wrists. "Fine. My headache is gone."

Lamkin's tape job and the bracing of Trish's and her mom's wrists had kept them from breaking bones in the wreck. Their worst injuries had come from the collision of their heads—concussions. Susanne especially had battled headaches and nausea, since the concussion had just made an already bad condition worse. Patrick was pretty sure that, before Lamkin had snatched them, Susanne had her first migraine, probably brought on by stress. He felt terrible that he hadn't been there to help her through it. Next time, if there was one, he'd be ready.

Patrick pretended to mull it over, but of course he was going to let Trish drive the Suburban. After she'd survived a brush with death, he was putty in her hands. "I guess it would be okay. Just for today."

"Come straight home after school," Susanne said. "I mean it. No matter how badly your friends want to hear about what happened on the mountain or to gossip about Coach Lamkin and what she did or Tara Coker getting fired because of her relationship with Brandon. You're your brother's ride."

"Ugh. If anyone asks me about Brandon, I have an easy answer for them." Trish held up both hands in a rude and very unladylike gesture.

"No, ma'am. Not in this house." Susanne shook her head. She hastened to add, "And certainly not at school either."

Trish kept her fingers up. "I can't believe he met Ms. Coker when he was in Laramie for basketball camp last summer. That they were together. And that she moved here to be with him. Yuck. I'm glad she was fired, but I wish they would kick Brandon out of school, too. I don't ever want to see him again."

"Young lady, put those fingers away."

Trish dropped her hands and adopted an angelic tone. "If we had another car, I could help out like this every day."

Patrick snorted. "Get a job this summer. We can talk about it in August."

"That's so far away!"

"Says the girl who was skipping school earlier this week."

Trish made a sheepish face, like she'd been caught out. Which of course she had been.

"Come on, Trish," Perry said from the front door.

"You're just in a hurry because your picture was in the paper. 'Hero boy saves mom and sister.' Gag. It doesn't make you any taller, and girls still think you're a dork."

"They do not."

"Do too."

"Trish," Susanne warned. "Don't tease your brother. Perry, you're my hero."

The kids disappeared out the door, still bickering, but without the sound of any real hostility.

Patrick stood in front of the picture window, stretching his arms over his head and arching his back. He searched the trees along the creek for traces of his mountain lion, but he hadn't seen the animal since she'd finally gotten her message through about his family. *Thank you, Lion,* he thought. He wondered if she'd ever be back, or if she'd just keep wandering up the creek into the mountains as the weather grew warmer. The creek was already high against its banks. Green grass and daffodils had sprung up in the last few days between the patches of rapidly melting snow. How different the world looked since the blizzard on Tuesday. And how much safer it seemed with the bad guys off the street. Bad guys who he had learned about from his wife and kids, because Lamkin had spilled everything she knew to them, about her own crime, and her plan to involve the other players in her cover-up. Stamey, the hitman hired by the Kemeckes. Peters, Judge Renkin's blackmailer. How could one small town have been harboring so many merciless criminals?

Susanne lifted the percolator. "Want the last of the coffee?"

Patrick knew that last cup would have been hers if he was at work. "You take it."

"If you're sure."

The doorbell rang. "This early in the morning?" he grumbled.

"Every day, although it's usually the phone."

"I hope it's not another big city reporter." He winked at her. They'd been fielding lots of calls and a few visits from journalists eager to write their story.

He walked over and opened the door.

Max Alexandrov stood on their front stoop. He brushed thin blond hair off his forehead. His blue eyes twinkled in a lively way Patrick hadn't seen in quite some time. "Hello, Dr. Flint."

"Mr. County Prosecutor." *A home visit from the prosecutor can't be good.* He twisted his wedding ring around his finger, then gestured for Max to enter. "Good morning, sir."

Max wiped his boots on the mat, then stepped inside. "There hasn't been a good one all week. Jesus, Mary, and Joseph."

"Sorry about how I look." Susanne appeared with a mug in each hand. Patrick thought she was the most beautiful woman in the world, even with the stitches, black eye, and bruises. Then he realized she was referring to her thick velour robe. He was glad he'd put on jeans and a long-sleeved shirt before he went to feed the horses earlier. "Coffee for you, Max?" she said.

"I'm the one who's sorry. I dropped in unannounced. But I'd love the coffee. Thanks." He cradled the cup in both hands and blew on it. "You keep the coroner in business, Patrick."

Patrick closed the door behind him. "It wasn't me. In fact, I saved one of your suspects. Lamkin."

The mere mention of the incident started a sequence of horrific images in Patrick's mind. Lamkin's inhuman screams at the first blow of his ax. Their escalation at the second blow. And how, at the third and final strike, she'd lost consciousness, which was a blessing, because getting her out of the truck would have been even more difficult if she was in pain and struggling.

No sooner had he dragged her back to his family and his emergency kit than the truck had exploded, raining burning debris and ash on all of them. The canopy of tree branches had provided some protection, but it had still hurt. He'd started emergency treatment on Lamkin seconds later, ignoring his own pain while he flushed her wound with alcohol, fashioned a tourniquet around it with tow rope, and bound it with bandages like she was a mummy. He'd had time to inject her with morphine for the pain before the ambulance arrived. The extensive job to repair her arm he was happy to leave for someone else.

He still wasn't sure whether he was glad he'd done it. Susanne hadn't been, when she regained consciousness and heard tell of it. His butt was a little smaller after that chewing. But if he had it to do over again, he would have to make the same choice. Patrick Flint wasn't in the business of death. Death didn't give a fellow a second chance. Patrick would rather leave that up to God, anytime he could.

Max laughed. "Thank you, although the state might have preferred us to forego the expense of her medical bills and trial. Deputy Harcourt saved my other suspect."

"She may have saved the judge, too. He's probably not feeling very grateful to her, since all of his misdeeds have come to light. We sure won't be calling him Senator Renkin."

"Or Judge Renkin either. Governor Rawlins has relieved him of his position, and seems to have disassociated himself from Renkin entirely, faster than you can say lickety-split."

Susanne smiled. "I'm not disappointed to hear that."

Patrick wasn't either. "I suppose this means another change of venue for the Kemecke trial?"

"Possibly, unless Rawlins gets a new judge in here quickly." Patrick knew Rawlins could work fast when he wanted to. He'd gotten his security guy there when he said he would, only for Morales to discover the excitement was over before he started. He'd gone back to Cheyenne pretty dejected. Max shrugged. "Either way, it will mean a delay. Which will keep you Flints out of the hot seat for a while."

Patrick blew air out through his lips. "I think at this point we just wish we could get it over with."

Susanne nodded vigorously.

Max said, "That's why I came by, actually. Don't hold me to it, but there are rumblings Kemecke will take a deal for life now that he's facing additional charges."

Susanne's face lit up. "No trial?"

Patrick smiled, too. "But he was in jail when it all happened."

"Conspiracy. Same as doing the deed."

"What will they charge him with?"

"The murder of Judge Ellis and the attempted murder of Judge Renkin. Although it's been dicey figuring out who did what to whom and when."

Patrick shook his head. "Who's on first."

"What's on second, I Don't Know's on third." Max shook his head. "Don Peters was blackmailing Judge Renkin. Peters killed Stamey. And we think Stamey was the hitman hired by Donna Lewis to kill Ellis and Renkin."

"Have you figured out exactly what Peters was blackmailing Renkin about?"

"Neither party has been entirely forthcoming on that point,

although that may change now that Peters is charged for murdering Stamey."

"That's good motivation for disclosure."

"It is. But based on what you told us you overheard about a title dispute in a mineral rights case, I've done some digging and found a case Renkin presided over early in his time on the bench. It appears he helped an attorney cover up evidence that would have meant millions to a family that had an ownership interest. And you'll never guess who that family is."

"Well, I know it's not the Flints. But other than that, I have no clue."

"Martin Ochoa's parents."

Patrick and Susanne shared a surprised look.

Patrick said, "Mayor Ochoa?"

"Yes. But keep that under your hat. The investigation is ongoing, and, if I'm right, the judge will be facing charges. For obstruction of justice, for starters, and for his misconduct toward the Ochoas."

"What will happen to the Ochoas?"

Max sipped coffee then lifted a grin from his cup. "I plan to get them their money."

Susanne put a hand over her chest. "Oh, Max, that would be so wonderful. They certainly need it."

"It would be great. The hardest thing we have to prove, really, is what Stamey did."

Patrick said, "And Stamey's dead."

"As a doornail. But one of his drinking buddies came in and told us all about Stamey's relationship with Donna Lewis. He backed up what Lamkin told you, Susanne, only with more detail, like how Stamey was hired on Kemecke's behalf to shoot Judge Ellis up with phenobarbital and leave him in his garage with the car running."

Patrick whistled. "That drinking buddy is either really brave or really foolish to cross the Kemeckes. Are the tox results back?"

"Yes. They confirm the phenobarbital."

"So, it definitely wasn't suicide."

"It wasn't. Which will make a big difference to Mrs. Ellis and the kids."

In more ways than one. "It's still tragic, but that's good news."

"The drinking buddy also credited Stamey for the attack on Judge Renkin and you in the hospital parking lot. Apparently, Kemecke and

Donna thought they could delay the trial indefinitely and arrange for him to make another escape."

"Stamey was a busy man."

"Hopefully this drinking buddy witness will be enough to tie Stamey to Kemecke and Donna directly. Because with Stamey gone, we have no confidence that Kemecke or Donna will confess. And anything Lamkin has to say is just hearsay."

Susanne started another pot of coffee. "Trish told us something that makes me think Donna's nephew Ben could do that."

"Oh?"

"Apparently Donna tried to recruit Ben to help Stamey kill the judge. And since Donna kicked Ben out, I don't think he'll have reservations about testifying against her and his uncle."

Max pumped his first. "Yes! How did I not know this? Thank you. Do you know how I can get hold of the kid?"

Susanne nodded. "Henry and Vangie Sibley. He's living with them, working as a hand on their ranch, and restarting school in Buffalo."

It was a deal Trish had brokered. Patrick and Susanne had serious reservations about the budding friendship between Trish and Ben, but they couldn't fault her good intentions. Henry and Vangie seemed thrilled about the arrangement. Everyone had their fingers crossed it would work out.

Max pulled a pocket-sized flip pad with a clip pen from his shirt pocket and made a note. "Unfortunately for your family, even if Kemecke pleads, there may still be more testimony in your future."

Patrick rubbed his forehead. "Barb Lamkin."

"Yes. We'll get her charged as soon as she's released from the hospital in Billings and sent back down here to us. I hear that may be awhile. Something about a messy hatchet job."

Patrick groaned. He might never live that one down. He'd done the best he could under the circumstances, but it had been ugly. If he never had to do another field amputation again, it would be too soon. In fact, he wouldn't be jumping to the front of the line if the opportunity to do one in a controlled clinical environment came up either.

"Did Barb lose the baby?" Susanne asked.

"No. She didn't."

Susanne's expression was sorrowful. She put her head on Patrick's shoulder. They'd talked about the fate of the baby until late the previous night. "She'll have a child while she's in jail. What will happen to the baby?"

"Assuming Lamkin's convicted of first-degree murder and the other lesser crimes she committed against you guys, and unless Judge Renkin wants custody, the baby will go into foster care. Possibly adoption."

Patrick didn't have high hopes that Renkin would step up. Or if he could. He might be incarcerated, too. "Well, let me know what we can do to help. On any of this."

"Just keep your family safe. It appears our justice system depends on you."

Patrick chuckled. Max bade him and Susanne goodbye, then departed. When Patrick had shut the door behind him, he turned to his wife.

"Wow," Susanne said.

"Wow," he agreed.

"It's been quite a week." She set her freshly filled coffee mug down on an end table by the couch, then slipped into his arms. Dollars to doughnuts she'd forget it was there and fill three more cups before the day was done. He'd find this one a week later with an eighth inch of mold scum on the surface of the liquid. The thought made him want to kiss her. "I feel so dumb for having trusted Barb Lamkin," she said.

"Don't beat yourself up. No one suspected her."

"But I made friends with a woman who tried to kill us."

Patrick thought of Tara Coker. "And another who was sleeping with your daughter's boyfriend."

Susanne half-groaned, half-laughed. "From here on out, you and the Sibleys are all the social life I need." She tilted her head back without letting go of him. "Speaking of social life, whatever are we going to do with our whole day off together, Dr. Flint?"

He grinned down at her. "Oh, I think we can come up with something."

She rubbed her cheek against his beard. "I already have." She pulled a razor from one pocket of her robe and shaving cream from the other. "Time to lop off your face fur, mountain man." She slipped a finger between the buttons of his shirt and tugged him gently down the hall.

Walking behind her with small steps, he appreciated the sway of her hips below the waist that was as tiny as when he'd first fallen in love with it as a teenager. He put a hand on either side. "Sounds dangerous."

"We've had enough danger to last us a lifetime. This will just be a peaceful, boring shave."

"But you could slip and cut my neck. Or it might rob me of my strength. Like Samson."

"Samson had long hair. This is just one patchy beard, Patrick. You'll hardly notice it's gone."

Ouch. "What will my reward be for submitting to this torture?"

She threw him a wink over her shoulder with the eye that still sported the shiner. "Oh, I think we can come up with something."

The phone rang. He'd never realized how busy the house was during the day. Bad timing, from his point of view. He didn't want to answer it, but he was conditioned to always be available, just in case. Susanne had her hands full of torture implements, so he hustled into their bedroom and picked up on the bedside table phone. Their room in their Texas house had been lavender and white—her preferences. Their old house in Wyoming had been western—his. Susanne had transformed this new bedroom into something he thought of more as "mountain," with pine furniture and bedding in forest green and brown. Theirs.

"Hello?" he said.

Henry's voice was droll in his ear. "You picked a nice day to play hooky, my friend."

"Why's that?"

"Vangie and I are at the hospital. She tried to wait for you, but she couldn't. Dr. John delivered our son."

Patrick laughed. "Good job, Sibley. Congratulations."

"You and Susanne need to come meet Hank."

"We'll see you in a few minutes, then." He put the receiver back on the hook.

Susanne walked in, waving the razor and shaving cream. "What was that about?"

He grinned at her. "I'm delighted to inform you that my shave is going to have to wait a little while longer."

***

Next up: When his son is critically injured on a river trip, **Patrick Flint** finds himself in a race against time and outlaws determined not to let the Flints make it out of the Gros Ventre Wilderness alive. *Scapegoat* (https://www.amazon.com/dp/B089CKF3J1).

Or you can continue adventuring in the *What Doesn't Kill You* mystery world:

---

*Want to stay in **Wyoming**? Rock on with Maggie in **Live Wire on Amazon** (free in Kindle Unlimited) at https://www.amazon.com/gp/product/B07L5RYGHZ/.*

*Prefer the **beginning** of it all? Start with Katie Connell in Saving Grace on **Amazon** (free to Kindle Unlimited subscribers), here: https://www.amazon.com/gp/product/B009FZPMFO.*

*Or **get the complete WDKY series** here: https://www.amazon.com/gp/product/B07QQVNSPN.*

***

And don't forget to snag the **free** *What Doesn't Kill You* **ebook starter library** by joining Pamela's mailing list at https://www.subscribepage.com/PFHSuperstars.

To my dear, darling, baby brother, Perry, er, I mean Colonel Fagan, who has always been heroic.
And, as always, to my own knight in shining armor, Eric.

OTHER BOOKS BY THE AUTHOR

Fiction from SkipJack Publishing

The *What Doesn't Kill You* Series

Act One (Prequel, Ensemble Novella)

Saving Grace (Katie #1)

Leaving Annalise (Katie #2)

Finding Harmony (Katie #3)

Heaven to Betsy (Emily #1)

Earth to Emily (Emily #2)

Hell to Pay (Emily #3)

Going for Kona (Michele #1)

Fighting for Anna (Michele #2)

Searching for Dime Box (Michele #3)

Buckle Bunny (Maggie Prequel Novella)

Shock Jock (Maggie Prequel Short Story)

Live Wire (Maggie #1)

Sick Puppy (Maggie #2)

Dead Pile (Maggie #3)

The Essential Guide to the What Doesn't Kill You Series

The *Ava Butler Trilogy*: A Sexy Spin-off From *What Doesn't Kill You*

Bombshell (Ava #1)

Stunner (Ava #2)

Knockout (Ava #3)

The *Patrick Flint Trilogy*: A Spin-off From *What Doesn't*

Kill You

Switchback (Patrick Flint #1)

Snake Oil (Patrick Flint #2)

Sawbones (Patrick Flint #3)

Scapegoat (Patrick Flint #4)

Snaggle Tooth (Patrick Flint #5)

Stag Party (Patrick Flint #6): 2021

The What Doesn't Kill You Box Sets Series (50% off individual title retail)

The Complete Katie Connell Trilogy

The Complete Emily Bernal Trilogy

The Complete Michele Lopez Hanson Trilogy

The Complete Maggie Killian Trilogy

The Complete Ava Butler Trilogy

The Complete Patrick Flint Trilogy #1 (coming in late 2020)

Nonfiction from SkipJack Publishing

The Clark Kent Chronicles

Hot Flashes and Half Ironmans

How to Screw Up Your Kids

How to Screw Up Your Marriage

Puppalicious and Beyond

What Kind of Loser Indie Publishes,
and How Can I Be One, Too?

Audio, e-book, and paperback versions of most titles available.

ACKNOWLEDGMENTS

When I got the call from my father that he had metastatic prostate cancer spread into his bones in nine locations, I was with a houseful of retreat guests in Wyoming while my parents (who normally summer in Wyoming) were in Texas. The guests were so kind and comforting to me, as was Eric, but there was only one place I wanted to be, and that was home. Not home where I grew up, because I lived in twelve places by the time I was twelve, and many thereafter. No, home is truly where the heart is. And that meant home for Eric and me would be with my parents.

I was in the middle of writing two novels at the time: *Blue Streak*, the first Laura mystery in the What Doesn't Kill You series, and *Polarity*, a series spin-off contemporary romance based on my love story with Eric. I put them both down. I needed to write, but not those books. They could wait. I needed to write through my emotions—because that's what writers do—with books spelling out the ending we were seeking for my dad's story. Allegorically and biographically, while fictionally.

So that is what I did, and Dr. Patrick Flint (aka Dr. Peter Fagan—my pops—in real life) and family were hatched, using actual stories from our lives in late 1970s Buffalo, Wyoming as the depth and backdrop to a new series of mysteries, starting with *Switchback* and moving on to *Snake Oil* and *Sawbones*. I hope the real life versions of Patrick,

Susanne, and Perry will forgive me for taking liberties in creating their fictional alter egos. I took care to make Trish the most annoying character since she's based on me, to soften the blow for the others. I am so hopeful that my loyal readers will enjoy them, too, even though in some ways the novels are a departure from my usual stories. But in many ways they are the same. Character-driven, edge-of-your-seat mysteries steeped in setting/culture, with a strong nod to the everyday magic around us, and filled with complex, authentic characters (including some AWESOME females).

I had a wonderful time writing these books, and it kept me going when it was tempting to fold in on myself and let stress eat me alive. For more stories behind the actual stories, visit my blog on my website: http://pamelafaganhutchins.com. And let me know if you liked the novels. I have three more in my hip pocket, waiting to be written if you want them: *Snaggle Tooth*, *Scape Goat*, and *Stag Party*.

Thanks to my dad for advice on all things medical, wilderness, hunting, 1970s, and animal. I hope you had fun using your medical knowledge for murder!

Thanks to my mom for printing the manuscript (over and over, in its entirety) as she and dad followed along daily on the progress.

Thanks to my brother Paul for the vivid memories that have made Perry such an amazing fictional kid.

Thanks to my husband, Eric, for brainstorming with and encouraging me and beta reading the *Patrick Flint* stories despite his busy work, travel, and workout schedule. And for moving in to my parents' barn apartment with me so I could be closer to them during this time.

Thanks to our five offspring. I love you guys more than anything, and each time I write a parent/child (birth, adopted, foster, or step), I channel you. I am so touched by how supportive you have been with Poppy, Gigi, Eric, and me.

To each and every blessed reader, I appreciate you more than I can say. It is the readers who move mountains for me, and for other authors, and I humbly ask for the honor of your honest reviews and recommendations.

Thanks mucho to Bobbye for the fantastic *Patrick Flint* covers.

Sawbones editing credits go to Karen Goodwin. The proofreaders who enthusiastically devote their time—gratis—to help us rid my books of flaws blow me away.

SkipJack Publishing now includes fantastic books by a cherry-picked bushel basket of mystery/thriller/suspense writers. If you write in this genre, visit http://SkipJackPublishing.com for submission guidelines. To check out our other authors and snag a bargain at the same time, download *Murder, They Wrote: Four SkipJack Mysteries*.

ABOUT THE AUTHOR

Pamela Fagan Hutchins is a *USA Today* best seller. She writes award-winning romantic mysteries from deep in the heart of Nowheresville, Texas and way up in the frozen north of Snowheresville, Wyoming. She is passionate about long hikes with her hunky husband and pack of rescue dogs and riding her gigantic horses.

If you'd like Pamela to speak to your book club, women's club, class, or writers group, virtually or in person, shoot her an email. She's very likely to say yes.

You can connect with Pamela via her website
(http://pamelafaganhutchins.com)
or email (pamela@pamelafaganhutchins.com).

PRAISE FOR PAMELA FAGAN HUTCHINS

2018 USA Today Best Seller
2017 Silver Falchion Award, Best Mystery
2016 USA Best Book Award, Cross-Genre Fiction
2015 USA Best Book Award, Cross-Genre Fiction
2014 Amazon Breakthrough Novel Award Quarter-finalist, Romance

Patrick Flint: Wyoming Mysteries

"Best book I've read in a long time!" — Kiersten Marquet, author of *Three Reluctant Promises*

"SWITCHBACK starts at a gallop and had me holding on with both hands until the riveting finish. This book is highly atmospheric and nearly crackling with suspense. Highly recommend!" — Libby Kirsch, Emmy award winning reporter and author of the *Janet Black Mystery Series*

"A roller-coaster ride from the first page to the last!" — *Amazon reader*
"A Bob Ross painting with Alfred Hitchcock hidden among the trees." — Terry Shepherd, author *Retribution: A Jessica Ramirez thriller*
"Edge-of-your seat nail biter." — *Amazon reader*
"Absolutely unputdownable wonder of a story." — *Amazon reader*

What Doesn't Kill You: Katie Romantic Mysteries

"An exciting tale . . . twisting investigative and legal subplots . . . a character seeking redemption . . . an exhilarating mystery with a touch of voodoo." — *Midwest Book Review Bookwatch*
"A lively romantic mystery." — *Kirkus Reviews*
"A riveting drama . . . exciting read, highly recommended." — *Small Press Bookwatch*
"Katie is the first character I have absolutely fallen in love with since Stephanie Plum!" — *Stephanie Swindell, Bookstore Owner*
"Engaging storyline . . . taut suspense." — *MBR Bookwatch*

What Doesn't Kill You: Emily Romantic Mysteries

"Fair warning: clear your calendar before you pick it up because you won't be able to put it down." — *Ken Oder, author of* Old Wounds to the Heart

"Full of heart, humor, vivid characters, and suspense. Hutchins has done it again!" — *Gay Yellen, author of* The Body Business

"Hutchins is a master of tension." — *R.L. Nolen, author of* Deadly Thyme

"Intriguing mystery . . . captivating romance." — *Patricia Flaherty Pagan, author of* Trail Ways Pilgrims

"Everything about it shines: the plot, the characters and the writing. Readers are in for a real treat with this story." — *Marcy McKay, author of* Pennies from Burger Heaven

What Doesn't Kill You: Michele Romantic Mysteries

"Immediately hooked." — *Terry Sykes-Bradshaw, author of* Sibling Revelry

"Spellbinding." — *Jo Bryan, Dry Creek Book Club*

"Fast-paced mystery." — *Deb Krenzer, Book Reviewer*

"Can't put it down." — *Cathy Bader, Reader*

What Doesn't Kill You: Ava Romantic Mysteries

"Just when I think I couldn't love another Pamela Fagan Hutchins novel more, along comes Ava." — *Marcy McKay, author of* Stars Among the Dead

"Ava personifies bombshell in every sense of word. — *Tara Scheyer, Grammy-nominated musician, Long-Distance Sisters Book Club*

"Entertaining, complex, and thought-provoking." — *Ginger Copeland, power reader*

What Doesn't Kill You: Maggie Romantic Mysteries

"Murder has never been so much fun!" — *Christie Craig,* New York Times *Best Seller*

"Maggie's gonna break your heart—one way or another." — *Tara Scheyer, Grammy-nominated musician, Long-Distance Sisters Book Club*

"Pamela Fagan Hutchins nails that Wyoming scenery and captures the atmosphere of the people there." — *Ken Oder, author of* Old Wounds to the Heart

"You're guaranteed to love the ride!" — *Kay Kendall, Silver Falchion Best Mystery Winner*

OTHER BOOKS FROM
SKIPJACK PUBLISHING

Murder, They Wrote: Four SkipJack Mysteries,
by Pamela Fagan Hutchins,
Ken Oder, R.L. Nolen, and Marcy Mason

The Closing, by Ken Oder
Old Wounds to the Heart, by Ken Oder
The Judas Murders, by Ken Oder
The Princess of Sugar Valley, by Ken Oder

Pennies from Burger Heaven, by Marcy McKay
Stars Among the Dead, by Marcy McKay
The Moon Rises at Dawn, by Marcy McKay
Bones and Lies Between Us, by Marcy McKay

Deadly Thyme, by R. L. Nolen
The Dry, by Rebecca Nolen

Tides of Possibility, edited by K.J. Russell
Tides of Impossibility, edited by K.J. Russell and C. Stuart Hardwick

My Dream of Freedom: From Holocaust to My Beloved America,
by Helen Colin

CPSIA information can be obtained
at www.ICGtesting.com
Printed in the USA
LVHW081325031021
699374LV00010B/1216